We Carry the Sea
in Our Hands

We Carry the Sea in Our Hands

◆ *A NOVEL* ◆

JANIE KIM

alcove
press

Published in the United States by Alcove Press, an imprint of The Quick Brown Fox & Company LLC.

Alcove Press and its logo are trademarks of The Quick Brown Fox & Company LLC.

Library of Congress Catalog-in-Publication data available upon request.

ISBN (hardcover): 978-1-63910-753-7
ISBN (ebook): 978-1-63910-758-2

Cover design by Amanda Shaffer

Printed in the United States.

www.alcovepress.com

Alcove Press
34 West 27th St., 10th Floor
New York, NY 10001

First Edition: July 2024

10 9 8 7 6 5 4 3 2 1

*For Goolgeum, and for contentedness in the present,
in things to come, and in things past.*

"There is a white flower with a single central purple petal. Can you explain how that purple petal got there?"

—ESTHER LEDERBERG

I.
ALL AROUND, WATER AND POISON

I have two lab notebooks. The regular one is for observing life as a biological phenomenon. The second one is for observing life as a personal experiment.

This is the second one.

★ ★ ★

Here's the beginning of all life's stories:

Life on Earth started in a planetary mosh pit with a lot of water and also a lot of poison.

No longer a cosmic fireball, Baby Earth cooled off from its hot-tempered terrible twos and the steam condensed into water and thus, seas were birthed from the skies. Enter a waterworld. Enter radioactivity and cosmic rays and gaseous ammonia and other maternal nondelights. There is lightning, too, and where it lances it leaves behind molecules that have the inklings of building blocks of life. From the space blackness beyond, throw in a spattering of meteorites speckled with more.

Regardless of how exactly this prebiotic potluck began and who brought what, what matters is that the right molecules made the scene, and that was good enough for the chemical reaction party to begin.

◆ 1 ◆

ONE WEEK AGO I learned that I was a drop-box baby. In that moment, the first thing I thought of was sea slug mating rituals.

When *Siphopteron* slugs mate, blissful unawareness comes first, followed by the stab. When two sea slugs decide to mate, horny sea slug chemicals coursing through their little sea slug bodies, things take an interesting turn of events. First, they engage in an intimate dance, curled around each other and spinning and swaying in the water. It's invertebrate intrigue. They embrace, wiggling the winglike ribbons of membrane running down their backs as seductively as sea slugs possibly can. Then the one that decides to act male the quickest will stab an accessory stylet into its partner's head, right between the eyes, and shoot in a cocktail of mind-controlling chemicals.

All is fair in love and war.

Much like violent sea slug mating habits, the drop-box-baby news cuts through any of my soft delusions real fast.

Over the past week, I'd called the San Oligo registry of vital records, ended up redirected to the U.S. Embassy in South Korea, was bounced to a ward office in Seoul, rerouted back to the embassy, and after a long wait and equally long email chains and deliberations over whether I could better convince the officials overseas to help me if I tried to compose my emails in choppy Korean instead of English, I was given the contact info for a little Presbyterian church in Seoul. The pastor on the other end of the phone told me in a voice gravelly with age and care that he has run the baby drop-off box attached to one wall of the church for many years. I heard children playing and laughing in the background. I was once one of them, he told me, before a couple in America adopted me.

He wished me well, told me that he loves all of his drop-box children near and far, and to please come visit if I am ever in the vicinity. In the distance marked by phone static came the voice of a toddler, begging the pastor to play with him, and then our call ended.

★   ★   ★

But I already knew that I was adopted at the end of fourth grade, thirteen years ago. I'd mailed a tube of my spit, plus secret swabs of my mother's and father's toothbrushes—and that was how I learned that they weren't my mother and father after all. The idea came from reading a book at the library I frequented after school, while waiting for my working parents to pick me up. It was a book on genetics. It talked about DNA and about companies that can peek into the family history written within those loose-lipped strands.

I spent the years between then and last week in a self-inflicted purgatory. I didn't go digging any further.

At first I didn't know how, and then once I figured that out, I found that I no longer wanted any more of it. For once in my scientist life, I didn't want to know more. I let things sit, and the longer I did so, the more I became afraid of what I would see once I finally lifted the lid off that fermentation jar.

But as myths will tell, restless creatures are not contained inside of jars or boxes or other enclosed spaces for very long.

Last week, I read an article that sent me back in time. Scrolling through the news on the morning bus ride to the lab, I came across an article about an adoptee living in Denmark who reunited with her Korean birth parents. She had a little tattoo on her inner left wrist, a cross with two dots, and it turned out to be a family tattoo—when she posted a picture of it online, the picture made its way to her birth family and they reunited.

I scrolled down the page and stared at the photos of the daughter reuniting with her sister, her parents, the small white dog. Something in me strained at the mélange of emotions filling their faces. A small but persistent tug in the heart for something that I don't have but want, something that feels like tachycardia with no physical cause.

And so, one week ago, I called the registry and wound up talking to the Korean pastor who runs the drop box into which someone had once placed me.

It was in those moments that sea slugs became part of my identity.

Invertebrates were on my mind. That day marked three months since the start of my unsuccessful sea slug-breeding campaign. In the lab, I study the molecules of bacteria that live within sea slugs, where there is a connection to the origins of life on Earth. I needed more slugs for a new set of experiments, but it had become expensive to hire someone to scoop them out of their natural habitat a thousand miles away and ship them live to the lab every single time. So I'd begun a long and arduous series of attempts to breed my own.

Turns out invertebrate love can be just as finicky as human love, right from the get-go.

"You'd think that it would be easy to get them to have babies," I told Iseul—my best friend, sister, partner-in-crime—that day. "Sea slugs are hermaphrodites. They've got both male and female reproductive organs. So you just throw two slugs into a tank, give them some privacy, and *voila*, baby extravaganza, right?"

I pressed my cellphone between my shoulder and cheek to unscrew my thermos, and the smell of tomato sauce filled the lounge area outside the lab. It was only after three hours of cleaning aquarium tanks that I remembered I hadn't eaten yet.

"Wrong," I continued. "Tragically wrong. It turns out sea slugs are picky about their love lives. It's ridiculous. I can't believe I've spent three months trying to get slugs to have sex."

I took a bite of my pasta, which was unpleasantly soft, because I had left it on the stove too long last night while distracted by an email—*It's been three months now,* said the email from my lab head, as if I weren't acutely aware and equally impatient with the sea slugs.

"If they're hermaphrodites, you can keep trying different combinations of them, right?" Iseul said. "How many do you have?"

Iseul is an investigative journalist. This means that she is perfect to bounce ideas off of when I've run up against a wall in my research: distant enough from the lab bench to be emotionally detached from failed experiments, but able to think logically.

"Twelve. That's what I've been doing. Combinatorials with sea slugs. Maybe I should put three of them in a tank together. Do you think jealousy will do the trick? Or it could also end up as a gastropod threesome."

"A win for you either way."

This was stupid. "Maybe it's just something to do with slippery marine organisms," I said. "You know that Freud started off studying eels? He spent weeks trying to find where in male eels the gonads are located to crack the mysteries of eel sex, and then he gave up." I stabbed a piece of bowtie pasta, and my fork clinked against the metal rim of the thermos.

"Abby, are you eating lunch right now?"

"Funny Freud."

"Abby, it's three forty-five p.m."

I chewed my pasta. "I guess after failing to use eels as a model organism, he moved onto humans."

"Abby, I thought you were supposed to maintain a regular meal schedule to fix your insomnia. Isn't that what the sleep disorder specialist said?"

I visualized Iseul leaning against the break room counter-top in her office, cellphone in one hand, pinching the bridge of her nose with the other.

"My god," she said. "It took me three years to finally get you to see a specialist. That's a whole lot longer than your three months. And you're still pulling this off."

"Yeah, well, we can blame the sea slugs and their libido deficiency."

★ ★ ★

Home from work, I am thinking about the drop-box baby news again—I find that I do after days dealing with my sea slugs. It's all hunky-dory while in the lab during the day, joking around with labmates about equivalents of baby gender reveal parties but for hermaphrodite invertebrates.

Then when I get back to my apartment, alone in an evening silence broken by the sound of passerby pedestrians three floors below and of cars sloshing through rainwater, the sea slugs remind me of my drop-box origins.

I am curled around the glowing screen of my phone where the light from those decade-old DNA test results spears through the midnight darkness in my apartment. My face bathed in the light of the screen, I've lost track of how many times I've viewed this page, how many times I've lingered on each number. The name of each DNA short tandem repeat, each percentage, as though burning these backlit numbers into my retinas will force out more answers and untie the knot in my gut.

Tonight I am mirroring the position I adopted over a decade ago, curled inward on my bed, all acute angles, leaning my head on the wall feeling the stucco spikes prickle against my scalp and thinking, why had no one told me?

I'm woozy all over again.

I remember I haven't eaten dinner yet. I get up and trip over the lamp cord that I never secured to the wall since moving in for undergrad over four years ago. Even with a biochemistry degree in hand since June of last year, seventeen months ago, still nothing has changed. I make it to the kitchen and go through the last of my off-brand milk chocolate hearts.

Some memories are mildly abrasive, like pepper flakes caught between teeth to the tongue.

It was not like I didn't have suspicions before sending off my tube of spit. Years of brushing my teeth in front of the bathroom mirror had wedged into me the unflickering truth that I do not look much like my mother nor like my father—whom I associate with the adjective *adoptive* in the way I am associating powdery-cheap chocolate with the word *dinner*. My adoptive mother is from Korea and my adoptive father is a born-and-raised American with great-great-grandparents'

Scottish blood, and I look the mix, but that is where the physical similarities end. The hard edges on my face, rounded nose, fuller upper lip, these are all wishy-washy brushstrokes that I could not locate in the other two faces around my childhood dinner table.

There was also that one page of a biology textbook back in middle school. Widow's peaks are a dominantly inherited genetic trait, it had said, next to some colorful Punnett squares. If either parent has one, then their child will too.

To lay my hands on the truth, it only took returning from school and seeing both parents' hairlines—so glaringly unlike my arrow-like own.

So that was how I learned that biology can be so exquisitely, unrelentingly precise. That science had answers for things that people would not tell.

There are lots of things that people will keep locked up in their voice boxes. Such as why an angry man kept showing up banging on my childhood apartment's rickety door and demanding money. Such as why my father began to hide his phone whenever it buzzed. Why he looked angry when I saw it one day and asked him who Natasha was. Why my mother seemed to spend less and less time in the home until she faded away entirely—I do not believe in ghosts, but she was a ghost if I ever saw one. Why my father flickered between days of silence and days of anger and then in a whirlwind made of liquor bottle shards, disappeared, too. Why social workers will give you boilerplate smiles and pat your head but keep their words sealed away behind pearly teeth. Even at their emptiest, youth shelters will always be overflowing with what is unspoken.

It is true that my adoptive mother hadn't always been so silent. She had talked to herself in Korean often, a long time ago. My father spoke no Korean, and my mother spoke broken English at best. The days she slept out on the living room sofa, she sang to herself in Korean the way some birds coo themselves to sleep. I'd thought it sounded like pebbles moving in a creek, something with rounded waves and little staccato notes. When she came home from work, I could hear her footsteps approach the thin apartment door, and she would stand outside for a couple minutes murmuring to herself in Korean—if my father wasn't around, I'd press my ear against the cracking paint to listen. There, the language had sounded urgently robotic, like a practiced prayer, or maybe an incantation to ward off demons, and once she was done, she would sigh—a long and juddering thing like exorcised spirits being flushed out—and then the door lock would turn, and I would run away to pretend that I hadn't been listening, and she would enter, slowly, carefully.

At a point when the angry shouting in the apartment had long since grown from an oddity to a daily occurrence, I'd heard my father's voice in the other room. "For god's sake, speak English, woman," he had said.

She used to teach me some Korean at night. That was before the *speak English, woman* incident. After that, she stopped. No more teaching, no more singing. But she did keep up with the urgent murmuring each time before entering the apartment. All the way up until she left for good.

Later, after Iseul and her family pulled me from the youth shelter, I would learn that unspokens run the gamut on the scale of how-hard-to-come-by, from rent money (hard) to affairs (easy). Everything is pulled along in the slipstream of silence.

But science talks. Cells and molecules and atoms will talk as long as you know how to coax their stories out, and when they talk, there are no euphemisms, no pearly-white lies.

Why had no one told me? Why the silence?

I roll over onto my back because my side is losing sensation. When I close my eyes, against the blackness of my inner eyelids I visualize my biological mother and my biological father, both a chimera of human and sea slug parts, swirling around each other in midair in some damp Seoul alleyway smelling of stagnant water and *makgeolli* rice wine, their elbows scraping along the tight concrete walls. There is a tangle of telephone lines and electric cables hanging low above them like gritty urban mistletoe. There is a box somewhere in that darkness, the lid maybe left ajar by whoever put an infant inside, like a little surprised mouth, as though the box itself is bewildered at its unexpected fate as a bassinet.

The world is full of strange conglomerates, I think, as I look again at my glowing phone, at the solicited pie charts about my unsolicited DNA.

Unlike experiments involving genes in sea slugs in glassy tanks in the lab—which await me for a change of water tomorrow morning, the reminder alert pings on my phone—this is not a science. This is foreign terrain upon which I have already lost my footing and am scrabbling for purchase, slick like slug slime.

I lie in bed for a long time trying again to fill the ragged-edged hole in my head. Accessory stylets are merciless. I have a furious internal debate about whether I would rather be the horny sea slug stabber or the stabbee.

Also, that variant of mating in the animal kingdom is referred to as *traumatic mating*. Evidently popular enough among living organisms to warrant a name.

My blankets get uncomfortably hot and sweaty around four in the morning. I sit up. I reach for my laptop, hover my fingers above the keyboard. To track down the source of my dominantly inherited widow's peak allele, there is an answer somewhere with clean, sharp edges, à la sea slug accessory stylet. So I string together keywords: *Korean drop box baby find birth parents. Drop box baby birth record. Anonymous adoptee find birth parent.* Among the Internet pages that pour forth is the article about the family-tattoo-based reunion I read last week. New pages include an exposé of adoption agencies whose falsified documents erased babies' connections to living relatives; the webpage of an organization founded by a Korean adoptee whose mission is to make birth and adoption records more transparent; a blog post by an adoptee living in New York who, upon entering college, suddenly remembered his birth mother's face and then flew to Korea on a wild-goose chase to search for her . . .

Then there is an article about a baby who appeared in a drop box years ago—with a copy of her Korean birth registration. This folded square of paper, slipped away between blanket creases, whether by accident or by intention, followed the child to her adoption in America and was quietly filed alongside other paperwork—years later to be discovered by the now-adult adoptee, during a visit to her local vital records office for a copy of her marriage certificate.

I stare up at the ceiling. What a long shot it is—and yet, as I look up the address for the San Oligo office of vital records, I feel a giddy surge in my chest, in the curiosity that has been smoldering for the past week since officially learning I was a drop-box baby. I will visit tomorrow to shake out any scraps of information about my birth parents.

I close my laptop, scoot to the edge of my bed, draw back the curtains, and peer out at the motionless dark.

Back in my adoptive parents' apartment, when I woke up in the middle of the night, I peered out the window and watched for the stray tabby cat that liked to emerge from the thorny hedges around the base of the building. Every night, it crawled out and leapt onto one of the marble pedestals, and perched there, eyes glowing, tail twitching like dancing starlight, it kept moonlight vigil with me.

This was also how I sat for hours, that night I ended up at the youth shelter. History repeats itself. I look up at the skein of clouds around the moon, and in their washed-out color I see that one girl's gray eyes all over again. That little gray-eyed girl on the upper bunk of my bed at the shelter. I still think about what she told me that night. It's hard to shake it off, even all these years later—it's as though a part of me is still lost somewhere within those few minutes, and I don't think it is the kind of lost that is retrievable.

I look away. I think about all the factors that could possibly compel a mother to leave her child, draw up elaborate hypotheses for which I have no empirical evidence.

At four in the morning, the world is so still and quiet, dotted only by streetlights further below my apartment complex. It is an otherworldly time. At four in the morning, it is okay to just sit in bed with arms wrapped around folded knees and to look outside the window and say nothing and appreciate the quiet darkness. It is okay to wade into dream logic, where I can glimpse streaky dream-things in passing, idea trails that dip between science and irrational thought. I record these on a document on my laptop, in a secondary lab notebook that chronicles the observations of a moonlighting self who is just slightly more unhinged.

I don't tell Iseul this, but I don't mind insomnia.

There are things far worse than a present-day inability to sleep.

I think again about the upper-bunk girl from the youth shelter, what she told me that night washing over me again, and again, and again. I imagine her words crusted over my skin like sea salt.

Tonight, I write with fingers smeared with cheap chocolate.

DNA is overhyped. Turns out you can tweak bits of it and it will still work fine. Like K'NEX toys but for grown-ass scientists. Pluck out the pentagonal sugar and replace it with a hexagonal sugar. Shuffle around some oxygens and nitrogens, or nix them completely. Replace the chemical backbone with a different line-up. The poster child of genetics is not an untouchable. It's a Franken-molecule of disparate pieces that happened to come together and to function just well enough. Sometimes there is a limit to logic. Sometimes there is only how the molecular dice land on the prebiotic table.

Sometimes there is only how chance decides your DNA and how your life will play out.

2

WHEN I HEAD OUT to the bus stop in the watercolors of early morning light, it is already a day of November rain's sticky cling. In San Oligo, the summer-to-fall transition drags its heels all the way into Thanksgiving.

The humidity masks the nerve-induced moisture that gathers on my palms, at the thought of visiting the office of vital records later in the afternoon.

It's part of a past I wanted to cut cleanly away, a buried thing that might just crawl its way out of memory into present-day. I watch the warm rain bead on my pilled sweater. I talk only about the past that came afterwards. So when I call *Umma* and *Appa* and Ha-joon on the weekends—always a juggling act to find a time that works with the seventeen-hour time difference, ever since they moved to Korea four years ago—I talk about this rain a lot.

This kind of rain is a lie. Potato-chip-bag rain, Iseul and I have always called it: like the lie of chip bags, mostly empty air, it's a false promise of sweet relief, only briefly cool against the skin before becoming indistinguishable from sweat.

It's the kind of rain that stirs up memories.

Iseul's family took me in after I wound up at the shelter, at the start of fifth grade. Iseul and I had been best friends from first grade on, and I was so often at her house with her family that my adoption this time around felt only like a formality.

I wasn't at that shelter for long—only overnight. Sleepless, by the dim nightlight plugged into the outlet by the head of the bed, I had lain on my side staring at the lines and shapes printed on that thin fleece blanket. A bedspring was loose, so I used one wire end to carve those patterns onto the wall beside me until the sun rose, and Iseul and her parents showed up, and I waved bye to the little gray-eyed girl who'd been on the upper bunk of the bed, staring red-eyed at me, for whom I'd felt a little sorry realizing that I'd kept her up with all my scritch-scratching on the wall paint all night long.

The September rain was warm and wet, as the four of us hurried out to the sedan.

The same rain was falling my first *Chuseok* with the Yoon family that September, tapping at the glass like fantasy fairy fingers, saying, *Can you believe it? Can you believe your luck?* Korean Thanksgivings, I would learn after my first, are threaded with a hope for luck. Luck, like the symbolic pine tree upon whose needles the *songpyeon* rice cakes were steamed until the house smelled of sweet rice dough and sesame and the needles' aromatic volatile, terpene. Luck, like the pyramids of stacked fruit and like the flutters in my chest when a fifth chair appeared at the dinner table and never went away, when we decided that my unknown birthday would now be the day I officially became part of the family. Koreans have two birthdays: the day you are born, and Lunar New Year. *You're twelve years old in American years, and thirteen years old in Korean years,* Iseul said. *In February, the whole family will be one year older. All of us together!*

After that dinner, I stopped saying "*Umma* Yoon" and "*Appa* Yoon" and started saying "*Umma*" and "*Appa*."

When I feel this rain on my skin, I think of the years that followed—a time period cast in sepia overtones like warm nostalgia and like the vintage film reels that *Appa* liked to collect. The film reels were one of the first things I noticed upon arriving at their home—the shelf in the living room lined with old film reels and their canisters, a peculiarity amid the books that filled the other floor-to-ceiling shelves.

Their home was full of incongruities like that. They didn't hit me all at once. I noticed them bit by bit at sporadic moments—sometimes in the morning, when I would wake up not to the sound of shouting and blaming, but to silent sunlight filtering in through the fabric curtains beside my bed. Sometimes in the afternoon, when Iseul and I would come back after school and the whole house smelled like spices and chopped scallions and garlic, nothing like the empty odor of reheated takeout that seemed a permanent fixture of my old apartment. Or night times, which were full of family dinners where everyone sat together at the table and ate together and laughed and talked about their days and took second servings. Things that I had never seen before.

Or the time *Umma* and *Appa* were arguing. Iseul did not go to hide in her room the way my instincts urged me to. She said instead that *Umma* and *Appa* often got worried about her little brother, Ha-joon, who had recurrent melanoma, and they also worried about their immigrant status. She said big worries sometimes become loud. She said it wasn't something to be afraid of, and I noted that I couldn't hear anything smashing in the next room over. No one was throwing beer bottles or furniture around. Iseul kept prying at the cracked wainscoting panel beside us in the entryway—we were convinced it opened into a secret passageway. When I peeked into the next room over, eight-year-old Ha-joon was still in bed propped up with pillows against the headboard, flipping through the book that never left his side, a secondhand field guide to North American birds.

But the most foreign of all was the golden lens through which the family viewed the country. They came of their own free will from a small village in rural South Korea, traveling to a place that seemed so heavily ripe with liberties and romanticized hope and an egalitarian opportunity to righteously work your way into comfort with enough education and dedication. That was why *Appa* collected film reels, I learned. The film industry is iconic—Hollywood and Highway 1 are at the level of mythology back across the Pacific Ocean—and so the reels were *Appa's* metonym for the American Dream.

I, on the other hand, had ended up in the same country, from the same country, through no act of my own volition.

Once or twice in middle school and high school, I tried to sit down and think about it all. It was often during final exams period, and I thought I knew what I was doing, because school was easy: in school, to understand how everything learned slots together, you just looked over the entirety of the material and drew connections between all of the different points.

But unlike the ease with which I skimmed through my science courses, I found myself overwhelmed. I thought about the pictures of embryos I saw in library books and textbooks. A human starts out as a little ball of cells that keeps dividing over and over, and eventually each of those cells commits to a very specific fate. *Here now, you will become the eyes, and you will become the spinal cord, and you will become heart muscle.* It's a delicate balancing act, but there is randomness. What draws the exact line between two adjacent cells that become distinct is itself often not so distinct.

Who am I to have met such a turn of events, such a stroke of fortune? I thought.

And so I stopped dwelling on the past, stopped trying to make sense of everything, and I decided to live in the moment and try to find happiness in each of those sepia-toned movie stills, in the smell of pine needles and the self-made luck that *Appa* saw within the film reels. *Umma* and *Appa* taught me the Korean that had been so abruptly cut off in my old home, until I could speak a chimeric "Konglish." With Iseul and Ha-joon, it was always English, of course. I learned to spit out the seeds in Korean grapes, to peel a whole *chamoe* melon with the yellow skin in one long piece, to knock on watermelons with my knuckles and deduce which were the summer-sweetest.

Within that apartment, I found a way of life that seemed to fly back and forth across the Pacific.

"*Appa* likes this bird the most," Ha-joon said one night. He pushed his field guide across his blankets to Iseul and me, and pointed at an illustration of a flying white bird with long angular wings and a cap of black feathers.

Ha-joon is a bookworm. Because of his health condition, he couldn't run outside and look under mossy rocks and chase after fence lizards the way Iseul and I did, so books were his muddy running shoes instead. High-fantasy novels, science fiction, biographies, popular science books, textbooks, obscure encyclopedias, university digital archives—being the son of a mechanical engineering professor has its perks.

That night, Ha-joon tapped a finger on the white bird. "That's the Arctic Tern," he said. "Look, it says here it has the longest migration of any animal. Over its whole life, it flies a distance equal to the moon and back."

Like moonlight, my stroke of fortune was otherworldly.

But I can't forget the longing I saw in the eyes of the girl in the upper bunk, when Iseul's family—my family—came for me after my night in the shelter. Her eyes were gray, and they had moved quick, flitting between the wearable call buttons on both my wrist and Iseul's wrist. Iseul had brought them to school one day—*Umma* worked at a group home for schizophrenics, and Iseul had found a few lying around their car. *When you're in danger, you press it, and it alerts me,* she'd said. *If I press mine, it alerts you. Easy.* What had been our neat strategy for schoolyard games of hide-and-seek tag became my ticket into a new life.

I had pressed that button that night.

What luck.

★ ★ ★

As I step onto my bus, shedding raindrops like memories, Iseul calls.

I drop my tumbler of coffee from my mouth.

"He what?"

"He died. He passed away."

Iseul repeats the name, and it's my adoptive father's.

"My colleague showed me his draft about the circumstances surrounding his death. The police suspect foul play."

I blink. It's wrong, it all seems wrong. Not his death, but how I feel, it's this emptiness, I realize: to learn of the death of a parent and to feel no sadness, like opening a chip bag to find nothing inside, an assembly-line defect in a moment of expectation.

I'm distressed at the realization that I'm more worked up about not being worked up than I am about his death, and then I'm confused why I should even be upset at all.

"You said there was foul play involved?" I finally say.

"They suspect it. My colleague writing the article talked to the police and dug around and it turns out he owed money, big-time money, to some Korean lenders. Loan sharks, who followed him." Iseul pauses. "He died by—" She stops again, a litmus test for my emotional reaction.

"It's fine. Tell me."

Iseul clears her throat. "He died by drowning. They found his body along the Hattepaa River, with bruises and grip marks."

I find that any words I had wither away on my tongue. Funny, how even in death he continues to steal words away from people's mouths.

He was not a parent to me. And I realize that I'm less empty than I'd thought: that heat in my head that I'd attributed to the muggy weather is actually twisted gratification. *He had it coming.*

What comes out is carefully modulated: "That's quite a story for your colleague to write on. That must be a lot of work for him."

"He interviewed his wife, too." Iseul says, gently, "You want to know what she said?"

I hesitate.

The names of my adoptive parents are so unfamiliar as I mouth them soundlessly—a consequence of having known them only through observation rather than interaction. The time we had spent in the same physical space was sparse and threadbare, and so were any conversations following the end of fourth grade. After becoming friends with Iseul early in elementary school— the two oddball children who preferred to sit in the dirt a ways from the playground writing fantasy stories and making magical wreaths out of the tall grass—I was most often at her home or at the library after school. These were the places where the learning happened, where I learned Korean beyond what my adoptive mother would teach, learned about plants and animals and the chemicals of life beyond what I learned in school.

She was always hoping, my mother. She tied herself to loose hopes and to superstitions the way she used to string red chilies onto cotton threads and hang them around the apartment. To ward off bad spirits, she'd said. My adoptive father used to call it "cute," this outdated Korean superstition that his wife had somehow picked up, but then once the lenders started demanding payments and his phone began to light up with messages from mystery faceless Natasha, he called them "stupid." Stop this nonsense, he would say. For a while, my mother left them up. *To ward off bad spirits,* she said to me, more firmly than before. Then when my father started his habit of throwing things, she took them all down.

Sometimes, when it was just me and her, she would say, "With enough hope, things will change."

I never knew if she was talking to me or to herself. Maybe it was to fill the still air between us.

When my father developed a drinking problem, she said to the air, "Things will change."

When he was laid off work and started throwing pens and then bottles and then one bad night, the coffee table, she said to the air, "Things will change."

When she too found that alcohol could be anesthesia, she said to the air, blurrily, "Things will change."

She always said that, with her heavy accent.

"Things will change, won't they, Abby? If we just hope enough, everything will change for the better."

So we waited.

But they never did.

My father was still yelling, blaming, throwing things. Words and other things were often in the air. Our apartment was zero-gravity.

He never threw anything at me or my mother, but we all knew it was only a matter of time before the dents in the plaster walls weren't showing up in just the walls anymore. Only a matter of time before all his *vitriol* began to bite like the sulfuric acid the word also refers to. Wordlessly, my mother and I wondered when the dents would appear in our pale skin.

I saw her smile once. My mother, changed out of her nurse scrubs and, wearing all-white pajamas and smelling of wine, gave me a wobbly smile when I walked into the kitchen to make myself a sandwich for dinner. She was sitting at the kitchen table. She was alone underneath the single hanging light bulb, hands clasped, chin resting on top of her knuckles. I was so startled by the cheerless smile on her face, a frightening incongruity, that I barely processed the half-English half-Korean words that left her mouth: "They say that it's the bride who smiles on her wedding day who suffers hardships the rest of her life." She spread her hands out beside her paradox-smile in self-referential peekaboo position, her hands flat on an imaginary glass wall like a pantomimist, and in that moment I was so certain that there really was a glass wall that had always divided her from me—*that* was why she could never tell me what was really happening and why I could never understand her, and come to think of it, perhaps there was also a glass wall separating me from my father, many glass walls separating all of us from each other. I was so sure that these layers and layers of glass were real that I wondered why I could so clearly hear the sound of her quiet crying through it all.

Vitriol: a word derived from the Latin for "glass."

And then one day, she left. After all of that feverish hoping that some magnanimous invisible hand would save us from the whole predicament, some spectacular deus ex machina, she never came back.

She never really did anything other than hoping, murmuring to herself outside of the door before entering. Passivity is a straitjacket. Because of her, I know what desperation is.

I never want to be in a state of desperation. I never want to be called desperate, nor thought of as desperate. I will never allow myself to be in that position.

This has become manifesto, and I can't decide how to feel about it, this piece of my adoptive mother still lodged in me, embedded so deep that it has become part of my identity. Even as my lot in life changed from my first adoptive parents to the Yoons, to *Umma* and *Appa,* even as I learned to love, as I felt for the first time that special kind of sadness that can only be borne from love—when Ha-joon grew ill, when the family moved away—I still think about this.

I'll admit it: it hurt, that my first adoptive mother left without me, without saying anything to me. It's the kind of hurt that easily pierces through eleven years' time, and I still long for a sign that she'd cared, that she thought of me as she left. And so Iseul's news of her present-day silence last week— salt into an ever-open wound.

★ ★ ★

Iseul repeats her question. "You want to know what she said?"

"Sure," I say, and I'm not being honest.

Iseul tells me that my adoptive mother is still working as a nurse, but not in San Oligo. She's at a hospital in Irvine. She said many times in her interview that her husband was violent. She feared for her life. She has a lot of regrets. She still hopes for her future. None of this stirs anything up in me. A hearse of dead memories just passing by. But there's one stone that catches its wheels, even as I tell myself that I have no obligation to concern myself.

"Did she mention me?"

Against my will, my heart is fluttering. I repeat my question, and Iseul's silence tells me the answer.

I figured as much. I figured as much, but even so, I'm embarrassed to feel the cinching of bitterness. Ersatz emotion, I quickly label it, discard it, what a waste of a heart's precious finite space. I have no concern for this person who discarded me—me that she sloughed off her hands into a youth shelter. In my mind's eye, she was tearless.

Iseul says gently that she thought I should know what happened. I agree. I take a sip of my scalding-hot coffee, but I don't feel its burn over the sudden resurgence of past memories— drop-box, adoptive parents, youth shelter—that is already searing its force-fed way down my throat.

★   ★   ★

I mostly think of that night at the youth shelter as a formative experience in my scientific career. I think of the geometric-patterned fleece blanket I curled under that single night. In seventh-grade science class, I would recognize the geometric patterns from the blanket that I had traced on the wall to comfort myself. They were molecules. Hexagons and pentagons and zigzag lines. I was twelve years old when molecules first began to mean something to me. Since then, molecules have become my career.

I am an origins-of-life scientist.

At San Oligo's biggest research university, I work on the chemical oddities within a bacterium that lives within a sea slug, which have connections to the origins of complex life on Earth. That's what I tell any nonscience person when they ask. Go any further and eyes glaze over and expressions grow slack. I tell people that I work with rare sea slugs from the Great Salt

Lake and the bacteria within them that help them survive. Can you believe that answers to how life began are locked away inside of bacteria locked away inside of sea slugs? That seems to intrigue people just enough to say, *Oh that's nice*, but not so much that they go asking for details and find themselves in the awkward situation of trying to pry themselves out of a science lecture.

So, some personal histories are like long-winded narrations about science—a lot of the time, you really don't want to know too much. There lies the commonality between the origins of cells on Earth and the little calamities that add up all cell-like into a person. It's all a nesting-doll set-up. In my sea slugs, within their own cells, there are little bacteria, and in these little bacteria, there are special Houdini-like RNA molecules. These can't sit still, they are proactive and bullheaded, they move as they wish.

The molecules are a reflection of a possible past.

The molecules are from a place where poison begets life.

The bus trundles to a stop. I hurry umbrellaless to the biosciences building, a stained concrete block half-buried in the grass lawn like a gray tooth. There is a fine line, I think, between brutalist architecture and nuclear bunkers. Next fall, the entire department is relocating to the shiny new building across the street, mauve brick layered high with aluminum and glass and stratosphere, christened with the name of an old-money alum nobody cared about until he whipped out some tax-deductible millions from his rear pocket.

But if all goes as planned, I will be long gone and settled in a different university by then, pursuing a PhD because I haven't quite had my fill of science yet. With the money I am making by continuing as a tech in the lab post-graduation, I will be able to travel somewhere else.

When I told Iseul the winter of undergrad junior year that I wanted to keep doing science through a PhD, the next day she gave me a store-bought sympathy card. The gilt script "With deepest sympathy for your loss" was left untouched, but she had scrawled "of sleep, free time, and peace of mind" underneath in ballpoint pen.

"A couple years later, we'll see if it's as much of a joke as it is now," I'd said.

"It's going to be prophetic." Iseul had laughed. "You're already a lab rat as it is."

The blast of air conditioning as I push past the lab doors is icy against my rain-filmed skin. Nadia, a fifth-year student in my lab who is somehow juggling her final year of experiments and a one-year-old daughter, is whistling as she wheels a cart loaded with flasks out of my lab's hallway and into the next. She gives me a friendly wave.

"Good morning to the Mother of Salt Slugs!" she says. We call my little invertebrates "salt slugs," because they are from the Great Salt Lake and are not technically sea slugs, although closely related.

My lab moniker resurrects last night's mental amphitheater filled with images of mating sea slugs in Seoul alleyways. I try to block it out as she tells me that my slugs were looking chipper just half an hour ago when she walked by.

Nadia is extremely protective of the salt slugs. She doesn't even work with them—I'm the only one—but she keeps a hovering eye on them like they are her adopted invertebrate children. Once she told me she was worried about them because they were looking pale and moving sluggishly. When I told her that sluggishly is how they're supposed to move by definition, she gave me the cold shoulder for the rest of the day.

It must be her new-mother instinct, I think. Nadia's got so much oxytocin coursing through her veins that it spills over from her one-year-old child onto everyone in the lab, slugs included. But then again, I am no expert on motherhood—on either the receiving or the giving end.

Once I get the salt slugs to breed successfully, Nadia will have grandchildren, too. "Such beautiful creatures," she'll say every day, vowels stretched long with affection.

And no one would disagree with her. The thumb-sized creatures are a muted green with white speckles, like honeydew melons with seeds, and they pale into cream along their bellies and darken into rust-red on the winglike curls along their sloped backs. The *Siphopteron* salt slugs look nothing like garden slugs. When they move, layered membrane ribbons rippling, they look like the littlest flamenco dancers.

I hurry down the hallway and card myself into the lab. The air smells faintly of bacterial cultures, the *Pseudomonas* like corn tortillas, and—because the autoclave around the corner is being finicky and pumping out angry ringlets of steam—vaguely like rice cookers. There is a comfort within these smells and sounds, within the familiarity. In the background, the fridges and chemical hood and sonicator buzzing at each other, LCMS machine click-clicking away, low purr of serological pipettes sucking up pink media, that one section of vinyl floorboard squealing underfoot.

In the corner with the aquarium tanks, Texan Simon, whose glasses wear his narrow face more than he wears them, sees me approaching and points at a salt slug floating limply in the tank nearest to me. It must have died between now and Nadia's watchful gaze half an hour ago.

"It's dead," he says.

This is his morning greeting. It's not atypical.

"Yes, I can see that," I tell him.

There are two Simons, one from Texas and another from Manchester in England. So we differentiate between them as Texan Simon and British Simon. I suppose we could have gone with Grad Student Simon and Postdoc Simon, but that would have been less illustrative of the stereotypes they occasionally embody. Sometimes we call them L and D enantiomers— Simon Liu and Simon Dawkins.

Nobody else in the lab has a name-duplicate. There are six of us total, plus the Very Famous PI, the head honcho who is currently away at a Very Important Conference. In addition to Nadia and both Simons, there's Tomás the lab manager and there's Petra, a postdoc who has been here for four years now and is in the process of applying for faculty positions at other universities. When I first joined the lab two years ago, I was convinced that Petra was an Amazonian woman reborn into the modern era, probably wearing a lab coat as she came out of the womb.

On my second day, Petra showed me where all of the reagents and equipment were located. Her impatience was as clear as the glass graduated cylinder she was holding—she was in between back-to-back experiments.

"That's where all the reusables and glassware are, and then we keep disposables over here. Easy enough. Come on." She strode to the side of the lab with the wall of shelves and boxes. "Some are in the unopened boxes on the floor here, and—"

She pushed aside some cardboard boxes, and something thin and black moved out into view on the floor.

"—behind these boxes—oh." She paused. She pushed her horn-rimmed glasses up the bridge of her nose, and with her graduated cylinder, slapped aside what I had just realized was a snake. It slammed into the wall.

"—and that's where the glycerol stock tubes are," she finished, pointing at the boxes just behind where the dazed snake had been seconds ago. She turned her gaze to me. "Got it?"

That was the first time I had ever seen someone use a graduated cylinder as a weapon. I will never forget the resonant *bonk* reverberating along the length of the tube. After we called animal control, the snake turned out to be a harmless garter snake on the loose from a lab further down the hall, but even so—it's not every person who slaps aside snakes and continues unfazed with their business. The episode is illustrative of Petra. You try to disagree with her, you get a slap. Usually verbal, but no one doubts her ability to make it physical if pressed. This is especially true if you have disagreed with her science. She is one of those people who have so interwoven their research and their sense of identity into one that it's all become a fine, inextricable meshwork. Try to peel one from the other, and it gets bloody.

I stop to wonder if this also applies to me.

There is a shuffling sound. Just outside the propped door is Kwan-sik, the third floor's janitor, all silent heavily hooded eyes and deeply creased face. She is staring in at us but does not speak nor acknowledge us in any other way as she pushes a mop along. I know her name because I once found her ID card fallen on the ground and returned it to her, but she has never spoken to any of us. I often see her bird-like frame moving through the building, and we have even stood in the glass-walled elevator together, but never once have we talked. She carries an immigrant's stoic melancholy.

Sometimes when I see her, an urge rises to ask her what would compel a woman to discard her baby, and what would compel another woman a few years later to do it again. It clambers up my throat. Maybe it's because she's old. Maybe it's because she's also Korean. Maybe—and I think of the office of vital records that awaits me after the lab today—it's because I sometimes feel that her silence and outward equanimity are more fragile than they appear, that the right prod would make it all collapse because I know from firsthand experience that such unsettled states never last.

Texan Simon waves a hand in my face. He points at the dead salt slug. "I'd get rid of it before Nadia comes back."

I look down at the floating slug corpse. With a mesh net, I scoop it out, toss it unceremoniously into the red biohazard bin, and unwrap a new tank filter to install for better luck.

The field of *origins of life* research is not so replete with all of the sparks glittering vitality that the name would suggest. In practice, death is an uncompromising mirror presence.

You could call origins-of-life research an elegiac science: we spin yarns and in circles around what's past.

Life on Earth did not burst into existence like the snap of fingers. It took its time through a slow and convoluted path of chemical evolution.

To make the molecules of life, you need some simple compounds: the likes of hydrogen, methane, ammonia, formaldehyde, hydrogen sulfide, hydrogen cyanide. You need a treacherous source of energy: ultraviolet radiation from the Sun, or lightning, or heat from volcanoes—perhaps news about baby drop boxes would suffice in a pinch. You need patience: the kind that can sit through eons of atoms wandering along chemical reaction roads, missing exits and making U-turns.

Rattle up the atoms, wake them from their slumber.

3

AFTER FINISHING UP MY experiments, I take the train to the office of vital records. The train is oddly full despite being before rush hour, and the whole ride I sit pressed between a dozing man whose unattended suitcase keeps rolling over my feet and an old woman who sighs and unsticks her thighs from her seat every ten minutes. The air conditioning has broken down and the heat is like molasses.

The best thing about looking permanently waiflike and wan no matter how much you eat or what clothes you wear is that people underestimate you. You relish all of the dark horse moments. The worst thing is that people think you take up less space than you like to have and public transportation is a matter of folding yourself up like origami.

The station closest to the office of vital records is a half-hour's ride away. I read on my phone that the original birth certificate should have the names of both of the birth parents. Or, if the father declined, then the mother at least. Soon I am feeling queasy, and I'm not sure if it's because of becoming carsick. When the train grinds to a stop at my station, it's been over an hour of alternating between anxiously perusing .gov and .org websites and watching sweat bead and roll on the sleeping man's brow. I too would have sighed and unstuck my legs from my seat had it not been for my long pants—the perks of lab safety attire.

From the train station, I cross a few sun-scorched blocks over to the office of vital records. The doors scrape along the floor when I push them open. This is the noise that I imagine bone on bone must sound like.

A clerk with droopy eyes looks up at me.

"Hi, I called earlier," I say. "I'd like to request a copy of my original birth certificate."

"Sure thing. Name?"

I open my mouth, but then hesitate.

"The one on my amended birth certificate?" I ask. Then I realize this is a dumb question. I don't have the faintest inkling of what my birth parents originally named me—if they had even named me anything.

The clerk nods.

"Abigail Rodier," I say.

He clacks on his keyboard a bit. He shakes his head. "Sorry."

"Sorry?" I repeat, stomach wilting.

He shakes his head again.

I pretend not to see the gesture. I pull up my DNA test on my phone, push it along the granite tabletop to the clerk who stares at it with a bemused blankness.

"I also have my amended birth certificate." I reach for my bag. "The one with my adoptive parents' names on it. That should help, right?"

He shakes his head. His droopy eyes look like unwatered plants. "There's no record. Sorry."

I stop ruffling through my bag for my papers. My palms are slick.

The clerk gives me a practiced look of sympathy.

"Some parents just forget," he says.

"Some might do it on purpose," I say. He immediately looks uncomfortable.

He fidgets. "I suppose so."

★   ★   ★

I take a roundabout route back home and pass through the business district. Wandering through unfamiliar paths seems to spark new ideas and solutions, I have found, when in a rut with my research, on walks through the arboretum north of campus.

The business district is utterly alien, a man-made complexity that outpaces any artificial aquarium ecosystem that I try to reconstitute in the lab. Everything in the city and in my head is thick and heavy. The city in heated nightfall is sticky-slow underneath orange sky and neon gas and glitzy billboards. It's the time of year when smog and sweat pool in clavicles. Women in tailored business gray clicking down to bus stops, daubing their brows. Men loosening their ties as they step out of glassy sky-high complexes. Girls with gold on the lids of their eyes, faces the color of pop art, high-heeled steps down the grimy sidewalks like strutting cassowaries. Cafés wafting fluorescent lights and the smell of all-day egg sandwiches. Somebody quiet sitting on the pavement.

Cities, aquariums, families. How hard it is to build any ecosystem from scratch. Harder still to understand it, once all the building is done. The origins are never clear.

I think back to over a decade ago, before my tree roots became so securely cemented in the Yoons, when I was terrified that they, like those who came before them, would kick me out.

At first, *Appa* had reservations about my joining the family. He tried to hide that from me, but I'd arrived trained in the fine art of eavesdropping on the inner dialogue leakage of parental figures. I overheard his quiet concerns to *Umma*. After dinner, after Iseul, Ha-joon, and I were sent to bed: Can we really raise another child? When we have Ha-joon's medical bills to pay? *Umma* shushed him, said, you're going to send away a girl like Abby? Where on earth would she even go, huh? I couldn't bring myself to do that. I couldn't. You know that.

Still, I was afraid of *Appa*.

When I stumbled upon various diagrams of egg-like shapes in one of *Appa's* many notebooks, some round, some oblong, some tapered, and stared at the numbers and foreign mathematical symbols curling across the page, scribbled out in places, accented by flocks of aggressive question marks drawn with a pen pressed hard into the paper, I knew he was in a bind. Having a *real* egg in those shapes would surely help.

This was how I found myself scrambling through the mangrove forests north of the apartment in the middle of a rainstorm. Three days before, I'd asked Ha-joon what kind of bird lays eggs the size and shape I'd seen in one highlighted corner of the notebook. He'd consulted his field guide, told me about a species of cuckoo, showed me a picture of its tapered blue egg, pointed at the fun-fact text inset that described it as the "rain crow" for its tendency to vocalize at the sound of thunder, and before Ha-joon could ask why, I'd slipped away.

I splashed between trees, listening, chasing after the raincrow cuckoo's puttering croak of a call, scrambling up rainslicked branches, teetering, sifting through swaths of leaves with shaking fingers. I only stopped trying to hold my breath once I found it: a sole pale blue-green egg, striking in contrast against the four smaller brown eggs tucked in that same nest. I scooped it out—thinking, where are the parents?—and began my descent when the branch under my feet snapped. With the precious cargo in my hands I couldn't grab the branch above my head and in heartbeats I was airborne, untethered, and then my legs hooked around a lower bough and sent me swinging upside-down by the crooks of my knees—that rough bark peeled my skin all the way to my heart—and hanging there, I closed my eyes and cradled the cuckoo egg against my chest.

Twenty minutes later I was back at the apartment soaked, shivering, bleeding, tracking mud, and I held the egg out toward a wide-eyed *Appa* sitting at his desk. He stared. I told him I saw his egg drawings. I watched him carefully as he ran a hand through his gray hair. The shock on his face was replaced with an undeniable amusement, as he shook his head and lifted the egg from my hands. He told me not to disrupt nature like that again. I told him it was a cuckoo's egg, it doesn't even belong in that other bird's nest. He gave me a funny look, at that. But even as he lectured me there was a softness in his face, indistinct but palpable, like an undercurrent, and I finally let down my guard.

I asked him, "But why do you care so much about bird eggs?"

So, to learn *Appa's* scientist origin story, it took a rainstorm, a cuckoo egg, and an incident with a falling tree branch. I still think about it often, hold it up against my own scientist origin story, turning both this way and that, as though there lay the clues as to how two very different people can be brought together into one family.

High-school-aged *Appa* had performed well enough on his entrance exams in Korea to be placed into an engineering program, to the bewilderment of his persimmon-farmer parents. It was that persimmon-farming that was the seed to their son's interest in science: the biology of why the white flowers of a female tree must sometimes be hand-pollinated with a paintbrush touched to the pink flowers of a male tree. The chemistry of why unripe persimmons placed inside a cardboard box will ripen faster—the ethylene gas they release and share. The mechanics of why the skin of a persimmon wrinkles when dried—the inside of a drying fruit loses more volume than the tougher skin, which then buckles and puckers inward and outward. In grad school, he developed an interest in architectural and engineering designs based on the curvature of eggs, those little epicenters of life.

Only later that night, tucked into a bed that felt even warmer than before, would I realize the irony of what I had said about the cuckoo's egg.

As a fact, *Appa* did not speak much, unlike *Umma* or Iseul. But things became different when he taught me about nature. By talking about nature, he would soon talk about other things. The way the October persimmon trees arced toward the earth with their ripe fruit, the way the bright-eyed starlings flew down after harvests to eat the fallen leftovers, which were the same fallen persimmons that he once caught nine-year-old *Umma* sneaking off with, that first time they met as children.

I felt the same warmth the times I woke in the middle of the night, when they sat together in the dim living room, sharing wine, unknowing that I was awake and eavesdropping on their conversations about their children—Iseul, Ha-joon, *and Abby*—with such a soft and full tenderness that I could almost taste the plump and juicy dried persimmon flavor of it in the air, that I knew that I was welcome here. On nights that sleep evaded me, I pretended to be fast asleep because I knew *Umma* would soon come into each of our rooms, still wearing her floral-print apron, and kiss us on our foreheads. I never grew tired of hearing her murmur "we love you" in that nighttime hush, and a glow seeped into my body like fireplace warmth and made my heart flutter so wildly that I wished I could protect it in that state with more than my ribcage.

I jolt out of my reverie at the hot squeal of tires as a nearby cab floors the breaks. Up ahead, a few pedestrians hurry to make the light. I steady myself against a streetlamp.

It takes another few seconds for me to register that my phone is vibrating. I fish it out.

"Hey Abby, can I ask a favor," Iseul starts saying, and then behind me there is loud tire friction on asphalt again. "Hey, where are you?"

"Out and about trying to get my birth certificate," I say. "With no luck."

I am passing by a botanica, and a smell like menthol and chamomile slips through the metal shutters that the shopkeeper is pulling closed over his storefront. It makes me woozier than I already am.

"Can I call you back?" I say. "I'll tell you more later."

The way that the smells slips out from between the steel slats reminds me that the barriers I and others put up around ourselves are also not impermeable.

"Make it back in one piece, yeah?"

"Yeah."

"Call me if anything happens. My phone's unmuted right next to me. I'm just editing my pitch to my editor. The one on the big pharma scandal with sea slug–derived chemotherapeutics. The one that made you spew half-chewed rice and curry from the couch to the other side of my apartment." She pauses. "We're both stuck on sea slugs, huh." I can hear her typing away. "Just write, and don't forget to cite as you go, I suppose."

Half a block ahead, a woman with a shock of gray hair hobbles out of a grocery laden with full bags. She stumbles on the curb to cross the street and autumn plums tumble from her bags to the hot concrete.

"Your carpet will never forget," I say to Iseul. I put my phone away.

I'm hurrying forward but someone closer has already stepped in, a taller figure in black who leans down and collects all of the scattered plums. He puts them back in the woman's bags, carries them for her, and they move together across the street.

I can hear the woman's words when I catch up to their slow pace.

"Thank you again, dear, thank you. It's not much farther, just across the street, the apartment above the pawn shop."

In this sweet little moment, a knot inside me tightens. *Not a plum is discarded*, I think. As I move past them, I find myself thinking, *If a plum is so valuable so as not to be discarded, then what is a baby to its parents?*

I feel queasy. I walk quickly.

But I always walk quickly. The faster forward the better.

★　★　★

I forget what a disaster my apartment is until I trip on something with painful inertia on my way in. When I flip on the lights, sitting there is the unopened air purifier that Iseul had insisted I purchase. I had forgotten that I dumped it by the door to deal with later.

Iseul had insisted many times. "Your apartment has zero ventilation, you never open your windows, and you're basically breathing inside a coffin."

"Yeah, and turns out miasma theory is correct."

"That's right, and your level of hygiene is only marginally better than Middle Age standards anyways."

And so I had become the unwilling owner of a fancy new air purifier.

Among other things I had also forgotten to deal with: mugs with coffee trails down the sides, pans encrusted in fried egg bits, books and papers strewn across the floor like an academic's rendition of a Jackson Pollock painting.

I pick my way gingerly across the floor to my bedroom, around the overspill of laundry that has ambitions beyond its hamper and is encroaching on the carpet, which I'll have to deal with soon at the risk of needing to borrow clothes from Iseul.

I text Iseul: *back. in one piece as always.*

Her response comes quickly: *one big piece of work*

It's in moments like these that I wonder where I would be if the Yoon family hadn't adopted me, all those years ago, after my first adoptive mother left for good, after the night at the youth shelter. Perhaps still in that shelter, still tracing outlines of chemical structures onto cracking wall paint, still talking to the gray-eyed upper-bunk girl. It is a strange feeling, what rises up in me each time I wonder. Some things cannot be articulated in words.

Umma still sends me parcels of homemade kimchi and *doenjang* every winter.

"Don't thank me, it's nothing," she says when I call her on weekends as I open her meticulously taped brown packages. "It's because you're terrible at taking care of yourself. Feed yourself well, okay? Even when you're busy, don't ever forget to take care of yourself, Abby-*ya*."

"Don't worry," I always say.

This past weekend, *Umma* held the phone off to the side, and I heard *Appa* in the background, and then *Umma* laughing as she brought the phone back.

"Your *appa* says this family wouldn't be the same if we weren't always worrying about you. I suppose it's true. From middle school, when you forgot to eat your lunch because you were too busy digging in the playground mud looking for earthworms, or high school when you were too busy doing extra science experiments with that nice teacher you had, all the way to now. You've never changed."

Even with the drop-box baby news hanging over my head, it was hard not to smile. "Ah, well, I keep you on your toes."

"Here, your *Appa* wants to say something before he leaves for work." A crackle of static as the phone was passed.

"Abby." *Appa*'s baritone voice. "Are you sleeping better?"

"It's better," I said. I am terrible at lying. I ignored thoughts of sleepless nights as I turned the image of drop boxes over and over and over in my mind like infinitesimal paper folds. I changed the topic, asked about Ha-joon. *Appa* said the new medicines were helping, but bad-stomach days were still all too frequent. He cleared his throat—he now had to leave to speak at a conference, but I should keep up with the better sleeping. I told him I would.

He always has to end calls with a lecture of some sort. It's the professor in him. It's his way of saying "I love you."

He passed the phone back to *Umma*.

"Love you," she said.

"Love you," I said.

I didn't end up telling them about the drop-box news.

But Iseul knows everything, of course. I made her promise to keep quiet.

"Both the drop-box baby info and my birth parents search are only between us," I said.

Every time I try to pick up the phone and tell *Umma* and *Appa,* my fingers freeze. I fixate on a newfound conviction that digging into the past will sever my ties with the present, and I can't override the cold fear. I wouldn't want them to know, I am convinced.

So much for thinking present and forward.

★   ★   ★

I'm at my computer before bed, crunching experimental data from earlier in the day, when Iseul calls again.

"About that favor I mentioned earlier," she says. "You're not running late-night experiments this week, are you? Can you come with me to the night market downtown Friday night?"

She sounds strange, almost warbled like she's nervous. It must be an artifact of blips in the phone connection.

"Sure," I say. I scroll through microscopy images of my salt slug cells. "Look at you, stopping me from holing up in the lab." To my amusement, if I squint at the arrangement of packed cells in the left corner, it almost looks like the Dropbox company logo. How timely and apt that my science mirrors my life.

"I'll pick you up at 11:30 Friday," Iseul says.

Again, that apprehensive murmur in her voice. She must be stressed out about work. Who is she to always nag me about overworking myself, I muse. "Yes, ma'am."

"Don't bring your wallet."

"Don't bring my wallet? But I don't eat night-market food with my eyes."

"It's a quick work thing. Wear something warm, too. We might be waiting for a little while."

This time, the edge of nervousness in her voice is as stark as a purple plum against gray concrete.

But I don't think too much of it. I'm preoccupied thinking about drop boxes again.

I DON'T HAVE MUCH time to dwell on Iseul's erratic behavior anyway.

My shipment of new salt slugs finally arrives in lab. I look at the things, swirling around delicately in seawater inside of their triple-layered plastic bags, as I carefully lift the bags out of the padded cardboard box. "Okay, you guys. It's time to get busy," I say to them. "Even my birth parents did it, and they didn't even want me."

The department facilities guy who delivered the box turns around by the door and looks at me.

I look back at him. I shrug. "It's their biological imperative." I open one bag and scoop out two salt slugs and push them into an aquarium quadrant. "All animals live to have babies and eat or be eaten."

And yet, here I am, still dealing with a metric fuckton's worth of unfuckable sea slugs. Stubborn, intractable, elusive, frustrating, the creatures are perhaps not so different from their wrangler. I transfer the rest into my freshly cleaned aquarium tanks.

The salt slugs are from the Great Salt Lake. Even in a lake full of salt and arsenic, things can still thrive. Their entire biology is based on *using* arsenic: the little microbes within the slugs' cells use arsenic for energy production, to make the energy-currency molecule ATP, and they also incorporate the poison into the lipid membranes that form their very cells. Arsenic infiltrating DNA molecules is how people die from arsenic poisoning, but the microbes are unfazed and their DNA happily incorporates the poison. This lab's success is built on microbes talented at playing with poison.

The slugs and I, we're both misfits. Before I stumbled through the drop-box news and then the office of vital records, I never tried to remember what came before the Yoon family. Misfits try not to remember their misfit days—the reason why people try to forget their gangly high school years.

It's a twist of fate, then, that both in and out of the lab I am now on a hunt for what came even deeper in the past.

Inside of the lab, I am trying to understand how a bacterium came to live inside of sea slug cells—what are the molecules of life that drive this Matryoshka doll set-up of cells? Like the origins of the mitochondria, inside of our own cells. It is an origins-of-life archaeological dig.

Outside of the lab, I am trying to find my own origins.

It's a bunch of prehistory, what I've become wrapped up in.

My head hurts as I think about it all. There's not enough crawl space in there for me to go searching and ruminating. I lean against the lab benchtop. I feel a sudden urge to scour my skin, to free it from a sudden sensation of unseen grime, and then decide to go splash some cold water on my face. I drape my lab coat on the backrest of my chair and slog past Texan Simon, who is dancing in place in front of the spectrophotometer as his earbuds audibly blast rock music into his skull, and then past Petra, who is muttering over papers at her desk.

Last night I read that birth registration laws vary widely country to country. South Korea, for one, simply asks its citizens to register the birth of a newborn—but if the parent forgets or, more important, intentionally neglects to do it, then there is no trace. Then you have a child in limbo. I glance at my reflection in the women's bathroom mirror of my lab's floor, which is flecked with evaporated hard water spots like the sparse freckles on my cheeks. I have always thought that I look like a bookworm reincarnated as a human being, still a little crumpled from all the time spent stuck between pages, some bony edges not quite unfolded or filled out. Tired eyes. I look away as I rinse my hands.

I once read somewhere that staring long into another person's eyes can trigger an altered state of consciousness. Dissociation from reality, hallucinating other people's faces, often faces of those close to them, sometimes their own faces, these were common experiences that the study participants reported after staring into each other's eyes for ten minutes or longer.

People often hallucinate the faces of their blood relatives, except they are fun-house-distorted all monster-like.

I am not afraid of many things, but I avoid looking at mirrors.

Even more than seeing gnarled caricatures of people I can't recognize, I can't bear the thought of seeing *nothing*. A cold emptiness where something, someone, should have been.

Last night I'd also read that the births of a quarter of children younger than five worldwide are not registered. All are children whose existences are unofficial—separated from legal protection by the negative space that a paper or electronic form should have filled.

★   ★   ★

I return to the lab and carry my microscope slides into the special darkroom, where I settle them gently onto the microscope platform.

A fact about negative space: it can be made by mirrors in science, too.

There is a type of microscope that allows scientists to see molecules inside of cells, by lighting them up in fluorescent colors. This is called a confocal microscope, and I use it often to peek at the whereabouts of RNA inside of my salt slugs' microbes. It uses a special mirror to filter colors, sifting out the ones you don't want into blackness. You see only what you want to see.

I look into the eyepiece, and it's as though each cell has swallowed the cosmos. It's all DAPI-blue nebulas, and when I switch the filter and the brief dark is filled with yellow constellations, I think that a Lilliputian from *Gulliver's Travels* must have wandered through and spilled a handful of stars.

In this field of yellow dots, there's no difference between cells, space, and pointillist art.

Each dot marks a place where a messenger RNA is born. It moves on, it is tweaked and snipped and adorned with chemical baubles, it gives rise to protein progeny, it dies of old age— in the company of proteinaceous companions that were once written into these genetic ribbons themselves.

But RNA can do much more. Some are in the business of molecular magic tricks, cutting themselves free Houdiniesque and jumping to new locales. Some finesse energetics, sweet-talking atoms into finicky chemistry. Some are missionaries sent to the extracellular beyond. Some recruit proteins by atomic siren songs. Some are contortionists. Some glow.

I switch the microscope filter again, and the cherry-red spots that light up mark my bacteria's Houdini RNA.

When I do stop to think about it, it is stunning that I can see all of this with mirrors and a little trickery of light. The origins of life are hidden within a slippery kind of luminosity.

Here, negative space is something beautiful.

When I look into microscopes, I think of negative space, and I imagine the kaleidoscopic multitudes within.

EVERY SCIENTIST HAS AN origin story. Some are tender, like *Appa's*, or stories I've read about Nobel Laureates who started off playing with toy chemistry kits in the furnished basements of their childhood homes. For Texan Simon, his parents were both engineer immigrants from Taiwan who encouraged him to play with numbers early on. Petra grew up in rural Louisiana, went to college because she wanted to set a good example for her younger siblings, and then fell in love with a physics class halfway through. Nadia left Honduras as soon as she turned eighteen and worked her way toward scholarships and fellowships for undergrad and grad school. When I asked Tomás for his, he snorted and said he's so old that it doesn't matter anymore, even if he did remember.

My own scientist origin story emerged out of things like unwanted widow's peaks and tubes of spit and blankets from youth shelters.

Middle school was when I decided that I was going to be a scientist. *When I grow up,* child me wrote onto the slip of paper that the homeroom teacher handed out to each student, *I am going to be a scientist. I am going to discover everything there is to discover about life. As a scientist, I will find out things that people will not tell me.* That was the first time I put those thoughts onto paper. As I dropped the paper slip into the box at the front of the room, the sheen of graphite on the pinky side of my writing hand, it felt heavy. That slip of paper had the weight of a blood oath.

Like all other inquisitive children, I'd wanted answers. But when I said this out loud to Iseul once, she responded, "Yes, but there's a different kind of underlying hunger."

She'd called it hunger.

It still feels like a fitting word.

In the rare moments when I stop to think about my past life choices, such as weird hours of the night when my brain is filled with too much static to sleep, or when I am standing in an elevator with no will to make small talk, I think about this hunger. Only the science I could do with my own hands would yield truths unaltered and unfettered, free of half-truths and embellishments.

I don't dwell for long. I prefer to think present and forward.

This has happened to be very good for quick progress in science. Thinking present and forward got me into a good undergraduate school, where I could learn to make said quick progress in science. I chose a technical university. I only applied to schools where I could breathe the objectivity of science. I told myself that I didn't want any of the wishy-washy humanities fluff.

"Dismissive, aren't you," Iseul had said, after I enrolled in my school and she enrolled in the other university in San Oligo, a liberal arts school. "You can't avoid history class forever."

I avoided history courses like the plague. I didn't want to read about other people's histories and see an unsavory reflection of my own, but even at a science-obsessed school like mine, the humanities still leaked through, like the second-hand smoke from the cigarettes that littered the Rodiers' apartment.

Then came the decision to pick a lab, my senior year. It was a snap decision. I chose Stanley Lenner's lab because the lab works with the origins of life on Earth, secrets locked away in molecules from invertebrates. When poring over the list of many labs to pick from, I had just two things in mind: one, the chemical structures drawn all over the blanket from the youth shelter, and two, my own inscrutable biological origins. So I chose the lab that revolved around the molecules made by microbes and by invertebrates, RNA molecules that give clues into the evolution of multicellular complexity.

It's a scientific obsession with the origins of life.

It was also the only lab that was taking work-study students at the time. I needed money quick for my tuition—I refused to let *Umma* and *Appa* pay. I didn't know anything about Stanley Lenner himself other than that he was a Famous Bigshot. Not that that mattered to me. When I walked into his office for the first time, my first thought was that he looked like a flounder fish, with bugging eyes and crooked down-turned lips, a tall skinny flounder with a ramrod spine, checkered shirt rolled up to his elbows, Rolex glinting at the wrist.

It was only upon joining that I realized the level of pressure associated with his Bigshot Fame and Bigshot Ego. Not that I needed his cattle-prod demands to work harder, faster, longer. *In this lab, we make groundbreaking discoveries.* I was already working at breakneck speeds, even by his standards, and he knew it. He didn't come after me like he did other members of the lab. And his sexist insinuations, racist asides, things that pigeonhole people that I could never decide whether to label as intentional or habitual—they all fell on deaf ears. I stuck through it—*present and forward*—and I quickly found that the science was interesting and fellow lab members good company.

And so, unlike the long list of former lab techs I've learned about from the stories whispered by senior lab members, Stanley never fired me, and I was able to pay tuition.

Why did you join this lab?

I was asked this, and I asked it of everyone else. Petra said she wanted Stanley's famous name to spur along her own career success. Nadia said she liked the research topic and the project Stanley offered her—but wishes she hadn't focused on that so much in the end. Texan Simon said he got along with everyone else in the lab. British Simon said that it was always his boyhood dream to be one of two Simons in a room—*Oh I'm just kidding, it was the only lab where I got a postdoc offer.*

An observation: camaraderie builds particularly quickly and tightly and very desperately under the chokehold of a shared bad situation.

My ears were trained solely on my science, my eyes seeing dancing images of the geometric patterns on that fleece blanket.

It was always forward, forward, forward, even as my research dug into the past histories of life itself, backward, backward, backward.

There is irony here.

My science isn't a dive into history, I had told myself, pretending that I wasn't talking about two sides of the same coin.

♦ 6 ♦

THE FRIDAY NIGHT AIR clogs with the smell of fish. Iseul and I squeeze our way through the throngs of people flocking to the midnight downtown San Oligo night market scene.

Iseul's strange favor turns out to be accompanying her on some nighttime rendezvous at the market. Her appearance is in stark contrast to the colorful stalls festooned with cords of little lights and pennants and sausage link garlands, booths stacked with fruits and lace-trimmed blouses and mahogany sculptures. She is dressed in dark and unobtrusive colors, as she does when she gets a good lead or tip-off and goes off quietly to do some sleuthing for her investigative article.

"He said he would be wearing a black puffer jacket with a rip down the left side," she says.

"Wonderful. Black jacket in the nighttime, super easy visual." I sometimes come with Iseul on her dicier nighttime meetups for investigative journalist work, masquerading as her aide.

Iseul grabs my wrist to pull me forward faster. "Come on, hurry up. We're meeting him by the stall with the hanging filleted fish."

The air here is thick with the smell of fish and brine, a clear sign that we are approaching the stretch of the downtown night market lined with seafood stalls. We may not be able to see the vendor stalls well past the sea of people, but we can guide ourselves by our sense of smell. I strain upward, and beyond the faces of a couple who look college-aged, the girl with her head nestled in the space where the guy's skinny neck and shoulder meet, maybe slightly younger than Iseul and me, I see the tall cover tarp of a vendor stall lined with lights and hanging filleted fish.

We make our way to the stall with the hanging dried fish, which sway in the slight wind like morbid tinsel streamers. I bounce on the balls of my feet. In the open air, away from the heat of all the moving people, the nighttime cold slips in through our coats.

Iseul checks the time. She's nervous. I see all the usual signs: arms crossed, the untucked hand massaging her other arm, jaw squared to the left, sniffing frequently, and not just from the cold air.

The last time I saw her this nervous was when she was interviewing a year ago for an editor position, at a news outlet that has never had a woman as a top editor in its one hundred fifty years of existence. She'd gone into the room half an hour before, and I was waiting for her in the lobby where two deputy editors standing by the coffee machine were making jokes about which of the women interviewees would be seductive enough to make the first cut.

I thought it was hilarious, too.

"Well *you* were certainly not hired for your looks," I found myself saying, just as the door opened and Iseul reemerged. She stopped dead in her tracks, heels clicking to a halt on the tiled floors.

The editors stared at me blankly. The one in the tweed jacket said, "I can't believe it."

"People who believe in nothing will believe in anything," I said, and Iseul let out a hushed cough of indiscreet amusement. "Fucking amateurs." They'd looked at me like I was the Antichrist.

Iseul didn't get the job—would they really have hired a woman, and a woman of color to boot? When she opened the email, I said apologetically, "I probably cost you the job," but she told me my comments made the experience entirely worth it and that she wouldn't have it any other way.

I am watching nervous Iseul again as we stand under the dry fish.

"So, where's this hot shot of yours?" I ask.

"Any moment now," Iseul says. She stands on her tiptoes, leaning left and then right to peer into the sea of people. "He said to meet him here by the hanging hairtail stall at half past midnight." She checks her watch. "It's thirty seconds past half past midnight."

"You know," I say, "you still really never told me who this guy even is." My fingers and nose are really starting to feel the cold now, and I bounce a little harder on my feet. "For starters, which piece is this for?"

She doesn't seem to have heard me. I nudge her. "Which piece?"

"Shut up, shut up, I think that's him."

Iseul cranes her neck upward, taking one more glance to confirm she had caught sight correctly, then comes back down to Earth and rubs her arm even harder.

It's a young man, maybe mid-twenties, in a black jacket with a tear and a baseball cap. He draws closer, looking down at his phone and then looking up at Iseul as if to compare and confirm with a picture. Under the curved shadow cast by the rim of his cap, I can make out dark rings underlining his eyes, like umbral offspring of his cap's shadow.

"Who is she?" he says, tilting his chin in my direction. "I thought it would be just you." He is clearly a born-and-raised Korean, or at least someone raised there since a very early age. The sound of a Korean-speaking tongue trying to navigate the pronunciation of "th" is a giveaway.

The guy looks unconvinced when Iseul tells him I'm her aide. He squints at me through gray eyes. "Halfie, huh," he says.

With the extra light from the fish stall behind us, I realize that he is the person who helped the old woman cross the street the other day, bearing her plums and groceries. He now carries himself so differently. Tonight, he is the living embodiment of *taut*, body all tense like a cocked gun, something about him like the pictures of shrunken heads that Iseul showed me last year, when she was writing a piece on peddlers of twentieth-century counterfeits. His sunbaked skin is stretched taut over his skull, and I swear I can make out stress lines from the sustained tension.

He takes a quick step closer. I notice then that he has a brown paper bag with him, one bony hand gripping the folded top. His body is angled to block the bag from the night market crowd's line of sight.

"So?" he prompts.

Iseul fishes around in her purse, all shaky motions. She pulls out a wad of folded paper towel, hands it to the guy, who puts it in a pants pocket. A corner of paper towel lifts away as he does so, and I catch sight of the green and yellow of 10,000 and 50,000 won banknotes. I stare as he touches the bills in his pocket with one hand, feeling for the plastic holographic security strips.

"The real deal, yeah?" he says. It is an undirected statement; he's staring unfocused at the dried fish above Iseul's head, but Iseul freezes up, assures him that they are.

He grunts, passes her the folded brown paper bag, watches as she takes it from his outstretched hand and draws it to her chest in one jerky motion. There is a growing look of amusement on his narrow face.

"First time?" A statement that could not be more obvious.

"Thanks," Iseul mumbles.

A thin smile breaks across his face. He shakes his pocketed hand nestled among the bills.

"You will hear from me if these aren't real." He nods at the cellphone in Iseul's hands.

★ ★ ★

A few hours of deliberate meandering later, we are back at my apartment. Iseul's apartment, which she shares with two other roommates, is out of the question. We strip off our night-cold layers, change back into our pajamas (I have a pair reserved for Iseul for these impromptu nights she stays over), spread some blankets out on the wooden floor, and sprawl out, soaking up the warmth from the warm floorboards. We are beginning to thaw out, our skittery heartbeats have gone down a notch, and the brown paper bag, upon Iseul's insistence, is safely in my mini fridge nestled between a package of tofu and a jar of Nutella that I like eating cold by the spoonful late at night.

"Okay, spill it," I finally say. "What on earth sort of article is this for?"

"It's not for any article."

Unexpected. I think again. I wave in the direction of the mini fridge. "What is that then? Weed? Coke?" I can't believe

I'm asking Iseul this. Iseul, the organized and composed and upright one.

Iseul rolls over on her side, her back facing me. She mumbles something.

I miss it.

"Weed?" I ask.

She rolls slightly back.

"Sea slug," she says.

I am silent. Then I prop myself up on an elbow and stare at her.

"Say that again?"

"It's a sea slug," she says, a little louder.

I flop onto my back. I start laughing, and it's absolutely raucous laughter, roiling in my gut and pouring out unsightly, like orange cantaloupe-barf. It feels and sounds like the laugh of a full-bellied early-balding middle-aged man holding a stein of half-finished beer, I think, not the laugh of a young woman fresh out of college.

In that moment, I catch myself wondering if this is the laugh of my biological father. Something carefully preserved in all my cells now slipping out through the cracks when I cannot help it. My laugh snags in my throat, but Iseul hasn't noticed.

"Okay," she says, "I know that this is all a little strange."

That dislodges my laugh.

"That," I say, "may be the biggest understatement of the year."

She snorts, sighs. I hear her pull her blankets all the way up to just under her nose, where she likes them.

I wait, but she doesn't say anything else unprompted. I get myself back up on one elbow, head propped against my knuckles. "You can't just leave me hanging like that."

"Okay, it's not an actual whole sea slug, it's this chemical from it that's chemotherapeutic. It's what insanely expensive products from big pharma are derived from."

I laugh. "So you really did get drugs off the black market."

Iseul's blankets stir. "It's the kind of thing that we can't afford but Ha-joon really, really needs."

I sit up. Neither *Umma* nor *Appa* had told me anything the last time I called, nor the last time Iseul and I called together.

Iseul continues. "It's . . . not been good. He's entirely bed-ridden now. His current chemo regimen isn't working any-more." Her voice wavers. "I'm going there for a week."

"To Korea? Now? When?"

"I'm leaving next Sunday. I didn't tell you because I know you're under a lot of pressure in the lab. I'm going to bring that"—she gestures in the direction of the kitchenette and the mini fridge—"and I want to see him when he's okay." She turns her head toward me, eyes evasive. "Sorry for breaking it to you all of a sudden. I told *Umma* and *Appa* not to tell you. You didn't need anything more to worry about, between the lab crunch and the drop box."

"No. No, Iseul, of course I need to know. You should have told me. He's my brother, too." I knead my blankets between my fingers. My upset is replaced by guilt when I think of how I, too, told Iseul not to tell *Umma* and *Appa* about my birth parents search, and realize the hiding of truth is bidirectional. I look toward the kitchenette. "You think it'll work? The sea slug juice?"

Iseul's blankets rustle when she shrugs. "Hoping."

"But how do you know if it's the real thing? You trust some clear liquid from some random guy?"

"That's where you come in. You're a scientist. You can find a chemist who can identify exactly what's inside of it."

"Wow. That's your plan? Way to ask me beforehand."

"You've got scientist connections. Tell them what it is, a potential profitable chemotherapeutic lead from a sea slug, the blue dragon nudibranch. That'll motivate them to work fast."

Iseul's conviction in the value of artless stubbornness, which she holds out before her life's path like a lamp through the dark, makes me feel an inward sob today, as though some small organ under my heart is spasming. She is always aggressively hopeful when she senses a lack of it in those around her. I don't think that she really believes this black-market drug can be given to Ha-joon; I think that she believes—*hopes*—that if she does something as crazy as jumping through all sorts of hoops to get ahold of it, then something just as crazy, like a spontaneous remission of melanoma, can happen too.

If there were organs responsible for human attributes, the one that allows people to hope must share space with the one conferring the capacity for delusion. It's self-deceit in a socially acceptable wrapping, and is something not rooted in logic or vigorous empirical evidence or intense scrutiny, the stanchions of modern science. There's a waffling air to it, like a tree rooted in clouds. I like my trees rooted in soil.

It unsettles me to think that there are some things in the world that work on the sheer basis of belief. But some nights like these, as I stare up at the blackness above with Iseul beside me, I wonder about unrelenting belief and stubborn hope. Not everything can be driven by my own hands, all gung-ho. Not everything can be anchored to the Earth. In the interstitial space between topsoil and far-away sky, a space inhabited by dreams and, briefly, by balloons that have escaped children's hands, we can sometimes hide out, hang out, and be okay, I suppose.

We lie there together staring up at the black space where the ceiling is.

Then Iseul says, "I really hope it helps. Actually does something."

I reach over for her wrist and squeeze it gently.

"I do too," I say.

Iseul falls silent again. Then she rolls closer, and the meager light catches on her wide eyes.

"I really hope you find your birth mom and dad," she says. Then she adds, "I really hope we find everything we're both looking for."

I squeeze her wrist again. "Sea changes."

She sighs and rolls onto her back. "We'll make sea changes, won't we?"

Soon Iseul's breathing turns deep and steady.

I lie on my side, listening, unable to find sleep.

Iseul's love for Ha-joon, for me, for her family, is a blinkered kind of love—that being all she can see, feel, know, in times like this. That terrifying clarity of purpose that comes with this kind of love during the murkiest of critical junctures . . . I saw that in her today, her eyes entirely clouded over with it. I feel guilty; is it something I'm capable of? I don't know. I'm an embodiment of the reality that many worldviews are constructed from flight and fright, but whether those pieces are layered into something other than a wall is a matter of the individual.

I don't know. I just like to think of myself as more rational.

★   ★   ★

When night oozes onward and I still lie as awake as ever, I reach for my phone and open an incognito tab. I type in *blue dragon nudibranch pharmaceutical*. The search results are not good.

There is an exorbitantly priced chemotherapeutic pharmaceutical derived from the little blue dragon nudibranchs, which are shaped like tiny versions of their namesake. It's outrageously expensive—half a million for two dosages, out of a six-dose regimen. Not only are the nudibranchs a rare species, but the pharma compound they naturally produce is immensely difficult to synthesize commercially, hence the international rings of smuggling and trafficking.

To think that Iseul has gotten herself entangled in this poaching-to-black-market ring, an arena littered with shady mercenary types and muffled violence . . . I'm not sure if I would have been more surprised by this or if the nudibranch pharmaceutical had really turned out to be recreational drugs.

I look at her dark blanket-covered outline rising and falling.

Dumbass. How could you put yourself in this kind of danger?

All these years since leaving behind the youth shelter blanket and the girl on the upper bunk with the wide eyes, everything filmed in a slick of warm rain, I had found the anchor for my own tree roots in Iseul and the Yoons. Now thinking of Iseul in danger, that earth seems to shake and shift and crumble.

What do you do when solid earth starts to give way underneath your feet?

The curdling feeling in my gut tells me that this whole affair has its own roots in Iseul's investigative journalist forays gone too far: she's fallen too deeply into her big pharma corruption piece. Snooping around the deepest recesses of the Internet and making contacts with burner phones is always the prelude to her breakthrough investigative pieces. Acting on birdlike twitchy impulses and snapping up clue trails in a flash and sniffing after smoking guns obviously makes her an excellent journalist. Except this time around, her moral resolve buckled and instead of disbanding the poaching rings through her writing, she has put down her pen and become complicit.

I let out a sigh into my cupped hands, quietly. We always knew she would grow up to get into some kind of muckraking business, even as two wild-haired girls playing in elementary school recess, the same way we always knew I would grow up to become some kind of scientist. At one lunch break in the playground's grass lawns, I had found that my Ziploc of extra cheesy crackers was missing from my lunch sack. Prowling around the playground, we found it fallen on the ground under the monkey bars, spilled like a stranded shoal on the wood mulch. Little Iseul spearheaded the sleuthing for the thief, insisting that all of the seven-year-olds hold their hands out and demonstrate that their fingers were not laced with orange cheese dust, while I trailed along announcing that it did not matter anymore because the five-second rule is fake and that bacteria and other microbes can stick onto your food all the same.

I put my phone aside and pull my blankets up to my chin but I'm afraid to close my eyes. I don't want the insides of my eyelids and my wayward imagination to show me Iseul being shot by masked men. *Dumbass.*

As I think about the danger Iseul has now put herself in, as I think about my family not telling me about Ha-joon, and about *me* not telling them about my search for what came before them—all of these glass walls that have suddenly rematerialized in present-day—I realize just how much I have gained in twelve years and just how precious it is and how I could not bear to lose any of it.

This is the first time I have fully appreciated the magnitude of it all, and it's huge and overwhelming, like trying to drink a whole ocean.

I'm sick with fear. Am I being selfish? Nausea, vertigo, a distortion of such bewildering emotions—it's all chimera-like as it climbs up from my gut into my throat, and I rush to the bathroom and then my dinner is in the toilet water, and I stare, blinking, thinking, *What was past has been regurgitated into present, literally.* Dizzy, heaving, I almost laugh.

Later, when I do close my eyes, it turns out that the overhead projector there has clicked forward from worrying about Iseul onto the next slide and now on the insides of my eyelids there are the familiar images of half-human half-sea-slug chimeras in the stained alleyway.

The invertebrate-vertebrates are back at it, and, dreamscape-frozen, I watch the borderline bestiality.

✦ 7 ✦

I GET UP BEFORE dawn the morning after to brew tea and fry eggs. When Iseul slogs in, a night of tossing and turning caverned under her eyes, she veers for the mini fridge, grabs the brown paper bag, peers inside—freezes, her eyes wide—and then she presses the bag to her chest like it's an infant. It would have been amusing, if I hadn't been so utterly, furiously worried.

"Satisfied with the customer service last night?" I flip two eggs—Iseul likes hers over easy.

Iseul puts the bag back in the fridge, closes the door firmly. She is not looking at me.

I hit the spatula against the rim of the pan twice to get her attention. She still doesn't look over. I purse my lips. "You're never going to do that again. Never. First the sex-trafficking article fiasco last year, now this. You have to stop putting your life on the line for work. Yesterday's stunt—it was something for your pharma corruption article, wasn't it?"

"It was for Ha-joon," she says with a lilt of protest.

"Well, you've got the thing for him now. Done deal. Now you can just sit safely at your garden-variety desk in your garden-variety office with your garden-variety colleagues and not go messing around in shady circles anymore." I wave my spatula at her, trying to get her to meet my eyes. "Iseul, I'm not joking. You're never going to cross paths with that guy again. Right?"

But Iseul doesn't say anything.

The last time she did anything this risky was for her investigative piece last year on American soldiers stationed in Seoul who were involved in a sex trafficking ring. The officers were shipping local women out on ships into sex slavery and patrolling the brothels to ensure that nobody escaped.

Iseul had told me that she was going to go visit the family in Korea for a couple days. I was back-to-back with planned experiments, trying to churn out the revision requirements for a submitted manuscript. I'd told her to send my hugs to everyone, to which Iseul had nodded very quickly and smiled—with a speed that I would only later realize was relief.

It turned out that she had instead slipped into one of the harbors at night to get video footage and interview some of the women. She only told me the truth after she returned, when we found nails in her car tires one day.

Not that that deterred her from her work. Standing outside of her office building in the receding evening light, all Iseul had said to fill our initial shock was, "Well, it was going to happen at some point. Milestone in my career!"

All these years as her talent for fishing out gritty truths grew, as she turned over varnished façades to reveal the truth clinging desperately underneath, her name was gaining recognition, and I was growing increasingly worried.

"There are bound to be some vendettas against you out there," I fretted.

"The origins of democracy are in the free press," she said simply. I knew that. It was like her verbal tic.

"Free press protects lives," she said. As always. "An origin unto itself. Plus, I'm lucky enough to have a boss who doesn't edit my writing to death. She never tells me what not to investigate. That's enough for me to keep at it."

And that was that. Each time I tried to bring up my concerns, she shook her head and shushed me, in her typical, gentle but insistent Iseul way.

Not that I could bring myself to argue with her desire to expose truths. That would be hypocritical of me. Her desire to ask questions and put out answers is a mirror—I am in the reflection, doing the exact same thing except with science.

Iseul is the one who guided me in searching for the identity of my biological parents. She knew all the ins and outs of sleuthing through Internet wormholes. Knew about the drop-box babies that sprung from military base canoodling. Once, she delicately suggested that I try phoning some of the well-known baby box locations around Seoul. I couldn't bring myself to do it. But my hot-potato phone trail led me there all the same.

Iseul is still quiet, so I try pushing her harder. "Why aren't you saying something?"

She shrugs, drifts over to sit down at the table, on her face a distant expression. *So fucking stubborn,* I think, *but I can never seem to get mad at you.*

"Iseul, if you're not going to stop getting yourself involved in this pharma black market business, at least tell me why."

The moment I put a plate of eggs and buttered toast before her, she scrambles back up to her feet to snatch the paper bag from the fridge again, all wild-eyed, and she pulls out the tiny glass vial of clear liquid. She waves it at me.

"It's real, right?" Her breath comes out panicky-fast. "It has to be real? This is supposedly six doses' worth."

I grab Iseul's wrist. What is wrong with her? "My god, Iseul. We can hope, but we won't know until I run it by someone in chemistry. Put it away for god's sake. I think you just need to get some food into your system, stat."

I wait until she's downed her eggs and half a mug of tea before I ask again. But she's fidgety and quiet and terse—*"It's for Ha-joon. Like I said."*—and avoids my eyes.

Then she leans over and gives me a light shove. Her touch is calibrated, carefully playful. "You wouldn't want to lose a chance to help him, would you? Abby, you don't want to help him?"

And that is when I know she is hiding something. Even in jest, Iseul would never guilt-trip me with people she knows I would protect at all costs.

★ ★ ★

So when she invites me over for dinner two days later, I can't help myself when I spot her laptop wide open on her desk. What could she possibly be writing? If she's not going to tell me what she's up to, I need to find out for myself.

I glance out the open bedroom door, down the narrow hallway still lined with the birthday bunting and garlands from her roommate's party last week. Iseul is still busy in the kitchen around the corner. I hear her slippers on the floor tiles, the sound of the fridge opening, the buttery smell of sautéing shrimp. Her two roommates are out this evening.

I lean over her desk, careful not to move any of the pens and loose papers out of place, and reach for her laptop mouse.

"Abby, you good? You found the socks?" Iseul calls from the kitchen.

The crackling of shrimp being tossed over heat pauses, and I hear her footsteps cross the squeaky patch of carpeting by the kitchen entrance. I spring back from Iseul's desk, grab the pair of socks I'd pulled from her dresser moments earlier, strip off the pair on my feet soaked from the rainy walk to her apartment.

"Yeah," I call back, and Iseul tells me to toss my wet socks in the hamper and come help her with the beans.

I wait to hear her receding footsteps signal that she's returned to the kitchen, and then slide back to her desk, forgetting all about the socks. I carefully nudge a jostled piece of paper back into place, but then blink. It has my name written on it, in Iseul's handwriting. I pull it out. It has my name, with a line connecting it to other names in an erratic network. The drop-box pastor. My adoptive parents' names. Another line linking the pastor's name to "nudibranch smuggler sister." A list of other Korean names that have no significance to me. A flurry of absent-minded scribbles off the side, next to "birth parents??" circled in lazy looping lines.

I riffle through the papers underneath. There are printouts of news articles covering the smuggling circles, some about the delicate little sea slugs from which her illegal compound came. Articles about drop-box babies and that pastor, who apparently runs one of the largest drop-boxes in Korea and cares for many of the orphans. An article from a Korean news outlet, dated last week: a man found to have links to poaching of the nudibranchs. And here's her coworker's article about the death of my adoptive father.

I set the papers back down, take a step back, confused. Iseul has been doing more investigations into my past. But she hasn't said a word about it to me. I think about glass walls again, and suddenly the smell of shrimp scampi in the apartment is nauseating.

I move quickly now. I click through the open files on her laptop. More articles about drop-box babies. The draft of her current article isn't among those open.

I scroll through her documents, neatly organized into folders ordered by year. She still has files dating back to high school, even middle school. She's the type of person who keeps all of her old files no matter what—*why do you cling so much to what's past?*

Maybe that's why I started listening to seventies music so much in high school, why I feel so attached to pieces of a bygone era that I never knew. There's a comfort in a shrouded past that I never knew and can never know, because I can imagine it to be what I want.

I scroll quickly past Iseul's high school assignments. In these folders are some of her first published journalism pieces, too. It was around then that I'd started calling Iseul a story phlebotomist. Iseul's talent for drawing out human stories interview after interview was clear at that point. Her exquisite writing, lodged within the ragtag school newspaper, caught the eyes of people at big-name magazines and outlets. A diamond in the rough, said an editor of an esteemed newspaper, who had a very long and fancy email sign-off. Iseul and I were freshmen in college when Iseul showed me the email that invited her to intern. This woman is her current boss, and Iseul is her boss' youngest full-time journalist as a now-twenty-four-year-old with an extraordinary gift.

When Iseul calls out from the kitchen—"What's taking you so long?"— my breath catches like static between ribs and I leap away from her desk, unsuccessful in finding her article draft.

I can feel blood rising back up into my face as I hurry back to the kitchen, where Iseul waves me toward the unopened cans of beans by the sink. She stares at my feet. I look down and realize that in all my dazed rush, I'd forgotten to put her socks on, the reason I'd been in her room in the first place.

Iseul laughs. "Addle-brained, you." She pushes a mug of hot chocolate along the countertop toward me. "That's for you. Go put some dry socks on and then come back to warm up your wet, miserable self. Wipe away that rain-soaked frown of yours and I'll cheer you up with dinner."

This Iseul is so different from the wild-eyed Iseul of two nights ago.

There's something numb and buzzing in my head. I had never thought of the possibility of glass walls existing between me and Iseul, and it's disorienting like I've been put inside one of my salt slugs' aquarium tanks. I move stiffly down the hall back to Iseul's desk, where I'd left the socks. Why hasn't she told me about the snooping-around that she's clearly been doing? I can't decide whether to be angry about Iseul's silence.

She knows well that this is the kind of thing that makes me mad. I'd told her before about that one frog dissection, from around the time I coined "story phlebotomist." I was doing something in the same vein as phlebotomy myself then. A biology teacher told me after class one day that I had a knack for science, and at her invitation, I stepped into the classroom again after school to try my hand at an extra experiment, which turned out to be a frog dissection—the little corpse was belly-up on a plastic tray the same shade of pale preserved white.

The American bullfrog's scientific name is *Lithobates catesbeianus*—the *litho-* and *bates* are Greek roots that stitched together mean "one that treads on stone."

I am sure my teacher saw my face, frozen like stone, when she made the first incision from its soft neck to belly.

I knew from library books that a frog's heart is three-chambered, but I did not want to see it for myself, tender skin flayed back to reveal it nestled within a dark and still cavity.

Seeing someone else's heart all exposed like that, it felt voyeuristic. I would never want my own to be seen like that, so vulnerable to the touch.

At the surge of anger that rushes all hot and red into my face, I realize that this part of me still hasn't changed. Even after all these years, even with family.

But I decide to wait. There must be a reason she hasn't told me yet.

If there's one thing that days spent toiling in the science lab have taught me, it's that there's no better detective than patience—the kind of patience with which to wait out infinities, time as interminable as the kind that governs things like tectonic plate movement, evolution, and family bonds.

Evolution: when a little bundle of proteins responsible for photo-copying your DNA screws up at its one job. Over and over again. DNA polymerase is not perfect. Check in at any point in time and what you have is different from what you started with, the mistakes accumulating each time, the universe's longest running, never-ending game of Telephone.

Life was made by a bunch of mistakes. Or sequential seren-dipity. Whichever way you want to look at it.

✦ 8 ✦

THROUGH MISTAKE OR SERENDIPITY, I have ended up a scientist who has never before felt so uncertain of her ability to find answers.

Here is the first practical law of science:

Experiments fail more often than not.

This is a fact.

This fact is the rare exception. Not much else in science is a fact. "Facts" are subject to revisions and rescrutiny and controversy over and over again. Science, when at its best, stays on its toes.

★   ★   ★

Up to this point, I had considered the glass-wall-less security of my place in the Yoon family to be *fact*. Something unchanging, unrevisable.

So it's a foul-tasting moment in my career as a scientist to learn so intimately that facts indeed are always changeable, revisable.

★   ★   ★

Umma once gave me a piece of advice: "You should not be a scientist because you should put family first."

It was winter break of freshman year of college, a week before *Umma, Appa,* and Ha-joon went back to Korea. Iseul and I were sitting on pillows in front of the fireplace, feet warming in the glow of the embers as though Southern Californian winters were really that cold, hands cupped around mugs of *yuja* tea, recouping from our finals exam week.

Umma said that there were specialists who could better treat Ha-joon's cancer in Korea. No need to keep dealing with the American healthcare system anymore, she'd huffed. Plus, it's closer to the rest of the family—wouldn't it be so wonderful to see them again, in person? And *Appa* got a better faculty position offer at a university there—isn't that right, *Yeobo?*

Appa was impassive. Folded into the quilted armchair older than both Iseul and me, the first piece of furniture they bought from a garage sale when he and *Umma* arrived in America, he didn't look up from his laptop. He had that expression on his face, the deliberate calmness that he slipped on whenever *Umma* called family at night curled around her cellphone like it was a lifeline, her voice and the longing in it wreathing out of her mouth into the air into the hallway and then under my bedroom door into my strained ears.

So they gathered up their belongings and made their way back across the Pacific. Except they didn't take everything with them.

Iseul stayed to finish a college education with me, and has since stayed for her journalism career.

Appa did not take his American Dream film reels with him. I saw the corner of a canister poking out of the top of the neighborhood dumpster the day the family left.

Umma left some words behind for me. Some parting advice. Always take care of your health first—and wear socks around the house, for goodness sakes, your hands and feet are always so cold. Try not to get so worked up over small details. Surround yourself with good people. Protect your heart—your heart comes first. And don't ignore my phone calls! And, really, think again about the whole science business. I am not so sure about it, and I worry about you. You overwork yourself already. When you have a husband and children, wouldn't all the science get in the way? Think about it for me, Abby-*ya*. I don't think you should be a scientist. You should not be a scientist because you should put family first.

I had been angry at that, so upset, the suggestion that I give up science for domestic life. What did *Umma* know about what science meant to me? What did *Umma* know about being a scientist?

Oh, trust me, she'd said quietly. Your *Umma* knows.

I had been too busy nursing my wounded pride to process what *Umma* had just said and to ask her what she'd meant by that.

★   ★   ★

When experiments don't work, I often find *Umma*'s words echoing inside my skull. *You should not be a scientist.* The words linger like specters.

When I walk into lab the next morning, half of my sea slugs are floating limply in their tanks, their soft curled wings unmoving.

So much for my esteemed title of mother of sea slugs. I can't seem to get them to stay alive. I've tried the works: changed the filtration system, moved the tanks closer to the windows, fixed an artificial sunlight lamp above. But no matter. It's always another little body floating limply on the surface of the water the next morning.

Experiments are a drag. It doesn't help that Stanley thinks that the solution to stalled experiments is more new experiments. Sometimes the brute force method doesn't work. Then you just end up with a greater number of simultaneously failing experiments plus a greater amount of scientist's sadness. *And where's the Utilitarianism in that,* says British Simon.

Stanley approaches with The Look in his eyes.

Oh I don't think that's how it works, said I, in internal monologue.

"Oh once you get the hang of it it'll be easy," said the PI, verbally. "Just a quick side project."

Just a quick side project. A classic knee-slapper. I fall for it every time.

It is only a matter of time before I try yelling at my samples. Maybe that will finally get them to crystallize.

Texan Simon is heading out when the yelling commences one night. He pauses by the door. "You okay?"

"Just working."

Maybe I should also turn in for the night. Bring everything tomorrow to that one postdoc with the beard in the lab two floors up. He does everyone's crystallizations there. He has a knack. There's weird voodoo in his neckbeard, they swear. Feed RNA input into the bearded black box model, receive perfect crystal structure output. You don't ask questions, you just trust the system.

Texan Simon is still here.

"Maybe take a break," he tries again. "Get something to eat?"

"I have the nutritional requirements of a cactus," I tell him. "I'm completely fine."

He doesn't look convinced by either of those statements.

"Okay. Sure," he says, and leaves me to my yelling.

Just a quick side project. Just take it step by step.

Step one is superstition, step two is sacrificial animal rituals.

I hear a janitor's key ring jingle down the halls just outside the lab. It's Kwan-sik doing her final weekday nighttime rounds. With the door propped open, she has definitely heard me. What a nutjob, she is probably thinking—but not thinking too much of it because she already knows that all scientists are nutjobs at a very fundamental level.

★ ★ ★

I keep fooling myself that science was my gateway out of my old life with my first adoptive parents, that the existence of science itself is entirely at odds with that past. But that is not quite true. Once, for example, I heard about experiments in my old home.

"Let's try an experiment, shall we," said my adoptive father one day.

This was before my adoptive mother left for good. It was a Friday evening. He had come back from work late, and my mother was not yet home—she was working a night shift at the hospital. I had walked home from elementary school after a few hours in the library. By fourth grade, I knew exactly how late I could stay among the books and still make the half-hour walk back before sunset.

My father had a strange look on his face. He was smiling, and he didn't smile unless he was looking at texts on his phone from the Natasha that he never explained to me. Smiles looked unnatural on him, made his face look damaged. He tossed aside his briefcase and sat on the raggedy paisley sofa, spread both arms across the backrest.

"Your mother always says she's working a night shift."

He didn't move his large eyes from me.

"It's always a night shift. Why is it always a night shift? She never took night shifts before. Why is it always a night shift, Abby?"

From where I stood in the narrow hall that led to my room, I couldn't smell beer. Usually that meant he wouldn't be having a fit and throwing things around. But I was still cautious. I wouldn't be walking by him to go into the kitchen to get a glass of water anymore.

"Why is it always a night shift, Abby?" he repeated.

I shrugged carefully. When I was asked questions, I tried not to answer. My father, the only questions he ever asked were ones with just a single correct answer—the opposite of science—or ones with no answer that could ever satisfy him. All questions were tripwires.

I never revealed that I knew where my mother was. I had once looked out my window into the night dark, hoping to see the stray cat that liked to sit on top of the marble pedestals by the apartment entrance, and instead saw my mother's slight frame wrapped in a beige shawl I had never seen before. To her left was another woman also dressed in nurse scrubs—the owner of the shawl, I realized—who put an arm around my mother's shoulders and hurried her over to a car stirring in the loading zone, those too-bright headlights knifing the darkness. That was how I learned that someone who worked with my mother at the hospital sheltered her when things with my father got tense.

"It's always so quiet in here," my father said. "Let's try an experiment, Abby, shall we?"

He stood up abruptly and opened his briefcase and pulled out a short chain the length of his hand, with a clasp at one end and a sliding lock at the other. He spent the next few minutes hammering the ends to the door frame. Then he turned to me and gestured at his handiwork, the way kids at school did at show-and-tell.

"Where is your mother tonight?" he said. "We'll find out. We'll hear when she comes back. She'll have to make some noise." He threw the hammer and box of nails to the ground and slouched past me into his room, where I could hear the bedsprings squeal a few seconds later.

My mother did not come back that night.

She did not come back the next day, either.

Then late Sunday night, I heard a key being pushed into the other side of the door, heard the unlocking, heard the ungreased doorknob turning. The door chain made a click as it was drawn taut. My mother, on the other end, tried the lock again, tried pushing. I heard her murmuring in Korean.

I didn't want to hear her raise her voice. I didn't want to hear loaded questions or raised voices.

I unfurled my arms from my folded knees, climbed down from the sofa where I had been sitting all day with my ears strained, and slid the door chain bolt.

When my mother opened the door, she didn't look angry. She looked gray. "Hello, Abby," she said absentmindedly. She glanced at the newly installed door chain, then at the hammer and nails still on the ground.

"Why is your father like this, Abby?" she said.

I had no answers to her questions, either.

She drifted past me into the apartment. She wasn't wearing her usual pastel nurse scrubs. She was wearing unfamiliar clothes, clothes from that coworker who helped her into a car and drove her away when my father had his outbursts. She had that beige shawl draped lifelessly around her shoulders like the skin of a dead animal.

She drifted like a ghost, I thought.

★   ★   ★

As a scientist, *I* am the one who now asks all the questions.

I am the one who designs the experiments.

The origins of my own life as I know it are tied to the chemical origins of life.

So I ignored *Umma*'s advice to not become a scientist.

I RECEIVE NOTICE FROM the U.S. Embassy and the ward office in Seoul that my request for birth certificate access has again come up with a blank. This time, instead of a plain-text email, it comes as an email formatted with a fancy serif-font header and golden seal, with the message also appended as a separate attachment, as if I needed that news twice.

I'd hoped that perhaps the Seoul registry might have some sort of record, but it's been countless emails with no information, just red tape and redirected phone calls and shaking heads.

I close my lab notebook, pull my hair out of its bun and run my fingers through it. I spin in circles in my chair, clicking my pen on and off.

There is no way that I will be able to find out who my birth parents are like this, trying to hound government officials into tracking my origins down.

I look over at my lab bench. Only half an hour ago, I was standing there extracting RNA from the salt slugs and the bacteria that live within them. I think back to fifth grade when I sent the saliva samples and toothbrush swabs to the ancestry genotyping service. I spin in slower circles. I wish there were again a way to science the information out myself.

When Petra calls me over, I am still spinning in circles. Today, she is teaching me a method for looking at RNA in my salt slugs. Petra developed a method for watching the movement of single strands of RNA in live cells—which is why she is about to go start her own lab. She had her breakthrough while studying the role of RNA in memory formation in California sea hares, where sticking little chemical adornments on RNA molecules affects the rate of synapse formation.

When Petra's methodology works, you can watch the entire history of a strand of RNA unfold before your eyes, from birth to death.

In many bacteria, there is a special type of RNA that likes to cut itself out and form a little lasso-shaped loop and move to other places. In humans, there is a bundle of RNA and proteins that cuts out pieces of other RNA and makes little loops out of them.

It's possible that evolution started with the former and ended up at the latter. The path is blurry. So with science, I am trying to go back in time to make clear the path that connects past and present.

How did a foreign transplant become so integrated in a new land?

I ask this of my science, I ask this of myself.

♦ 10 ♦

WHEN I CHECK MY cultured cells the next morning, it's abundantly clear that the experiment hasn't worked, again. It's a total bust. Again.

Something unstitches inside me as I, for the first time in the lab since starting on this salt slug project, realize that I'm afraid, afraid of getting kicked out—and suddenly I feel a little faint, because I don't think I could bear being sent away from any place in which I'd felt I'd belonged, whether the Yoons or the lab. Stanley is growing impatient with my lack of progress, and my chances left are running thin.

Petra is displeased.

"I do think it should have worked" is all she says when she sees the cells. She starts reorganizing her already-organized lab bench.

I toss the flasks. "Maybe we should increase the salt concentration?"

Petra doesn't look up. She sniffs and continues moving around bottles and racks.

"Or incubate at a lower temperature?"

"Well. I just think it should have worked the exact way we did it."

The whole lab is well aware that Petra recently received and accepted an offer for an independent position at a fancy university on the other side of the country. In the six-month limbo until then, she's finishing up projects and tying up loose ends. It's the lame-duck phase of her time as a postdoc, and she is more than antsy to get up and going. She is stressed out, and it shows.

It's enough to troubleshoot an experiment for weeks on end, to meet dead end after dead end with my own origins, never mind dodging snipes from a cranky labmate. In the wake of recent events, patience is in low tide.

"Lots unspoken between those few words of yours," I say.

Petra's backside says nothing.

"With this word count you've got going, you might instead consider a career as an editor for *Nature Brief Communications*."

"Say that again?"

"Oh, no. 404: this page doesn't exist."

Petra turns around. "You also need to stop cracking jokes every time you get upset."

She has really embraced the newly-minted-PI role. It went to her head real fast—a drug-like rate of absorption. The pharmacokinetics of recognized accomplishment are incredible.

I raise an eyebrow. "Really? I think jokes are the most polite defense mechanism, out of all options in nature."

"That's beside the point."

"Would you rather I shoot blood out of my eyes like horned lizards?"

Texan Simon overhears this. He stops typing and spins around in his chair, an earbud dangling. "Can confirm that getting shot by horned lizard blood sucks."

"Shut up, Simon," Petra says. I think she's lost it. She curses in Creole, and it's something new that I've never heard from her before. "We all know you're from Texas."

"C'est la vie." He sticks his earbud in and resumes typing.

In the silence as Petra turns back and tries to regain her composure, we can both hear electric guitar from Simon's headphones: Bon Jovi screaming about being shot through the heart, albeit not by reptilian blood. Why Simon even owns headphones is beyond me.

"You know what." Petra sighs like she's given up. "Tell me something about your science that will blow me away. One thing. Right now."

That's a good one.

I think.

I leaf through the options that come to mind. Eeny meeny miny moe.

"All the bigshots in oligo synthesis history had the same hairstyle as my dentist?"

Clearly I'm the only one who thinks it's an interesting trend. As I watch Petra's face, I draw the conclusion that she has reached her limit.

But today I'm not done. Something's unscrewed. I look over to Texan Simon.

"Hey, Simon, this is like a spaghetti western standoff. It's just your thing."

He doesn't hear me above Bon Jovi.

"Except nerd edition." I can't seem to stop—is this bordering on clinically pathological? "Because instead of antique Colt revolvers we have antique P1000 pipettes." Also, the air smells like methanol from the rotovap instead of millennia of wind-eroded feldspar and creosote and tumbleweed, but that is an unimportant detail. The same angst of *The Good, the Bad, and the Ugly* is very much thick in the stuffy air, and, based off of Petra's taut face, the same level of danger.

I have crossed a line today.

But, yes, Simon, c'est la vie. Life is all about crossing lines.

It's in this moment that I have a revelation: Today, I have empirically determined the limit of Petra.

I finally crack a smile. Whoever said I couldn't be a scientist.

★   ★   ★

On the door of one of the lab's −80°C freezers, there is an ongoing collaborative poem comprised of sticky notes. A header stitched together from seven stained sticky notes reads, *Mosaic of Exasperation in the Lab.*

> *I know why the failed experiment stings. ("I Know Why the Caged Bird Sings," Maya Angelou)*
>
> *I. PCR*
> *"Surely," said I, "surely I'll now have a correct-sized band." ("The Raven," Edgar Allen Poe)*
> *Quoth the PCR, "Nevermore." ("The Raven," Edgar Allen Poe)*
>
> *II. Cloning*
> *O positive clone! my positive clone! ("O Captain! My Captain!," Walt Whitman)*
> *For you they call, the praying scientists, their eager faces turning ("O Captain! My Captain!," Walt Whitman)*
> *It is some dream that on the agar plate, ("O Captain! My Captain!," Walt Whitman)*
> *one day you will appear.*
>
> *III. Gel Electrophoresis*
> *There is a place where the agarose gel ends ("Where the Sidewalk Ends," Shel Silverstein)*

My samples learned where, when I ran them for too long.
But O heart! heart! heart! ("O Captain! My Captain!,"
    Walt Whitman)
Where on the floor my dear gel lies, ("O Captain! My Cap-
    tain!," Walt Whitman)
fallen cold and dead. ("O Captain! My Captain!," Walt
    Whitman)
Gel electro-floor-esis.

IV. Western Blot
Bands, bands, not burning bright. ("The Tyger," William
    Blake)

V. Contamination
I give the flask a shake ("Stopping by Woods on a Snowy
    Evening," Robert Frost)
To ask if there is some mistake. ("Stopping by Woods on a
    Snowy Evening," Robert Frost)
Said I: "Thing of evil—prophet still, if microbe or devil!"
    ("The Raven," Edgar Allen Poe)

VI. Confocal Microscopy
The fluorescence has become quite mucky and dull ("Messy
    Room," Shel Silverstein)
And often is its gold complexion dimm'd. ("Sonnet 18," Wil-
    liam Shakespeare)

VII. Phage Transduction
I was angry with my phage. ("A Poison Tree," William Blake)
I watered it in fears ("A Poison Tree," William Blake)
Night and morning with my tears ("A Poison Tree," William
    Blake)

Thou art slave to fate, chance, desperate scientists ("Holy
    Sonnet 10: Death, Be Not Proud," John Donne)
Where are the colonies?
What happens to a dream deferred? ("Dream Deferred,"
    Langston Hughes)

When I first joined the lab as a college senior, it was only at stanza II, the work of British Simon.

British Simon had pointed to the pad of sticky notes on the shelf to the left. There, he also kept a roll of tape and a clustered handful of disc magnets.

"If you ever feel so inclined, add to it anytime." He reached over and pulled a pen from a box and put it in my lab coat pocket. "When science runs amok, we write ad hoc."

Since then it's reached VII with contributions from Texan Simon and Petra.

Petra wrote IV, after persistent nudges from British Simon.

When Texan Simon added VII, he said to me, "If you're ever wondering why I haven't graduated yet." He rapped his knuckles on it definitively. "When science runs amok, we write ad hoc."

★   ★   ★

I finish setting up experiments for tomorrow, and head to the campus soup and sandwich café for lunch, where I meet Iseul and tell her about the dead-end with the birth certificate attempts.

"What about your DNA test?" she asks. "You can submit that to different places to see if there's a match somewhere, right?"

"Yeah," I say.

"Have you tried that? You would know about it, you're the scientist."

"Yeah. It's already available for people to compare with, so I'll know if someone is a genetic match." The buzzing of café conversation around us is beginning to hurt my head. Why isn't she telling me that she's been digging around herself? Iseul looks so composed, all tucked in and neatly creased, her brow pleated in concern. This is an unexpected twist; I'd always thought Iseul was a bad liar. I'd thought that having a face-to-face conversation would crack her resolve, and she would spill everything. I almost want to laugh.

Iseul peers at me. "Something off?"

I stir my broccoli cheddar soup. "I don't know. I'm not sure I want to know about every other person who has a blood link to me. Maybe some things are better left buried."

"Sounds like investigative journalism. Finally sick of it?"

"Very funny."

"Early drive tomorrow?" She reaches across the booth table, takes my free hand and waves it around gently. "To lift the old spirits a bit?" She gives me her small asymmetrical smile, the single-dimpled one that emerges when she's apologizing or admitting something embarrassing or feeling guilty.

"Yeah," I say. "Yeah, I'd like that."

I can't stomach anything more, so I wait for Iseul to finish her sandwich and I sit there staring up at the Bauhaus art print framed on the wall. There are geometric shapes nested within other shapes. Circles inside of circles, squiggly lines inside of circles, like simplified cells. When I look down at my soup again, it manifests something primordial.

♦ 11 ♦

WE WAKE UP BEFORE the sun and drive up the dark coastline, singing badly to Elton John's "The Bitch is Back" because it reminds us of an inside joke from middle school. Not all memories from pubescence are acne-ridden and terrible, I suppose. Some are just acne-ridden.

Red-winged blackbirds sing at the sunlight creeping over the lagoon, and their breath and music notes purl into pink skies. Their cattail perches and pampas grass plumes sway as Iseul and I wade into the shallows. Eelgrass curls around our bare toes.

It feels like a personal welcome from the wetland, washing us over with childhood memories of paddling around the salt-licked coastline.

When I see nothing but miles of water kissing the sky, a continuity broken only by the stoic form of a white stork or the occasional fisherman in a wooden boat, I am put into a pocket in space and time where my shoulders know no weight other than their own. I know Iseul feels the same—in this place, the stillness temporarily hushes our awareness of Ha-joon's deteriorating state and of our inability to help because he and *Umma* and *Appa* are halfway around the globe.

Iseul has visited their new home in Korea once. I still have not. I argue that the plane ticket money should be spent on Ha-joon's treatments—I wire most of my payments from my lab tech work to their Shinhan bank account, against *Umma's* insistent "Oh, don't, Abby-*ya* . . ." I tell everyone: I'm chin-deep in lab work anyway. I tell everyone: I'll hold out with video calls.

I keep to myself. I am afraid of running into certain people unprepared, the two people whose spools upon spools of DNA gave rise to mine. I can't imagine it being a chance encounter—an unceremonious bump at a bus station or in the fish aisle of a grocery store, or someone who steps on my foot on the subway. I don't want it to be accidental. And how would I even know if it really was them, two random passersby? How do I know if their cells really mirror my cells? You will see what you want to see, after all.

Iseul sighs happily beside me, and I give up my thoughts to the water around us.

I point at a damselfly, perched on its stilt legs on a blade of glass, and wade toward it, trying to think instead about Ha-joon's unfaltering ability to stay in the honeymoon phase with life despite all the antilife cancer bullshit that life has thrown at him.

I come away with the damselfly cupped gently between my hands and wade over to Iseul.

"Take a picture for Ha-joon," I say.

Iseul pulls out her phone, and I lift away a hand and she snaps a picture of it sitting glittering blue on my palm. It flexes its light-sheet wings.

"Here she goes," I say.

Silent as a train of thought, it takes off.

"You know it's a she?" Iseul says.

"Females have a stockier build, and they've got a little bulb at the tip of the abdomen," I say. "That's what they use to lay eggs." The damselfly is a speck in the sky. I wonder how far it will fly, how many bodies of water it can cross. So I keep talking. I keep talking as though I can tie this string of words to the vanishing creature like a message to a homebound pigeon. "You know, a lot of female insects have bacteria that live *inside* of their egg cells and determine what sex the off-spring turn out to be. It's called *Wolbachia*, and it's the radical feminist of the microbial world. It's in flies, wasps, aphids, mosquitoes . . . It can direct development into females only and kill off larvae developing into males. It increases lifespan, makes them resistant to viral infections, some *Wolbachia* even have helpful viruses inside of themselves." I pause. "You want me to keep going, or nah?"

Iseul stares, laughs. "You nerd."

Then all of a sudden, I am thinking. Maybe, maybe this is the key to the salt slug bacteria's erratic behavior—a virus within? Perhaps this is the angle I need to consider, the piece I was missing all along. A virus within the bacteria—called a bacteriophage—might explain the unusual patterns I had been seeing, plus the failed experiments.

I might not be kicked out of the lab after all.

Iseul watches my face. "The cogs are turning again," she says, elbowing me. "Come on, we came here to relax. Forget your lab worries for a hot second. Let's go eat something."

We sit down a little way from the water, where low-lying squat trees spread their boughs over the ground like nesting birds spreading their wings over their eggs, and watch a dis-tant fisherman in a wooden boat pushing along with a long slender pole. I reach out for the sack of croissants. One for Iseul and one for myself. I'm reaching for the thermos of *yuja* tea that Iseul brought along when I notice that she is rubbing her upper arm, as she does when something is on her mind.

"What's up," I say. I wave my croissant at her incriminating gesture.

Iseul rolls her eyes. "You scientists and your need to pay attention to every detail."

"Come on, spill it."

Iseul makes a noncommittal noise.

"Oh, come on," I say. "How bad can it be?"

And then I learn that Iseul has met with the black-market man from the night market again.

"We talked one more time," she admits. "I interviewed him for my article. Anonymously, of course. He does what he does because he's trying to make ends meet to make sure his twin sister goes to college."

Iseul must have had a heart-to-heart with the guy.

Iseul is very good at coaxing stories out of people. There is something about her gentle mannerisms and expressive eyes that leaps across the normal period of time it takes for trust to stitch together the space between two people. It is near-instantaneous. People first tentatively trickle and then pour their life stories at her, and she sits and listens and swells an aura of comfort. It is a natural-born gift. I can't relate—this is why she is such a renowned investigative journalist and why I am not. Maybe that's because I have a permanent groove between my eyebrows that makes me look perpetually ticked off. I blame its existence on all the time lab work requires me to squint at cells and molecules and other small things, but sometimes I am glad that my presence does not elicit life stories left and right because, honestly, I could not bear that extra weight.

"But there's something else you should know." Iseul is still rubbing her upper arm. "He and his twin sister were also brought up by that drop-box pastor."

I stop chewing.

"The same drop-box pastor," Iseul says. "*Your* drop-box pastor."

"So they grew up in Korea?"

"The guy was there until his late teens. Apparently he and a number of other drop-box babies were likely children of U.S. Marines who were stationed on South Korean islands. The pastor told him that. So he and his sister wanted to come to the States to see what it's like here. Get to know the other half of their heritage."

Iseul shoos away a fly buzzing over my head. "You were probably born around the time he was. When we went to the night market, he looked like he was around the same age as you. So I wanted to talk to him again. And I did."

"How'd you get in touch with him in the first place?"

Iseul looks hesitant. "That article I'm working on—it started when I found a link between illegal poaching of the nudibranchs that produce chemotherapeutics and Marines stationed in Korea. Turns out that the pharma company that owns the license to the drug was involved in a hush-hush deal with the military bases in Korea, insisting that military bases were to be offered as collateral in order to make their product available to the country. You won't believe how deep this black vein runs; healthcare providers given kickbacks for prescribing the drugs more often . . . And then a month ago a man was arrested in Hong Kong for smuggling rare nudibranchs endemic to Korean islands. He confessed to having spent years in the business, colluding with Marines once stationed in the area. That's how it started. And then I got curious. I called that pastor not long after you did. He told me a lot of the babies who end up under his care are from—"

"Sex-trafficking," I finish flatly. "U.S. military bases and Korean women. So there's a link to your old article. That other one you risked your life for."

Iseul nods. "So I was interested, of course. Two worlds collide. That sort of thing. When you find a trail like that, you follow it."

"And so then?" I prompt.

"I was curious. I had a hunch that there was a common thread running through all that. So I contacted that smuggler." Iseul sounds defensive now. She eyes me reproachfully. "You look so angry. I'll admit it—at first, getting the sea slug compounds from him was both for Ha-joon and out of curiosity for what else I could find out. And then when I finally saw the thing . . ." She shakes her head. "I couldn't just stop there. Too much going on that needed answers. So I reached out to the guy again. Look, Abby, from a scientist's point of view—would you be able to stop at *that* kind of data? The kind of data that seems like it connects so many other unrelated data points—sea slugs, melanoma, sex trafficking, military bases, drop boxes, and . . ." She makes a little motion at me. "You. Just maybe."

This explains the papers I'd seen on Iseul's desk last week and all her evasive behavior. I say slowly, "And so then this guy told you his life story."

"Some." She shrugs. "There's still more I want to ask him, but he got skittish after realizing that I wasn't there to buy more from him and he ran off. Abby, you know you can't stop me. Stop giving me that look. This is my line of work. It's how it is. You know that. I'd never get between you and your science."

I'm not sure what to say. With what I know to be my base-line stubbornness it would seem reflexive to bristle at being word-sparred into a corner, but this happens often enough with Iseul that I've built up a tolerance for it.

So I shrug. I find something to say. "I can fetch sea slugs from the lab that you can woo him with. Maybe he has an invertebrate fetish."

Iseul rolls her eyes.

"Or maybe he's into having variety," I say. "Maybe he's got a taste for echinoderms. Sea slugs are mollusks, but we could probably find some other washed-up echinoderms from Strand Beach to complement his nudibranch sea slugs. Sand dollars, maybe." I sound like an idiot, half-joking words emerging out of a distortion of confusion and fear and curiosity.

Iseul snorts. "But actually," she says, "we should go sometime."

"I have to go collect local sea slug specimens for an experiment anyway and most are nocturnal. We'll also come back with echinoderms to last you a lifetime."

"Good, wouldn't settle for anything less."

"I'm glad you got an early return on your sea slug investment."

That gets me an elbow in my side.

Then a thought snags. I turn to face Iseul, no longer laughing, instead thinking of the papers I saw on her desk, that crude diagram she'd drawn that had my name circled in the center with more lines and names radiating out of it, thinking of the lengths to which Iseul goes to help me. I say, "But if you're doing this just to help me in my personal search, don't. You're not allowed to risk your own life for me under any—"

Iseul elbows me again. "I'm not doing this *just* for your sake. There. Okay?" She laughs, looking genuinely at ease.

"Stop worrying, I'll be fine. It's not just for you. Don't be so full of yourself, Miss Protagonist. Hubris doesn't look good on you. I have reasons for doing this."

I look at Iseul's sparkling eyes and try to believe her.

Once, in high school, I asked Iseul, "What's the worst thing about writing stories about people?" We were eighteen then, sitting on one of the concrete planters that dotted the high school campus and waiting for the bus. This was the first of two times I asked her that question.

"I feel like I have to help everyone. Everyone has something they want to say. It's hard to sift through it all. Savior complex, right?"

The second time I asked her that question we were twenty-two, months before college graduation, a little over a year ago.

This time, Iseul said, "The feeling that I can't help. I can't help Ha-joon at all with my writing."

She told me that there is much debate in the journalist community about how close or how distant you should stay from the people you write about. Deciding where to put your emotions when you talk to people and write about their stories is like deciding where to cut off a limb—there's not really one painless answer.

She laughed a little after saying that. Not that anything she said was funny.

Iseul's defense mechanism for pain and uncertainty is laughing, covering things up with a smiley-face band-aid.

I told her that.

She laughed a little again.

I asked her what she thought was mine.

She said, "I don't think you *have* a defense mechanism. I think it's all offense mechanism."

I thought about that.

"You're bullheaded," she said. "You never ask for help. You always have to be the one doing everything, solving all your problems alone." She paused, laughing, and not defensively this time. "You want me to keep going?"

"I'm flattered. Please do."

"You hate confrontation, so you hide your feelings to make the other person have to do the work. Plus, physical violence makes you throw up. But if you did throw up, you'd probably direct said throw-up onto the perpetrator."

"You know you're the only person who can say stuff like this and get away with it."

"Well, maybe cracking the odd joke is the one exception," she added. "But only to jab at the other person, which, again, is on the offense."

So I suppose that is why we became close in the first place, her with sunshine defense and me with my brass-knuckle offense. It's the stuff of mandalas. Like the mandalas that a high school counselor had me draw back in sophomore year. The walls in her office were a washed-out blue. I was there after a teacher got frustrated at the class and threw a dry-erase pen across the room, which made me freeze up in a nervous breakdown with my eyeballs rolling into my skull because I started having flashbacks of things flying across apartment living rooms. I sat in that pale blue room for hours. I think I would never have left had it not occurred to me that my adoptive father's eyes were a similar blue.

But Iseul and I, we have both always had a sense of direction. She was set on journalism as though it made up her cells. Myself, I knew that the cool objectivity of science needed to be a part of mine.

Later in high school, I made a microscope out of cardstock, tin foil, a flashlight, and carefully arranged single droplets of water that acted as lenses to channel light and magnify. Through this, I looked at rainwater and saw single-celled organisms with whip-like extensions called flagella that they used to propel themselves in the direction of their choice. In this microscopic realm, where haphazard Brownian motion will toss less-determined little creatures left and right, you can't just sit passively. You will be thrown off course. You must be on the offensive.

◆ 12 ◆

AFTER WE RETURN TO Iseul's apartment that evening, I borrow her car and drive straight back to the lab, making the excuse that I'd left my wallet there. The virus hunch I had while we were standing knee-deep in water never once left my mind.

By the time the concrete building is in sight, it's half past eight, late enough that the limited parking around the natural sciences drive has mostly emptied out. I pull into the loading zone at the entrance, fumble with the car keys, nearly drop them on my way in.

To know if there's a virus within the salt slug bacteria—a bacteriophage—I will have to retake microscopy images. The images I already have aren't zoomed in enough; phages are tiny, often only tens of nanometers long. That's already several hours of work I'm looking at.

But that doesn't matter. I just need to know.

I card myself into the lab. Texan Simon is still in, weighing out various powders and whistling *Bohemian Rhapsody*. He's having trouble reaching the higher notes, and he's not even at the "Galileo" portion yet. He nods at me as I walk in and make my way to the corner with the salt slug tanks.

It's routine. Scoop out a sea slug from one of the tanks, anesthetize with cold water and magnesium chloride, slice with a razor blade through to the tissue that wraps around the gastrointestinal tract where the bacterial endosymbionts tend to cluster, shave off a sliver and fix with paraformaldehyde and mount on a glass slide. Preparing microscopy slides of sea slug tissue used to bother me. I used to feel faint, and the issue was never squeamishness—as long as I don't think about internal secrets being flayed open to the world, the tide of queasiness never comes.

Across the lab, Texan Simon is drawing closer to the operatic parts of the song and I brace myself. He misses, off-key.

My finger stings, and I realize that I've cut through my glove in my distraction. There's a bit of blood that slips out onto the salt slug slices. Shit. I rush the slides over to the sink and rinse them off—my cut isn't the problem here—and I debate over whether I should toss all of the slides I've prepared and start from scratch.

I look up. Simon is still weighing out reagents and whistling and hasn't noticed.

This isn't as bad as the time Simon incompletely shut off the tap to his Bunsen burner. The valve wasn't turned all the way and kept leaking all night long and when everyone came into work the next morning, it smelled like gas for hours even with all of the windows propped open. Stanley's anger lasted much longer than the lingering smell.

By the time I've dabbed off my finger, Simon's whistling has reached the end. *Nothing really matters, any way the wind blows.*

Any way the wind blows, I agree, as I wrap a piece of lab parafilm around my finger and pull on a new glove and go ahead with my slides anyway.

When I bring them to the microscopy room, I realize quickly that my own cells from the cut on my thumb have indeed contaminated the slides: there are foreign cells floating around that lack the distinctive features of the salt slug cells that I'm so used to looking at. *Damn.* Should have trusted my gut and thrown out the samples and started afresh instead of plowing along. I'm leaning back staring at the ceiling, rolling my eyes, then stooping down to swipe the slides into the disposal, when I do a double take.

Inside of my cells, very distinctly outlined, are *more cells*. They're encased within thin membranous vesicles.

I rub at the computer monitor, but the outlines are not dust or grime. It's only a fraction of the contaminating cells—not the red blood cells, which are easy to tell apart because they are small and have no nuclei, but what I presume are skin cells. Each of them contains internal extra residents, some with as few as two, others with as many as eight, but no matter the variation in number, the fact stands that there is something *very strange* about my cells.

I lean back, woozy.

Any injuries in the lab are supposed to be officially reported, but I'm scared that might lead to someone else finding out about my strange biology before I myself have figured out what's going on.

I save the images onto my laptop, then carefully delete them from the microscope computer.

I make the decision not to file an injury report.

★　★　★

"Iseul, holy shit. You won't believe it."

"What?" Her voice is groggy.

"Holy shit. There are cells inside my own cells—maybe I've discovered an endosymbiont of humans. That's absolutely unheard of. That's unheard of in mammals at all. There are cells *inside* my cells. They didn't seem like pathogens, no signs of harm to my cells at all. They could be endosymbionts."

Hands shaking, face heated despite the night cold, I almost drop my cellphone.

"Holy shit. This could be huge. No one's heard of something like this before, this could be a major scientific discovery. This could singularly make up for all of my failed experiments. This could open up a whole entire new field of biology. Iseul, my hands are shaking so much."

"You found them in your own cells?"

"Yes! Yes. In my own cells. Iseul, what are they doing in there? How'd they get in there, am I the only one or are they in other people? I need to do so many more experiments, I need to figure this out—"

"Abby, I think you've again not realized it's past two in the morning."

"Oh god, is it?"

"Let's get some sleep first, yeah?"

"Okay. Okay. Holy shit. Okay. See you tomorrow."

★ ★ ★

Quickly after that, it becomes a game of squeezing in experiments on my own cells. My secret secondary project. I add a DNA probe lying around, and find out quickly that the cells within my own cells are bacterial.

A bacterial endosymbiont of a human, possibly—unbelievable. A cell inside a cell, like Russian nesting dolls.

I keep thinking "a human" rather than "myself."

It's like the case studies of individuals from classic psychology and neuroscience. A person singled out after a tragic incident that causes brain damage, to be studied and probed, like the guy who lost all sense of inhibition after surviving a metal rod that went straight through his frontal lobe. A medical marvel. A singular curiosity. Something like a museum artifact to be studied from all angles. An intellectual puzzle to be solved, as Stanley might be inclined to say.

I think to myself: I have discovered a bacterial endosymbiont of a *human*. I put protective distance into this murky space, because otherwise, I'm afraid I will feel more isolated and outcast than I have ever felt before.

Most of the following nights in lab I fidget at my desk rearranging my folders of to-be-read papers, watching Texan Simon's backpack from the corner of my eye—Simon is almost always in lab the latest, and the presence of his backpack is the indicator that he's still up and about somewhere. Until that backpack is gone, I can't get going on my secret work.

Come to think of it, no one would ask what experiments I'm doing (pipetting is pipetting), but I am too jittery. If I were in more control of my shaky hands, which are a clear emotional giveaway—*why are your hands shaking so much?*—maybe I would have the boldness to do my side experiments even during the daytime.

Shaky hands are no good for pipetting anyway.

★   ★   ★

It turns out that my shaky-handed inability to sneak experiments in during the day saves my skin.

One day in lab I am extracting RNA from isolated salt slug endosymbionts—but wishing I could be unraveling my own cells—when the sound of footsteps coming up behind me makes me jump.

"How is the work coming along, Abby?" Stanley asks. His left eye is twitching as it does when he is impatient, which means that his question is not so much a question as it is applied pressure to give him results ASAP. British Simon mentioned the other day that Stanley has a big grant deadline coming up very soon.

"It's coming along," I say. There are a lot of failed experiments behind the curtain of those three words. But my secret knowledge of my cells and their inner lives keeps me buoyant.

Stanley gives a noncommittal grunt, and continues down the lab.

He only makes that sound when he is displeased.

"The Lenner Grunt." Texan Simon gives a low whistle from his bench behind me.

"Not my first." Almost immediately I add, "And it won't be my last."

But there's no denying that Stanley Lenner is pretty good at being a scientist.

It was as a graduate student that he discovered the basis of his present-day lab. At the Great Salt Lake, Utah, October 2009—says the caption underneath a picture of young Stanley on the webpage bio featuring his recent research award. I count back the years in my head. The lab is an overachieving teenager. This month marks the sixteenth year since his lab has been up and running.

I scroll down, and there's another photo of young Stanley floating cross-legged in the salty pink water. I'm amused to see that Stanley once had a full head of brown curly hair. He's smiling for the camera, but even then it was only with his mouth. There is no warmth behind the eyes.

It's always the eyes that never change, years down the line. A person's skin sags as they age, or they develop a slight hunch, or their step becomes arthritis-slow, but the eyes are always the same. When I look at old pictures of Iseul and me from our middle and high school days, her eyes in the pictures glow with their present-day kindness and stability. My eyes still have the same nervous edge, a fragile kind of contentedness like spun glass.

Stanley's eyes are piercing. They will never have the crow's feet that Iseul's do.

All those years ago, he was supposed to be collecting specimens of microbes in the Great Salt Lake. Then he stumbled upon a living creature, what looked like a sea slug, and it changed his life. With the "salt slug," which he named *Siphopteron salina,* he started his own lab and reeled in lots of grant money and won awards and titles and invitations to give plenary talks at big-name conferences.

So yes, Stanley is very famous.

He was already wallowing in success and fame from early on. It's been so many years of consecutive achievement that I think he's entirely forgotten what it feels like to stumble, to doubt yourself, to feel small.

Texan Simon told me when I first joined the lab that Stanley was solving unsolved physics problems by the time he was out of grade school, and that it was only when child Stanley was pouring his brain into solving the unsolved that his restless leg syndrome temporarily went away. A textbook savant. Ever since then, I have kept an eye on his leg-bouncing. One-to-one meeting and his leg is bouncing as I present my data? He is not engaged. Simon also said that he is twice-divorced. The rumor transmitted through years of lab members is that in the heat of an argument with his wife, he would shout that problems in science were, unlike the woman in front of him, both solvable and beautiful.

And therein lies the difference between Stanley and me. He does science because it's an intellectual game for him, both his lifelong playground and the obsessive love of his life, the only thing that satiates his sweet tooth for brain candy. I do science out of a frantic desperation, a disarray of wanting to understand the origins of something else because I cannot understand my own. Deluded, perhaps, but I often think, if I can just understand the origins of life itself, the most fundamental pieces, then that will surely be the gateway to understanding mine.

"That's how science works, right?" I said to Iseul once. We were driving to the beach on a Sunday afternoon. "Reductionism. To understand biology, you have to understand chemistry. To understand chemistry, you have to understand physics. To understand physics, you have to understand math."

She was silent, watching the palm trees flying by outside.

"How is a person supposed to understand *all* of that?" I said. How am I supposed to understand the complex network of random events that make up a single person's history, my own? That make up this whole ecosystem branching through time? There may have been a shrill note in my voice.

I think about this again as I sit down in front of my computer, Stanley out of sight, and click through images of my own cells. The stained bacterial DNA is lit up like a flare.

A human endosymbiont? I still can't believe it.

What if I'm the only one with this? The only one with this unknown living inside her own cells?

The thought of being so alone, so singularly isolated is chilling: cold sluices down my spine like ice water.

The orphan child, abandoned by one family, picked up by another across the ocean, abandoned again—could it be that her status as an outcast is not happenstance, but one that is written into her cells?

A biological basis for her outsider status.

I can't bear to think about it.

I can't decide if I want to solve this puzzle or not. Maybe some stories should be left unspoken, unwritten, unthought.

Scary stories come from all sorts of places, far and near. Very near, even.

Case in point: a critical piece of RNA in the hepatitis D virus performs a bit of chemistry that is the spitting image of the behavior of some human-derived RNA. So, it has been proposed that HDV, the scourge of millions of lives worldwide, originated from the human genome itself.

Hits rather close to home. Who knows what these bacteria in my cells are doing, are capable of?

♦ 13 ♦

I'M SO JITTERY THAT I spend the night awake in bed pulling apart split ends under the glow of my bedside lamp. Once or twice, I look out my window in the hopes of spotting a stray cat in the moonlight, like the one that kept me company on sleepless nights in my adoptive parents' apartment, but all night long, there is no cat, and I am alone.

Iseul calls me in the morning, as I'm on the bus to the lab.

"Any luck getting sleep?"

"Nope. But I have enough black tea to last me a lifetime." I drink from said massive tumbler. "I don't know if I should tell someone in my lab."

"Are you thinking of the Simon from Texas? Or the hard-as-nails one. Petra, right?"

"Simon. Simon might know how to move forward with the science. He's worked with all sorts of endosymbionts, from insects to spotted salamanders." I raise my tumbler to my lips again. The bus rolls over a pothole and the jostle spurts hot liquid against the back of my throat, and I'm coughing violently. "God, I don't know, I don't know, I'm just scared." I cough again. "Why is it always me who's the odd one out?" I sound like a petulant child.

Iseul is quiet. Then she says, "You know, even if you turned into some horrific multi-armed, tentacled creature with fangs, you *still* wouldn't be free from my nagging."

"Oh yeah, you'd still nag me about not eating lunch at normal-people hours of the day."

"If you called me and said that you'd eaten only *one* random-dom passerby for lunch—"

"Oh god, imagine the horror, only one passerby? That's insufficient protein intake."

"Unacceptable." I can hear her smiling. She says, "Stop worrying so much, yeah?"

"Yeah." I look out the window and the concrete biosciences tooth rolls into view. Its familiar bulk is oddly comforting. "Why don't we drive to the beach later today? We can go hunt for echinoderms for you and your mystery man, and I can collect some local sea slugs for me and my science gig."

"I'll drive this time around?"

"I'll be out by four."

On the sidewalk where the bus rolls to a stop, there is a woman in a yellow sundress pushing a stroller. The green of the stroller and the blue-clothed baby nestled inside reminds me instantly of the microscopy images of my cells: the microscopic scaffolding of my cells, the intermediate filaments, stained bright green, and then the membranous bulwarks of the bacterial residents stained bright blue.

It occurs to me in this moment, watching mother and child, that many endosymbionts are passed along from parent to offspring. Vertical transmission, as scientists call it.

It next occurs to me that if the bacteria inside of my cells are indeed vertically transmitted, then it's possible that my *birth parents* might have them in their cells as well.

If this is true, I could science my way to my birth parents.

I almost fall over as I step down from the bus onto the sidewalk.

It's a possibility.

But whether an endosymbiont is transmitted vertically depends on the particular endosymbiont. I don't know enough about endosymbiont biology; I mostly work with some narrow biochemistry within my salt slugs.

But Texan Simon knows a lot.

★ ★ ★

In the lab, Petra is furious: she's ejecting her used pipette tips into the plastic disposal bin on her lab bench from higher above, so that the clack of plastic on plastic is loud. She doesn't look up when I walk into my bay, and it's just the two of us wrapped in early morning silence.

The last time she was silently fuming, the rest of the lab played a discreet guessing game. It turned out I'd guessed correctly, sort of—*Stanley didn't approve of one of her ideas?* We found out the next day that Stanley had told her that he wouldn't support her leaving his lab for her own independent research position until she finished her current project. Or rather, I saw the email exchange open on her laptop screen when I came around to return her stapler to her unattended desk.

An angry Petra is often best left to her own devices.

Half an hour of silence later, interspersed by aggressive pipette-tip-ejecting, Texan Simon arrives, and I leap out of my chair.

"That eager to see me?" He raises his eyebrows as he walks into our bay, and he points his chin questioningly in Petra's direction.

I shrug.

"Have you seen Tomás anywhere?" Simon sets down his backpack and pulls on a pair of gloves. "I'm collecting four hundred fly ovary samples today. Which will hopefully all contain bacteria. Tomás had mercy on me and said he would help." He pulls on a pair of gloves.

I shake my head.

Simon grimaces. "Looks like I'm doing it all solo then." He gathers up a box loaded with pipettes, tips, little vials.

"Hey, wait, Simon." I stop him before he heads out. "Are you sending any of those samples for 16S sequencing anytime soon?" 16S rRNA sequencing is a means of identifying bacterial species in a sample. The ribosome, a tiny molecular machine made of both proteins and RNA responsible for manufacturing most of a cell's proteins, has a sequence of RNA unique to each bacterial species. This bit is called the 16S rRNA, and can be used to identify species, including—hopefully—the bacterial endosymbionts within my cells.

"Later today, actually," he says.

"Can I submit one sample with yours?"

"Sure. What've you got? I thought we already had the salt slug endosymbionts figured out?"

"Yeah, this is a different bug."

Simon's eyebrows lift. "Cliffhanger. Not gonna tell me anything else?"

"I—" I balk. *They're from my cells. My own cells.*

Simon looks amused. "What is it, like really bad data?"

I turn back to my computer, pull up the colorful images of the endosymbiont bacteria within my cells, and carefully watch Simon's face.

"I mean, first off, that's a really nice image," he says, leaning closer to the screen. "I don't know why you were so embarrassed. Looks like some kind of eukaryotic cell that's got some endosymbiotic bacteria."

"Yeah, that's right."

"But they're not cells from your salt slugs, because the cell shape isn't correct."

"Right again."

Simon looks bemused, eyebrows rising above the wire frames of his glasses. "Keep going?"

"What kind of bacteria do you think they are?"

"You can't really tell just looking at them. Based off the thickness of the cell wall, I'm guessing it's a Gram-negative species, but really, I don't know." He shrugs. "We'd know after 16S sequencing."

I nod quickly. *Good.*

"Yeah," he says, "just prep the samples and leave them with mine, and I'll take care of the rest."

And then I leave before he can ask me where the cells came from.

Iseul comes to pick me up from lab after I finish prepping my cells for Texan Simon.

She is waiting by the lounge chairs just outside the hallway lined with labs, hair pulled up into a bun and typing away on her laptop.

"What's cooking?" I say as I approach.

Iseul looks up and grins. "The next grand slam article, that's what. Ready?"

I shoulder my backpack. Inside is a flashlight I added this morning, to scope out sea slugs and the sand dollars that wash up on beach shores at night. Beside the flashlight is a bundle of plastic baggies, for collecting sea slug specimens, and a small plastic aquarium tank.

"Never been more echinoderm-ready," I say. "But chicken first as always."

Iseul shakes her car keys in agreement.

We drive through our favorite chicken joint, pick up a box each of extra hot wings and honey garlic wings. The sweet, garlicky, sticky smell fills the car interior and, swaddled in nighttime darkness, it feels safe to ask:

"So, want to tell me more about black-market guy?"

Iseul doesn't flinch and doesn't take her eyes off the road. The light ahead changes to red and casts her face in a flushed light.

I press. "How'd you get in touch anyway?"

The traffic light changes, and her face is green, like ocean algae.

She speaks slowly. "I interviewed a local guy when I was writing that piece on sex trafficking linked to the American military base in Seoul. He talked about desperation. He talked about how it shows up in things like getting life-saving medications by any means and just banking on a lot of hopes."

"He had connections?"

"We all have questionable connections." Her words are almost snappish, quick to defend the sea-slug-juice guy. "Don't we all?"

I can't disagree. I know so well; my cells are full of them.

"So, can I read your article?"

Iseul never lets anyone read her articles until she has a full draft.

"You already know the drill. You can read it when it's done." Iseul is always gentle but doesn't budge. "I promise."

★ ★ ★

We pull up to Strand State Beach, the glittering cityscape behind us illuminating the night and throwing rippling lights onto the watery expanse ahead. We bring our food to the usual spot, the concrete picnic benches that dot the transition from city to sand. We trace the strip of cushion sand that cusps the soft dry hilly mounds and the quicksand-like parts that the ocean licks over and over. Prime walking sand, easy to traverse, peppered with seagull tracks and the pitter-patter steps of sea plovers.

There are not many other nighttime visitors. As we plod to the shoreline, we pass by an old man walking his dog, and then a couple lying together on the sand, and further off in the distance is a quiet figure silhouetted against the warm lights from the boardwalk shops.

The waters glitter with bioluminescence as though the ocean has reached up and engulfed the night sky.

"That's *Pyrocystis fusiformis* and *Lingulodinium polyedra* hard at work," I say.

We stand ankle-deep in water. The waves roll toward us and then draw back, tugging on the sand under our feet that sucks on our toes.

I look over at Iseul and she is utterly transfixed.

"Never doesn't feel amazing," she says, and I agree.

I click on the flashlight. Iseul reaches down into the water with a plastic disposable cup and lifts it back up full of seawater, where there is a tiny nickel-sized creature striped white and shades of blue with winglike fans running down its sides. It is the blue dragon nudibranch, and like its namesake it is a feisty thing that you don't want to touch; the little invertebrate eats poisonous jellyfish and stores the stinging cells in its own skin.

"Here's nudibranch number one." She moves back and sets the cup gently on the sand. "Beautiful, isn't it?" She wades in a little deeper, "Shall we look for some more then?"

The flashlight sputters out.

"Of all possible times for dead batteries," I mutter.

Iseul reaches into her pockets, jangles her car keys. "Is it AA? I have some more in the car."

I wave her in place.

"You stay and watch the waves," I say. I reach for the keys and pull them from her hands. She relinquishes them happily.

"Check the glove compartment," she says.

I splash out of the water and plod up the sand toward the outlines of the sparse cars pressed up against the sidewalk, outlined by the moonlight coming off their hoods. I get to Iseul's car, find the batteries, swap them into the flashlight. I click. The abrupt light beam is blinding in the dark interior of the car. I turn back to the sea.

That is when I see that something is wrong.

Traced in bioluminescence, there is a spot where the seafoam coasting on the tops of the waves is not heading into shore. An ominously foamless patch of sea. Troubled, I hurry across the sand, until I can make out Iseul's outline against the lack of foam. She has waded out farther since I left, she is stomach-deep.

I break out into a run. Sand flings up into my face.

"Iseul! Get out of the water!"

She does not seem to have heard me. I can see the foam patterns on the water now. They skirt toward the shore and then whorl inward into the bare seawater and draw back away before disappearing under the surface. These are rip currents, clear as day during the night.

I am only yards away now. I shout at Iseul again, my voice careening upward in panic. When she finally seems to hear, turning back toward me, a surging wave swells out of the water and plunges toward her. The wave does not break and barrel, and instead it rushes around Iseul and then immediately pulls back, sucking its swallowed contents out to sea. There is no whitewater, only lightless ocean being violently drawn down and away. Iseul is gone.

Something inside of me drops like ballast weight.

In the darkness, I think I see a hand break through the waves but it is submerged before I can blink. It is too far out, too far out already. Some rip currents move almost ten feet per second.

Blood pulsating in my ears, I cannot hear above the whooshing in my head, cannot hear my own shouting voice blindly spearfishing for Iseul. Tinnitus cancels thoughts. I regain control of my limbs and I fumble for my phone, call emergency. Rip current, rip current, I tumble into the phone. I look around, eyes rolling. Near Tower 9, yes, Tower 9.

The operator says to wait while he pings Tower 9. No one is there, of course, because lifeguards are only on duty from morning to dusk.

I only realize how hard my legs are juddering when my knees buckle, and I fall to the sand. The operator tells me that a dispatch is on its way. Okay, I say. He cautions me. Don't go into the water to find her yourself, that is the last thing you want to do, don't make yourself a victim too. Okay, I know. Hang in there, we'll be there soon. Okay.

But the motion picture in my brain is awful. I keep seeing hair fanned out in the water, like feathered black algae.

The dispatch comes soon and gets a water rescue boat out onto the dark sea, a little red inflatable thing buzzing along the water, its yellow floodlight slicing the ocean's surface like a butter knife.

I crawl across the sand. Iseul's phone is lying on the sand next to mine where we had placed them before entering the water less than an hour ago. I brush off the clinging sand with my shirt. I press the home button and the screen glows to life. A picture of me and Iseul, her lock screen. My hands quaking, I wish I had another pair to hold them still.

When I find that my legs can carry my weight, I run in the direction of the boat and its two-person crew still skimming around. The waves rush toward the sand, fail to reach the dry hillocks, withdraw, then mount another attack, over and over. I plunge my hands into the water, cup them, collect ocean between my palms and let it stream away. One of the rescue team members spots me there standing ankle-deep in water and shouts at me to stay away.

Once my legs give way and fold and I sink down to the sand, I begin to think. There is a keening pain in my core because I know that Iseul is a terrible swimmer. Has been since we were kids.

I stand up again and pace the strip of hard-packed sand with my numb head in between my hands until the boat draws in to shore and gives me the news that I knew was coming but still leaves me winded.

We're really, really sorry, one of them says.

When I try to look past her at the boat, where I think I see the outline of a large yellow zip-up bag, the woman sidles herself into my field of vision.

We can handle that later, yeah? the dispatch woman says.

They talk to me about my relation to Iseul, her nearest living relatives, forensics, everything that mixes into the muddied mess of my thoughts. Police arrive, ask a flurry of questions, which suddenly reminds me of my adoptive father—*who what when where*—and write down my responses as they leave my mouth, which reminds me of Iseul interviewing people for her articles. Where are her family members residing? They moved back to South Korea four years ago? One officer pulls a seashell fragment from the sole of his boot, glances at it, and throws it back into the ocean waves.

I look into that dark, dark ocean and I see all that I could not stop.

★　★　★

I drive home in Iseul's car. It is still full of her smell. Once or twice, something amoeboid moves up my throat, but I swallow it back down. The blue dragon nudibranch sits quietly in the plastic tank I have buckled into the passenger seat.

In my apartment, I put the little tank on the kitchen table, and I touch in Iseul's phone password—HotGoose, which is a high school reference to the look on her then-boyfriend's face when he came across her audio recording titled "sexy time," which was actually a recording of Canada geese mating calls. I open up the photos. There are pictures of us secreted away in here that I don't have on my own phone—pieces of life that so quickly went from present tense to past tense.

I am an idiot. Idiot. Idiot. How could you not see that it was rip current zone? You have been trained for this, for all the time you spent collecting sea slugs. Idiot.

What if I had just gone in and tried to find her and bring her back? I am a strong enough swimmer, stronger at least than Iseul. But I know that I am being an idiot. Never enter a rip current to save someone if you are not a trained professional. A fundamental beachgoer law. Drilled into me every trip I took to the shore to collect marine samples for the lab. But what if, what if. What if.

When I crawl into bed, I realize that there is ocean salt rimed white and powdery on my legs, but I leave it there to preserve what I can.

II.
SMALL WORLD, RNA WORLD

Until more recent years, people pigeonholed ribonucleic acid as a lowly intermediate between a cell's DNA and a cell's proteins. DNA is a template for messenger RNA, which is itself a template for proteins. mRNA conveys life instructions to proteinaceous progeny.

This is the establishment: mRNA starts a sheltered life inside the protective walls of the nucleus, the womb-like safe place where DNA is stashed away, a bulwark against the busy highways and nightlife and dangers in the greater intracellular beyond, a place unfit for the unlearned still green behind the molecular ears. Only once a smattering of enzymes snip and preen and bejewel a strand of mRNA is it sent out to the world. There, it reaches childbearing age, gives rise to proteins.

This is the Central Dogma status quo of biology.

But people have since discovered that RNA can do much more than produce proteins. Like DNA, it can store information. Like proteins, it can catalyze reactions. Perhaps it existed before both other molecules, sintered into existence within primordial bodies of water.

There is no debate that RNA incubates not only life, but also untapped potential.

◆ 15 ◆

ONCE THERE WAS A doctor who measured the weight of his patients while they were still barely alive and then after they were corpses. He did the same with dogs, and then claimed that only in humans was there a loss of precisely twenty-one grams when shifting over the cusp between life and death. And so, a Dr. Duncan MacDougall published his findings in 1907 that he had elucidated that the human soul, the elusive thing, weighs twenty-one grams and slips out of the mortal form upon the final exhalation, accounting for the loss in body weight.

This is, of course, bullshit. Modern studies refute his claim with plenty of evidence along the lines of water evaporation and measurement error.

One might also wonder why this doctor had so many almost-dying patients to begin with, and wonder how that reflects on his capacities as a practicing health-care professional.

But let me tell you. The human soul may not weigh twenty-one grams, but it also does not weigh nothing. Contrary to popular opinion, it also does not look like an ethereal gossamer outline gently glowing around the edges. No. It is shaped like an angry thorn-covered gremlin, and it weighs at bare minimum a ton, and, imbued with the newly liberated spitefulness no longer shushed *by a living person's good manners and civility, leaps up and out of its dead body to latch onto the shoulders of those who loved it the most in life, burdening them with a heavy and painful weight so that they can never, ever forget.*

★　★　★

The weekend is like picking out a footpath through broken glass.

I try very hard not to think, but of course I think of Iseul anyway, and then I have to nurse my shard-pierced heart all over again.

It's phantom limb pain, I think, as I percolate through the days.

The thin strip of carpeting between my bedside table and my yellow plastic trash bin becomes worn thin as I oscillate between deciding to keep Iseul's cellphone and deciding to throw it away. I put it under my bed. When not pacing back and forth, I often stand in the kitchenette on one leg with the other bent at the knee like a flamingo, basking in the increased pressure between my foot and the hard linoleum because it reminds me that the floor still exists.

My phone lights up with calls from the Yoon home phone at scattered intervals, pings with accumulating voice mail and unopened text messages. Lots of texts from Ha-joon. My logic is that if I let these sit longer, somehow it will be better, like wine and cheese.

When I called after Iseul died, nobody could say anything. It was a stretch of silence, until *Umma* was the first one to start crying, until I was the first one to speak. It's my fault, I said, the words dropping like featherless hatchlings from a nest. It's my fault. I was there, I could have stopped it from happening.

I was right there at the same beach. I went back to the car to get batteries.

★   ★   ★

The blue nudibranch swims slowly around in the plastic aquarium tank, for the first few days. I should have taken it to the lab, but I couldn't bring myself to remove it from my apartment, couldn't fathom having to anesthetize it and take it apart in order to search for my molecules of interest—because each time I look at it, I feel the same squeeze in the heart as when I look at photographs of Iseul.

One morning, I find that it is motionless no matter how much I jostle the tank or prod at it with a chopstick. It's clearly very dead, and yet I can't bring myself to throw it away. I move it into a plastic Tupperware and put it in my fridge, next to the Iseul's illegal little vial. On second thought, I take it out again to stuff inside a brown paper bag before putting it back—I won't have to see it each time I open my fridge.

★   ★   ★

When it takes two flustered cashiers and a store manager for me to realize that I have been trying to pay for Ritz crackers and a bottle of wine by inserting my driver's license into the chip reader, I decide that I will stay away from the lab for the time being for everyone's sake. If I cannot tell the difference between a driver's license and a credit card, then it is probably not a stretch to imagine that I will not be able to tell the difference between the hand soap dispenser and the sodium hydroxide wash bottle.

I am in my kitchenette searching for my toaster when my phone vibrates again.

I know it's always *Umma*. Nobody else has reason to call me over and over; lab people will flip-flop between calling and emailing. Looking at the homogeneity in the missed call contacts, I realize that I never took the initiative to contact much anyone else in these last few years. Funny, I think, how keeping living relationships is like speaking a language, whether science or a linguistic one, something that requires deliberate practice and upkeep.

Not today, I say to my phone, as I search through my fridge. Not any day. I wave my slice of white bread at my phone until it stops vibrating. Where is the damn toaster? Then I realize that I am searching inside the fridge.

As soon as Iseul died, my brain turned to autopilot. Like riding a bike. Purkinje neurons, those sneaky bastards.

So, yes, this is all like riding a bike. In the dark. While intoxicated. As the centerpiece of a game of reverse hangman characterized by poor guesses, so stick-figure limbs are dropping off left and right.

The authorities ascertain that the cause of death was accidental drowning.

Sometimes I become subsumed by sudden rage, suspecting that Iseul put dead batteries into that flashlight on purpose. Yes. She put in dead batteries and then had me return to the car to replace them so that she could sneak off and talk to that sea slug dealer again, and then by the time I returned with fresh batteries, she would already be back, smiling and laughing and acting like nothing happened, like she'd just pulled off something as inconsequential as a cheap card trick.

But these angry flares of accusation dissipate as quickly as they come.

Every night, the fight to pass between awake and asleep becomes increasingly violent. It never comes quietly—not that it ever has. It comes in amidst halting montages of people drowning that flicker across my eyelids like stop-motion. It's some kind of witching-hour juggernaut, hurtling through melatonin, doxylamine succinate, zolpidem, barbiturates, benzodiazepines, the works. Pill bottles and blister packs piling up like a cairn for sleep.

During this time, I get into the habit of wandering around outside searching for graffiti. Sides of buildings, storage sheds, aluminum backs of street signs. Everything is fair game.

I look at the graffiti up close, nose almost touching the cold surface. I can see where the spray can slipped in palm sweat and sent fine paint careening off to the side, where the first can ran out and the artist started a second but didn't close up the gaps completely—little patches of bare concrete bleeding through, like when you scratch your skin so hard that it breaks in scattered little red dots. Not that different from looking at fluorescent mCherry-tagged cells under a confocal microscope. Little kaleidoscope of mirrors.

★   ★   ★

Then I see Iseul back from the dead.

It's in the black-and-white TV screen static in the lobby of my apartment complex. I'm returning home after going for a graffiti walk—it's the first sunny day after a week of rain—when I stop dead in my tracks on the *Welcome!* mat at the entrance.

She's waving, in the flickering pixels. She's waving both of her arms above her head, the way she does when she's excited and calling me over from a distance, smiling, pausing for a moment to push back her untied hair.

I blink. When I let my eyes unfocus and then look again, the Iseul mirage is gone. I squint harder, trying to piece her form together out of the grainy static flecks, and then she's back again, waving.

"You okay?"

The lobby attendant is looking at me. He's holding the landline phone off to the side.

I glance again at the TV screen. I can see and unsee waving Iseul—by focusing just a bit more to make out her pattern from the static, or by not focusing.

"The TV is broken," I tell the attendant, pointing.

I move on toward the stairwell up to my apartment.

★   ★   ★

When I go out to graffiti-wander again, I see faces in the paint speckles up-close.

They're not just any faces. They're faces of people I know, in very specific moments.

There's graffiti-paint Iseul, laughing as she did in a mix of pride, horror, and amusement when I tripped walking up onto our high school graduation stage and ended up doing an awkward little shimmy trying to regain my balance. (That was my first time wearing heels over two inches, at her insistence: "Oh come on, you're valedictorian, don't wuss out on me now with *flats*.")

There's graffiti-paint Ha-joon. Made of blue paint speckles, he's smiling like he does on one of his good days, when his chronic pain has decided to subside, and he is able to walk around a bit and crack jokes and eat something not the consistency of *dakjuk* chicken porridge.

There's graffiti-paint boy-I-once-dated-in-high-school-junior-year, his face twisted in the same picture of embarrassment in the moment he took me out to see the migrating winter whales on the pier and spilled the hot chocolate he had bought for me all over his ironed white shirt.

Then there's the graffiti-paint version of the girl from the youth shelter on the upper bunk of our bed, staring at me, unmoving.

I'm shaken. This is like the lunatic conspiracy theorists who insist that they've seen Jesus in their breakfast toast.

I stop my graffiti-wandering habit.

Google tells me this face-seeing phenomenon isn't out of the ordinary. It's called pareidolia. The human brain is naturally wired to recognize human faces, and sometimes it pieces face-like patterns out of objects like clouds or grooves in a tree trunk or caramelization patterns on a piece of toasted white bread. And "bereavement hallucinations" are nothing uncommon.

But what Google does not tell me is why pareidolia has suddenly taken precedence over my sense of perception *now*. Never before had I seen faces in *everything*. Google also does not tell me why such specific memories are entangled in these patterns either.

It almost feels like a personal insult, this fact that order has begun to appear out of things with no order. Look, says the world. Look at all the order that appears everywhere you look. It's only your life that has been stripped of it.

★   ★   ★

When I accidentally pick up a call, my finger pressing the wrong icon, I learn that *Umma* and *Appa* have decided on cremation, a scattering of her ashes into the sea.

"Abby?" *Umma* sounds shocked.

"Oh," I say. I fumble with my phone but can't hang up now.

Umma collects herself, as though her lips have forgotten how to speak in the span of the past seven days of my silence.

When she does speak, the smallness of her voice frightens me. "Abby," she says. Her voice is so different, each word afraid as though it could crack me like fiberglass. "Tell me how you are doing. Can you tell me how you are doing?"

What have I been doing? Seeing strange patterns in everything, spending hours with my nose pressed up against street graffiti, developing leg pains from standing on one leg for too long, lying in bed at night seeing rewinds of the night at Strand Beach on the insides of my eyelids, all feverish, all hysterical.

But I don't tell her any of that.

I tell her that I'm okay. The words are like cuckoo birds all grown-up and flying from a robin nest.

Hidden behind that quiet "I'm okay" is the real reason I have avoided her calls. *Your biological daughter is dead but I am still alive.*

Saying "I'm okay" out loud drives the nail of fraudulence deeper into my heart.

I ask her how she and *Appa* and Ha-joon are doing.

She says, "We are okay."

Nobody is okay.

I'm silent the rest of the call as *Umma* walks on eggshells around the "I'm okay" glass wall that we have both thrown up in the liminal space between us. She is trying to tell me that they had her cremated remains sent to their home in Korea, she is trying to tell me that I should try not to isolate myself, that I should reach out any time of day, but I am having a hard time hearing anything over the tumult of *your daughter is dead but I am still alive* echoing in my skull.

I do hear her when she tells me that they have decided on scattering her ashes at sea.

Iseul is going back to the sea.

I think of the police officers who came to Strand Beach and asked me questions, so many questions. I froze up at first, and had to remind myself that these questions were not like the ones that tripwire-laced my old apartment with my first adopted parents. I think of the one officer who pulled a sea-shell shard embedded in the sole of his boot and tossed it into the waves. I couldn't decide what was worse, all of the *who what when where* questions, or the frenetic scritch-scratching of their pens, or the sight of the shell that made it all the way to the shore only to be thrown back into the sea.

It feels wrong, I think, to give Iseul up so easily back to the water that stole her away. It feels weak, like buckled resolve. If it were up to me, I would have Iseul buried in the chocolate-rich earth by the wetland, let the saprophytes transfigure bone and waterlogged flesh into food for the cattails and willows and the creatures that live in them. I would have her fade naturally as living organisms do.

Imagining her ashes being affixed with priority mail sig-nage and sitting in the underbelly of a FedEx plane flying across the globe and then bumping along in a mail van heading to her family's mailbox, I feel mortified on her behalf. On the day that the ash scattering ceremony happens, I sit in my apart-ment pulling apart split ends with long fingernails, staring up at the ceiling when my eyes get tired, making constellations out of the stucco.

★   ★   ★

Texan Simon and Petra both call me, and then text me, and then email me when I don't respond. Stanley emails, too. It's mild at first—*Abby. Where are you? You haven't been in lab for a few days.*—then irritated—*Abby. You cannot just quit when research gets difficult.*—then angry—*Where have you been, AWOL for near two weeks?? Respond ASAP. Nadia stepped in to take care of your salt slugs. They would be dead otherwise.*

I don't respond to Stanley, but I do send Nadia my silent thoughts of thanks. No need for more deaths.

In a voicemail, Petra tells me that she talked to one of Iseul's roommates—she had her number from the time we all carpooled to the LA Natural History Museum's free day. The roommate gave her the Yoon home phone number, and when she called, *Umma* picked up and told her what happened.

There's a silence. Then Petra says that she lost her father to pancreatic cancer eight years ago. There's another long pause before she tries again. *I know it's not the same, and everyone's grief is different, but I'm here if you want someone to talk to. Just so you know.*

I can't summon up the strength to respond to her. Another message comes in a day later. She says that reading books was her escape. *It could be worth a shot.* I almost smile at that. Unsolicited advice—it's classic Petra. The to-be-PI never misses a beat.

I take her advice and try to distract myself with YA novels—the ones that are quick, full of energy and fantasies and romance—but once the casts of characters are introduced, I find myself playing the game of *which character is the author going to kill off first?* It's only a matter of pages before the ink runs red.

Sometimes it's the loyal sidekick. He's too nice. His loyalty is going to be the end of him.

Or, the father figure—the orphan heroine trope is practically laid out from here on out.

In another book, I make the guess twenty pages in that it's going to be the childhood best friend—and that is when I stop.

If I turn out to be some biological monstrosity with strange bacteria hiding out within her cells, the only person in the country who would never turn against me is now gone.

★ ★ ★

A phone rings, the buzzing jarring me awake at my desk—the consecutive nights of sleeplessness are finally manifesting. Iseul's cellphone is pressed against my chest underneath my hands—*what is it doing there?*—and then I remember that I'd fished it out from under my bed after dinner and dared to look at old photos of the two of us. I'd fed my eyes with our terrible selfies taken from low angles, and I'd fallen asleep in a haze of ravenous affection that cut deep into my chest, my last conscious thought that maybe I could seal that wound if I just put the phone on top of it.

At the sound of the ringing, I wonder if this is Iseul trying to speak to me from the dead. I fumble across my desk with sleep-slow hands, tilt my phone up toward my face.

It's Texan Simon.

"Go away, Simon," I say out loud.

I let it go to voicemail. Simon tries calling again.

"Nope, Simon, not today."

A silence, and then my phone gives a single buzz to indicate voicemail.

Simon never leaves voicemail. I reach over and hit the play button.

"Hey, uh, Abby, this is Simon from lab. Hope you're okay." A pause as he searches for what to say. "So about your endosymbiont. The sequencing results. It's something new, it's not some known species." Another pause. "But more importantly, I, uh, wound up sequencing the host cell too, and . . . that came up as human."

Shit.

"I thought it was a mistake at first, since human beings don't have endosymbionts, so I resubmitted for sequencing. And it came back as human again. And then I couldn't help myself so I found your freezer stock labeled "WTF cells" and grew them up fresh and repeated the whole process. And yeah, the host cell is *definitely* human."

Shit, Simon, didn't anyone ever teach you not to dig through someone else's belongings without their permission?

I keep listening as a growing sense of dread weighs down my gut.

"That was a couple days ago. But I couldn't help myself, so I'm calling to ask you where you got those cells. Whose cells are those?"

None of your business. Private matter.

"It's a scientific marvel, to say the least. For a moment I'd thought maybe you'd somehow engineered it, but after spending some time tinkering with it myself, it doesn't look like it. It looks 100 percent natural to me."

100 percent natural is right. It's me, free-range, organic, untreated with synthetic hormones.

"So, uh, call me back. When you're feeling up to it." A pause, and then he adds, "And I hope you'll forgive me for digging through your freezer stocks."

I DON'T CALL SIMON back.

It's some kind of primal fear hemorrhaging in me that drives me up and out of the apartment to the lab in the middle of the night. How much could he have done with my cells, I think over and over. How much does he know about them? How much does he know about me that even I don't know?

My rush back to the lab is like watching horror movies—you cover your eyes with your hands because you don't want to see what has happened, but at the same time you do, and so you spread your fingers apart just enough.

I still can't bring myself to use Iseul's car, so I climb into the backseat of a cab that smells like the aftermath of too much drinking. I cannot see where the incident happened in the nighttime darkness. I sit gingerly on the edge of my seat.

The cab driver must have made out my face in the rear-view mirror.

"Yup, you can thank the couple from three rides ago for that," he says. "Picked them up from a dive bar. The guy had frozen daiquiri in his hat, and he and his girl were pouring it into each other's mouths. Strawberry. I could smell it. Still kinda can, though now it's mostly puke."

"Sorry," I say. His words are faint to me as I wipe my wet palms on my pants.

The cab driver is nonchalant.

"Don't be, this car's seen a hell of a whole lot worse," he says. "You can trust me on that one. Sixteen years on the job and on the road and you get a thick skin for most things. So anyway, where you off to this time of night?"

I give him the university biosciences building address, and he takes it in stride without batting an eye. Sixteen years on the job, and nerds going to lab at one in the morning does not strike him as anything worth a comment.

The rest of the ride, he tells me about the time a drunk passenger rolled down the window to moon the cop car beside them on the highway, and then about endlessly digging out peanuts and their papery husks from every imaginable corner of his car, and the one time he pulled out a hundred-dollar bill from underneath the passenger seat—and then the university and the gray concrete block of a building come into view.

"Anyway," he says as I head out, "moral of the story, you pay attention to where the peanuts are. Might turn out not to be just peanuts in the end, if you know what I mean."

I tell him that I will.

I press my ID badge against the proximity reader on the building and push the doors open. The air that meets me is freezing, the same as ever, even as everything else has changed.

When I reach the lab, the lights are off—no one is here this late tonight.

I head straight for Texan Simon's lab bench, and see nothing suspicious. I head for the −80 freezer and dig through my boxes until I find the one where I'd stashed the cryovial of my endosymbiont-containing cells, which I'd hastily labeled "WTF cells." Every slot in the box is occupied by a tube except for one. With fingers numb from the icy cold, I lift up every tube to read the label on their sides. The WTF cells are nowhere to be found.

Damn you, Simon.

I look through his boxes and find the tube there. I rub away the frost, lift it up to eye level, and through the transparent sides of the tube, it's clear that the amount of cell stock has decreased since I first made it.

Simon has indeed been busy.

I put everything back and slump into the rusty metal chair in the corner, lightheaded. From here, I can see the salt slugs in their aquarium tanks. The creatures are fine. In fact, they look almost better than they had when I had last been in lab. They're rippling their ruffled membrane wings happily, and they're greener, too. They're the color of thriving. It is almost maddening. How can they be doing so well when I have been withering away?

They make me think of Iseul. With the fresh wave of grief that hits me like a wall, as I steady myself against the chair, there is also another spark of anger. I can't fathom its target. Was it me or Iseul who suggested we go to the beach in the first place? Why did Iseul wade into the water so far? Stupid. Why did we go at night? Stupid, stupid. To feel something else, anything else, I kick my heel against a leg of the chair. I don't feel anything. Stupid.

I wander down to the kitchenette down the hall. Another lab must have had a party of some kind. There are soda cans lying around on the little table and a plastic catering tray of stale-looking cookies that no one has taken the initiative to throw away yet. I make a point of avoiding looking at the cookies—I'm certain that I will see faces on their surfaces. The irregular crumb-speckled surfaces and the random distribution of chocolate chips are a pareidolia land mine.

I pull out a beer from the fridge, pop the tab. I have an idea. I walk back to the lab, pour it all fizzing into an auto-claved beaker, stick the glass into the sonicator waterbath, let it buzz. Trade secret: this is how you get a pillar of thick, creamy beer head. Ultrasonic waves cause pockets of high and low pressure and release dissolved gases like carbon dioxide, so bubbles rise up to the surface and become stabilized by proteins in the mix.

I have actually never done this before. I wonder if I shouldn't have let my self-control and restraint hold me back all those times I had contemplated it before.

All the could-be's and would-be's spring to mind when people are about to leave a place, I suppose. And when people have left a place.

Before my staring eyes, the fine foam swelling up in the beaker begins to form people-like shapes. A likeness of *Appa* emerges, pointing at a flying bird larger than his foamy arm span, and I know in that moment that a foam Ha-joon will also appear, and so will I, because this is—once again—a pareidolia motion picture of a memory, the last bird-watching trip before the family moved to Korea.

There's cold against my fingers—my grip on the beaker has gone slack and I've spilled some beer over the edge. The foam-Ha-joon dissolves away into liquid. I lean back against the wall. Between TV-static Iseul from a few days ago and now foam *Appa* and Ha-joon, it seems that I really have been shaken up. Perhaps I've just lost it entirely, or perhaps there is a biological cause behind it. There is a biological motive behind most everything, I remind myself.

I should call Ha-joon. But every time I think about it, about what he will say, what he could possibly say, it feels like a punch to the solar plexus.

I wonder what would happen if Stanley saw me like this: all red-eyed, beer in hand in the lab. But I couldn't care less.

What would happen if Iseul saw me like this?

She would just snort, a sound that says, "Abby will always be Abby."

I can almost hear it, and I can feel the pain building in my gut, bubbling up like beer foam.

I walk over to the dim corner of the lab where the salt slugs are milling about in their tanks. I wave my arms above my head but the automatic ceiling lights in this section of lab must have burnt out. I keep waving my arms anyway. I pretend that I am undulating my parapodia. The salt slugs undulate their parapodia back at me. I stop undulating to catch my breath and tell them about my problems. They are good listeners. I ask each in turn whether it would like to be the stabber or the stabbee. I squint, but none of them give me a clear answer.

Iseul was the one who convinced me that I could use science to track down my birth parents. Perhaps I owe it to her to follow through on that.

I lift my beaker half-full of beer. A toast to that.

★   ★   ★

When I make it back to my apartment, in the hour-long sliver of night before the sun, I finally look back inside the brown paper bag with Iseul's blue dragon sea slug.

I lift the flimsy plastic container up to eye-level. There are spots of white mold fuzz cropping up along its sides.

I give the container a small shake, and the dead thing flops around and bumps against the side and makes a wet squelch.

I stand there, staring.

"Stupid," I say to it.

I still can't bring myself to throw it away.

I put the container inside of a larger Tupperware, wrap it inside of the brown paper bag again, and stuff it into the freezer compartment.

✦ 17 ✦

THERE ARE A LOT of firsts these days.

The first time someone close to me has died.

The first time I feel obligated to do science in the memory of said dead person.

The first time I have found myself piecing face-like patterns out of every rough and random surface, from graffiti paint flecks to my fake granite countertop to jarred marinara sauce. It's unsettling, and I'm no longer sure it's just bereavement hallucinations.

What is wrong with me?

★ ★ ★

The first time I find myself staring at pictures of Korean roof tiles.

I am reading about apophenia—the more generic form of pareidolia that refers to the human tendency to see and form patterns out of random and uncorrelated phenomena. I'm looking up geometric patterns, and come across images of the roof tiles. Traditional Korean buildings have intricately decorated ceramic roofs, with eaves that curl up at the ends like unanswered questions. Each row of tiles is capped by a circular disk called a *mak-sae*. I try writing the Korean characters out. 막새.

This *mak-sae* is what I find so absorbing. They are delicately carved with floral designs—lotus, lily, daisy, intricate geometrics—or sometimes smiling faces, so that there is a periodic rhythm to these roofs, all linear and neat and interspersed by these motifs. In these images I see overlaid ghosts of the fleece blanket and of my faceless biological parents.

I spend a great deal of time staring at pictures of random traditional Korean things. A nonscientific corner of me thinks that burning images of ancient historical artifacts into my eyes will help, somehow, as I long for a past in which Iseul breathed.

★ ★ ★

The first time I get a hug from Texan Simon.

I finally agree to meet him at the campus coffee shop near the biosciences building. On the bus ride to campus, I instructed myself very carefully to tell him about my cells and their bacterial endosymbiont, learn from him what exactly he has been doing with them while I was gone, and if he seemed nonjudgmental, to leave the option open to talk further in the future. I played out the scene in my head several times.

In reality, I do tell him about my cells and their bacterial endosymbiont. But then when he shows me more microscopy images he's taken, the delicate arrangement of the endosymbionts within the circular outline of their host (my own cells!) reminds me of *mak-sae*s. I don't see faces this time, just *mak-sae* floral patterns.

And then Simon is awkwardly offering me a paper napkin, and I become aware of the tears on my cheeks, and that's all followed by an awkward hug.

★ ★ ★

The first time that I'm the one to initiate a call home.

There's a note of shock in *Umma's* voice when she answers, and then she recoups quickly and is furious, the pent-up motherly protectiveness spilling out at last. Why hadn't I answered her calls, how worried they were, how I'd just about broken their hearts again, nobody deserves to have their hearts broken like that twice in a row, had I been eating enough. And then it breaks down into relief, and she's blowing her nose loudly into a tissue, *what am I going to do about you.*

I'm sorry, I tell her. I'm sorry. And then I'm blowing my nose into a tissue, too. Don't ever do that again, she's saying. I'm still saying I'm sorry. She's saying, Oh and here's your *Appa* too, and let me have you say hello to Ha-joon while I finally have you here. What am I going to do about you, Abby-*ya*? I tell her that I don't know either. Well, she says, first things first, I am going to send you a lot of kimchi so expect to do some heavy-lifting soon.

Then she says: Abby, please, don't make us think that we've lost you, too. Don't make us think that we lost both daughters.

Both daughters.

Hearing those words, feeling the way they include me in their fold, the guilt that had fastened its grip within my chest cavity seems to loosen.

★   ★   ★

The first time I run into Stanley since going AWOL after Iseul died.

I'm walking into lab to resume my work, grunting a greeting to Texan Simon (who turns, says, "You've come back to lab from the dead"), shouldering off my backpack, pleased to see that the mess of papers on my desk has not been touched in my absence, when Stanley rounds the corner.

He stops in his tracks.

After a tight pause: "Well. Look who showed up."

The periodic sound of pipette tips being ejected by Texan Simon working at the bench behind me has suddenly stopped. Everyone in the lab pretends to be busy. I know that Petra must be peering between the shelf bottles and racks in the next bay over. I can see in my peripheral vision that Nadia is keeping her head down, flipping a little too quickly through pages in her lab notebook.

The image of Iseul's unfinished journalistic piece comes to mind, her writing cut short and suspended in draft-stage limbo on her desk. By now, a thin film of dust would have settled on the various sticky notes and pens, a layer of passing time landing atop the flecking of eraser dust. A mise en scène of tragedy.

I had spent the last few days thinking about my adoptive mother, her passive silence, the desperation. I know what I want. I need the equipment and connections here to figure out my endosymbiont, to then use it to find a path to my biological mother.

I lift my chin and look Stanley in the eyes.

"I want to stay in your lab and do my PhD here," I say.

Stanley's eyebrows rise. "This is the first thing you're going to say to me?"

I continue. "I want to do my PhD here. I'm going to finish the salt slug endosymbiont project. I haven't shown you all of the newest data yet, but with that data and two more experiments, I'm in position to pull together the paper." The words are coming out slippery-fast.

"Well. With your recent string of absences, I have to say, I am not particularly favorably inclined."

"I'm willing to place bets that if I bring all of this data I've gathered to your competitors, they'll be more than happy to take me on." And the words are out before I register what I am about to say.

Stanley is open-mouthed now. "I cannot believe the *gall* you have to say—"

"You can talk to the admissions committee. I emailed them a file with all of the application components this morning. It's late, but I know you can pull some strings and make it happen. Nobody here would lift a finger against you."

It's a little funny. Stanley now looks more bewildered than furious. His left eye has stopped twitching, and now his thick white brows are pinched together. Never in his career did he envision someone coming up to him with this degree of chutzpah, never mind his lab tech, of all people. His lab tech, who worked tirelessly, meekly, always raising her pipette but never a finger nor her voice.

Up to this moment, Stanley has been very skilled at concealing any uncertainty—if someone asks him a question about science and he is uncertain about the answer, he always finds a way to weasel out of it or huffily give an evasive answer. (I've never understood why this phenomenon seems to be so common among men? What is so wrong with saying, "That's a good question, I'm not sure"?)

But now—he just doesn't know what to do.

It was the right move, placing my bets on his reluctance to kick me out of his lab, on his reputation's attachment to the highly productive lab member who generates the results that maintain his stature, even despite my recent lack of progress with the salt slugs.

With his resources, I'm going to figure out my endosymbiont, my origins.

Emboldened by his silence, I continue. "I'm going to start my own project. I have an idea that's related to the salt slugs and their endosymbionts—let me do some preliminary experiments first, and if they're promising, I'll show you what I'm going to do. There's no better lab for it, no place with more concentrated resources to figure it out. It's something . . ." I search for words. Terrifying. Startling. Unsettling. "Big," I decide.

Stanley is quiet. The left eye starts twitching.

"So this is what you've been doing all this time. Coming up with this?"

I shrug.

Then he just starts laughing—it's a slow build, from a guttural chuckle into an erratic sound, like a zipper in a clothes dryer machine. He's shaking his head as he says, "Well. We'll talk more later, yes?"

After he leaves, I stand there for a moment, wondering if the exchange really just happened. Simon ejects a pipette tip into the benchtop waste bin, and the little sound of plastic on plastic is like a thunderclap in the silence.

My knees are shuddering, but I realize that I'm grinning. It feels stiff and foreign—I realize that this is the first time I've smiled since Iseul died.

British Simon breaks the silence. "Well *shit,*" he calls out, from across the room by the storage wall. "She really just did that. She really just did that. Bloody hell."

Texan Simon has spun around in his chair. He's shaking his head. "You come back from the dead, and then you manage to cheat your way out of death a second time." He looks worried, and I try to ignore his are-you-sure-you-should-have-done-that expression.

I fall into my chair. "Yeah, I bet that gives Petra a run for her money. For a lifetime."

"What a way to end a conversation with the head honcho," British Simon calls across the room. Unlike Texan Simon, he was clearly delighted by today's public theatrics. "You know, one time some Romans tossed a priest into a gladiator fight, and his end was so bloody they called it his second baptism. Oddly reminds me of that."

Petra comes around to my bay, stands between Texan Simon and me with both hands on her hips. She just looks amused. I think there is almost begrudging admiration folded within her look.

"You've just set some kind of tiger loose," she says. "And now that you've set it loose, you're going to have to watch your back at all times."

I'm lightheaded, giddy, the adrenaline still thrumming through my veins.

It's intoxicating, being able to speak my mind. No glass walls here.

This was a complete detour from all of my demure emails to Stanley, carefully worded so as not to come across as demanding, not to invoke anger. I think about all of the time I have spent tiptoeing around, the way I tiptoed among bottle shards and flakes of fallen wall paint in my old home, with my first set of parents in America, scared that they would pierce my feet and reach my heart. I think about all of the time I spent treading carefully after leaving that apartment—fearful that one misplaced step would dismantle the newfound sense of security I had found in the Yoons, that the ground would melt away treacherously and I, too, would be flying through air like vodka bottles and small furniture. I think about the time I once walked past Stanley's office while he was meeting with another PI, the door half-ajar. *East Asians are quiet and work their butts off,* Stanley was saying. *It's excellent for lab productivity.* I'd turned a furtive glance and seen the backside of the other PI sitting across from Stanley's desk. Blue linen shirt, brown oxford shoes, all garden-variety old white male academic, it could have been anyone.

I shrug again at Petra. "I'll just cheat death another time." I'm surprised as the words leave my mouth. It's like being drunk.

Drunk on power. Is this what that is?

★   ★   ★

Some scientists say that life on Earth began when meteorites car-
rying live cells arrived from outer space.

I think that's a complete cop-out of a theory. Solving the sci-
entific mystery of how cells could have possibly arisen on prehis-
toric Earth is an enormous challenge—what molecules, what
location, what conditions, what reactions, what happenstance?—
and so some people choose to skim over all the brain-wracking
and frustration and failure to wave a dismissive hand toward the
sky and say that somewhere out there, far away in outer space,
life first began and made its way to Earth and now, look, here we
are.

It's the biggest deus ex machina ever.

Strictly speaking, the biggest deus ex machina in the history
of life.

But I admit, there is a sense of comfort in knowing that I'm
not the only one who is waving her hands around trying to make
sense of nonsense.

I wish you were here waving around with me so I could
express all the nonsense going on right now without having to say
a single word.

★   ★   ★

As I write tonight, I think about the family's pathetic goodbye
to Iseul, the scattering of her ashes at sea. And the night she
died—my own pathetic goodbye, too, a wordless stare and
trembling as the police on the beach carried away the body bag.

What was the last thing I said to Iseul? It must have been
"get out of the water."

Every sleepless night since Strand Beach, I have lain in bed
with my blankets pulled up to my nose the way Iseul always

did and tried to come up with the words I wish I had said instead. Still, nothing. Trying to come up with what I would have said is like trying to catch receding ocean waves. It's there, I can feel it, but when I try to grab at it, it slips out all the same. I don't know how I would have said goodbye. I don't think I know how to say goodbye.

I never said goodbye to my adoptive parents.

When my mother left, I knew it was for good because when I pulled the loose back panel off the broken clock on her bedside table, the cash and the red burner phone I'd once seen inside were missing. She had left in her work shoes, her heels cushioned by those secret savings from pawning her jewelry.

My father stuck around for a while longer, pacing the living room day in and day out and shouting at no one and everyone. People need their villains.

I often slipped out and sat outside in the hallway against the wall. I closed my eyes and hugged my knees because if I tried hard enough, it felt like it was Iseul hugging me and not just my own spindly arms. A neighbor must have sent in a tip. There's a little girl who always sits in the hallway while a man shouts inside. She looks about ten. She never cries, though.

But my father had already left by the time child protective services people came around. He left a note on the sofa, on top of a crumpled ten-dollar bill. "Goodbye Abby."

Saying goodbye means acknowledging an impending loss. It means agreeing that you are parting ways with something.

I wonder if that is why my mother never said goodbye. I wonder if this is why I am unable to say anything to dead Iseul.

I dedicate my moment in the lab earlier today to Iseul. She would be elated if she knew what I just did. I've dedicated the thrill of freedom to her and her journalist's heart. I dedicate my newfound sense of empowerment to her.

So, this is how I begin my PhD on the origins of life on Earth.

So, this is how I begin my PhD on my own origins.

★   ★   ★

This time period also marks the first time I speak to Kwan-sik, the silent and elusive third-floor janitor.

It is evening, when I have set up some experiments and head out to the communal lounge with the pasta dinner I remembered to pack this morning. I stretch out the kink in my neck from hours standing over experiments, sprawl out onto the lime sofa, and kick my feet up onto the journal-littered coffee table, the latest copy of *Science* crinkling under my heels. Then I notice Kwan-sik perched at the other end of the sofa.

She is staring off at the night sky, through the glass side of the building across the open atrium. With one rheumatic knee tucked up against her chest, she looks like a threadbare winter bird nursing a limp. She doesn't acknowledge me.

The silence today is peaceful. Maybe it is the moonlight filtering through the glass wall and spilling across the floor. Only when I open the lid to my pasta and the thick smell of cream sauce and tarragon seeps out does Kwan-sik turn and look at me. Her deep-set eyes are like water wells. Beneath their surface, I think, they are unfolding recursive fractals, dark as inkwells.

"Do you know what *han* is?" she says, in heavily accented English.

I'm startled by the discrepancy between her voice, chirpy like youth, and her wood-carved appearance. I'd begun to believe that her mouth was like tree bark, motionless in its bulwark made of lignin and cellulose and other fibrous and unbudging meshwork.

She repeats herself.

"*Han?*" I echo. "No, I don't."

She looks bemused. "You are Korean too?"

I nod.

She points at my name badge hanging at my hips.

"Your last name is Rodier?"

"I was adopted."

This seems to satisfy her. She looks away again, out through the glass.

"You should know what *han* is," she says. She hums to herself, and it is a tune full of an unfathomable sadness as deep as her well-eyes.

✦ 18 ✦

I QUICKLY FORGET THE odd and brief exchange with Kwan-sik, as I fall deeper into my science.

When I say "my science" now, it really is *my* science.

Every day, I prick my fingers for live skin cells containing the bacterial endosymbionts, and the acute sting briefly distracts me from Iseul.

The bacteria within my cells can grow outside of their confines, it turns out.

This was one of the quirks Simon discovered while I was gone. He managed to remove the bacteria from their cell cases by rattling the outer husks up with ultrasonic waves, and then passing them carefully through a filter to sift away the cellular detritus.

Simon found out a lot while I was gone. In fact, after all of his experimentation, he knows more about my cells than I do, which makes me feel foreign in my own skin.

He shows me a turbid liquid culture of cells, the flask an off-pink, like old Spam. I think about how *Umma* likes cooking with Spam. Iseul inherited that fondness.

"These are your cells."

Some kind of out-of-body experience.

He next shows me a turbid flask of reddish growth media.

"These are the bacteria that live in your cells, now grown outside of your cells. Took a bit of fiddling, but they're pretty stable now."

I nod. I try to shake off the thoughts of Iseul's cooking, try to focus on my science. The fact that the bacteria can be separated from their host cells and still survive means that they were probably acquired fairly recently—*recently* meaning later in time than chloroplasts in plants, which were acquired by plant cells hundreds of billions of years ago, or mitochondria, which were acquired 1.5 billion years ago. I rack my brains— some notably "recent" amoebal endosymbionts were acquired tens of millions of years ago. That's *recent*.

So far back in history. *Homo sapiens* first showed up on the African continent some three-hundred thousand years ago. It hurts my head to dwell so long on the past.

Simon has also sequenced the endosymbiont's genome in my absence.

I pore over its genome sequence that night, a mug of *yuja* tea piping fingers of steam beside my laptop. I find that the monotonic scrolling of one point two million As, Ts, Cs, and Gs doesn't blur before my eyes, and I can pick out motifs amongst the DNA bases. In minutes, it's clear to me that there are sequence biases and there are mutations sprinkled willy-nilly throughout genes that suddenly insert the equivalent of stop signs for a cell's protein-making machinery. In a nutshell, the genome bears key signposts that indicate an endosymbiont.

I pause, startled. This pattern-finding is what sophisticated bioinformatics software is supposed to do. Not the human eye. Especially not the sleep-deprived human eye within the span of time it takes to drink a mugful of tea.

When I paste the sequence into the software I used half a year ago with my salt slug endosymbiont's genome, the algorithms tell me the same story that I intuited myself.

This can't be bereavement hallucinations. No way. Hallucinating Iseul is one thing, and maybe hallucinating other people is another, but this? Pattern-finding not in graffiti paint nor cereal flakes nor my apartment's irregular carpeting, but a bacterial genome sequence?

I shake my head. I keep scrolling through the genome.

It's clear the endosymbiont is more closely related to pathogenic *Rickettsia*, but it's lost just about all of its genes for pathogenicity. It's a domesticated creature, declawed by the passage of time.

Historically, a number of endosymbioses have arisen from pathogens that slink their way into cells with the full intention of causing harm. But somewhere along the way, they change their minds and lay down their molecular arms and make peace with the host cell.

★   ★   ★

But even with the distractions of my science, I can't stop thinking about Iseul. The nighttime dream sequences have become intense. The images that seem to fill the space between cornea and closed eyelid are haunting, and I can't stop thinking about them even during the daytime.

When I get in bed after staring at the genome, it's not long before the blackness turns into a scene. There is something ensnared in the ropes of seaweed above me, a dark mass blocking the spears of sunlight that lance through the water's surface.

There are wavy protrusions like sea slug parapodia membranes, and my dream-drugged brain kicks into autopilot and

I will it closer. Like deceased lab sea slug after lab sea slug, I must fish it out of the aquarium and dispose of it—dead sea slugs give off bad vibes for the rest of the live ones.

As the mass approaches, I see that the wavering parapodia are actually curtains of human hair and the sick throb in my gut rises because I now not only know *what* it is but *who* it is.

I can't help myself, and I reach out a hand and part the black veil of seaweed and the movement causes the body to roll over onto its side, all bloated bulge, and then Iseul's wide eyes filmed green in half-decomposition are staring.

★　★　★

Sometimes I can't tell the difference between missing Iseul, my increased capacity for pattern-finding in everything, and general delirium. Perhaps they are one and the same.

During fitful insomniac dream sequences, my sleeping self is so resolutely certain that those nonsensical dreamscapes are reality that when I wake up, simply in bed and realizing the fiction of it all, I'm stunned at how I could have been so certain in what lacked any skeletal system of logic. I begin to doubt my waking ability to perceive and to think.

I'm often working in the cell culture hood sucking up my cells with a pipettor as the night falls—although I can't see the sun set nor the moon rise in this windowless room. The wall clock is also broken, so the passage of time is a grand mystery in here. In here, we passage cells against the passage of time.

"Late night in the lab?"

I look up from my cells. British Simon is leaning against the doorframe, carrying a large cardboard box of pipettor tips.

I shrug.

"Alright." He sets down the box along the wall, sending up a cloud of dust, and shoulders his packed bag over his coat.

"Well, watch out for the restless spirits of mastered-out PhD students. They still haunt the building."

British Simon thinks he's hilarious.

He gives me a two-fingered salute and then heads out. The door squeals behind him like a stuck pig—nobody has done anything about it for two weeks. The dust hangs in the air behind him, and the swirling of the faint speckles reminds me of the swarms of gnats that hover over the wetland in the summer, reminds me of the times that Iseul and I waded through the waters with our mouths and eyes closed. I turn away from the gnat-dust.

In the silence that follows, I finish my work quickly, and I become aware of the low background humming of the hood. The sound kicks up a queasy tightness in my throat as I think about how I used to get annoyed at Iseul humming, when we studied together in school. Retrospectively, it was such an insignificant inconvenience. My throat curdles. What I wouldn't give to bring her back, to hum and to annoy me one more time.

I find that somehow I am laughing as I put my cells into the incubator, and the dry sound reverberates in the reflective space. *An asthmatic walks into a recursive algorithm.* My chest hurts, and I am not an asthmatic.

When I close the incubator door, I see in the corner of my eye someone outside the TC room entrance.

"Back already?" I say to Simon as I turn the latch.

Simon doesn't say anything. I look over and realize very quickly that it's not Simon. It's a shorter woman. I squint through the gnat-dust in the dim light. Why didn't the automatic ceiling lights turn back on when she walked in?

I can't make out her facial features, in the shadows cast on her form, but she is certainly not a member of the lab, and I don't think I've ever seen her around the building. She's a visitor—the fact that she is wearing sandals is a clear giveaway. *Ah, an open-toed plebeian!*, British Simon would say. *Welcome to the lab. Here be dinoflagellates and dragons.*

But how did she get in here without the infernal squeal of the lab door? And then I think again: How'd she get in here *at all* without key-card access? In a startled moment of lapsed judgement, I say, "Well, hell, a mastered-out spirit," and regret it—I've just committed a probable netherworld faux pas—but she doesn't react.

I stare.

Her hair is dark and curly and shoulder-length, like Iseul's.

I realize then that I am hallucinating. This is my pareidolia acting up; I am seeing patterns in the motes of gnat-dust hanging in the air.

This has to be like the movies: once the protagonist looks away, the apparition is gone. So I turn my head away, close my eyes. But when I look back, she's still there. Then I cover my eyes with both hands, like a fool. When I lower them, she is still here.

What sort of botched peekaboo is this?

I can't unsee dust-Iseul. She's not moving, just standing and blinking.

I scramble for words.

"Hello?" Silence. "Can I help you?" I don't know what else to try. "Welcome to the lab, can I get you anything? Cheeseburger and medium fries?"

She says nothing, of course. Then she points at the incubator and shakes her head sadly.

I follow the invisible line from her finger. Is something just wrong with my cells? I open the incubator again. They look fine to me, cells being cells, wallowing in expensive pink slurry.

I just need to sleep. Should probably kick it up a notch to temazepam tonight.

"Milkshake?" I say weakly.

When I look back, she is finally gone.

I walk out into the aisle and look around. I wave my hand in the air and the gnat-like dust motes swirl lazily. The ceiling lights flick on.

Some people see Jesus in their breakfast toast. Others see their dead best friend in dusty lab air.

Here is a reason why a swarm of gnats is called a ghost.

★　★　★

I speak again to *Umma*, too.

When I ask how they are doing, she tells me that they took all of Iseul's photos down then put them back up, to make the motionless photos seem less motionless.

She tells me that they all hug each other a little longer than before, a little harder than before.

She tells me that *Appa* is the only one who hides his tears.

"Your *appa* hides them. From me, from Ha-joon." She sighs, and it's a dry rattling sound, like the wind after all of the rain has already fallen. "I wish he would not."

I hear the skittering of hard pills as she measures out Ha-joon's morning medicine.

Umma clears her throat. "I wonder if that is why he still spends time at his university office, where only he will see his tears. So that when he comes home, he has already run dry." A gas stove clicks on, and there is the sound of a heavy pot being placed on the grate. "What's the last meal that she ate? Do you know?"

I know what work-tunnel-vision Iseul is like. When sucked into writing a journalistic piece, she only ate the granola bars from the break room. But I don't want to tell *Umma* that—*Umma,* who threw a fit when she found out that I ate only instant noodles for four days one finals period in college— *That's not a proper meal. Where is the kimchi? Where are the rice and beans?*

"I don't know. I'm sorry," I say, the words coming too quickly.

There's a recoil of guilt when I think about how I have again hidden the truth, the same way the social workers did when they took me from my adoptive parents' apartment to the youth shelter, when I, too, asked them questions with unhappy answers.

Umma tells me that she is making soy-braised lotus roots, chive kimchi, preserved bracken fiddleheads. She will pack them up in a big box and ship them to my apartment when the post office opens tomorrow morning.

"If only we had been in the States," she says. "In coming here, to protect Ha-joon, we lost Iseul."

I shake my head. "No, I was there when she died."

This will never go away, both that truth and its icy cold. The permanence is terrifying, doesn't seem to fit inside my life story otherwise marked by impermanence.

"I was there," I say again. "That is fact. That fact will never change."

I can hear pills rattling as *Umma* puts their glass bottles back in their cabinet.

"My *umma*—your grandmother—says that Iseul's death will always be," she says. "But, there will come a day when we find that we are okay with that." She lets out a desiccated sigh again. "We are all trying our best to believe it, as hard as we can."

Ow far would you go to make a point?

There was a guy who drank *Helicobacter pylori*, to prove that it does in fact cause gastric ulcers contrary to the skepticism of all naysayers. There was another guy who drank *Vibrio cholerae* (and fed it to two other volunteers) to show how it could be that only some people got sick. He and the second person were fine, the third almost died.

How far would you go to make sure your experiment worked?

I have heard stories of grad students drinking suspensions of viruses to make more for experiments when they run out. It's easier to use yourself as a bioreactor than to toil with lab reagents. In one end, out the other. Viruses: I replicate, therefore, I am.

How far would you trust your gut?

The overarching theme is that there is a lot of drinking of things that should not be drunk. It is a recurring motif among the academe, it seems, in line with all the excess caffeinated liquids during the day, and then in the evenings all the excess beer and two-buck chuck and bourbon shots deployed to hand-wave away stressors.

But there are also stranger cases. Auto-brewery syndrome (ABS): when a person's gut microbes go crazy with fermenting consumed carbohydrates, producing so much ethanol that the person becomes intoxicated without touching a drop of alcohol to his or her lips.

I have read stories of families accusing ABS patients of closet alcoholism. Once, I almost convinced myself that my adoptive father suffered from ABS, that it was all something not of his own free will. In these stories I read online, there are accusations of lying—*your breath smells like alcohol, who do you think you're fooling.*

It's only through science that the families' suspicions are allayed and the patients regain their trust.

★ ★ ★

Very quickly, I lose myself in searching for my origins.

I'm not sure where the boundless energy comes from. I think it must be trickle-down from Iseul, all of her hope and vigor that went unused when she died. She invested so much energy into helping me with this search for my biological parents that it has percolated into my existence, I like to think. I have been swept up in her spirit, in my science.

By day I worked on sea slug genes, surrounded by my labmates. By night, I pried at the obscure mystery of my own genes, alone. Some nights I lingered behind after everyone else had headed out—"Don't worry about me, I just have to finish one more quick experiment and then I'll be home." But not every night—I mixed in some breaks to avoid stirring up suspicion. Other days I wrested myself from the building, had a bite to eat, and then snuck back in when I could see from the outside that the lab's three third-floor windows were all dark.

Stanley doesn't check the lab door's keycard access logs as far as I know, and even if he did, he would probably be pleased to see me working late. Tomás, who orders our lab supplies, never asked about my reagent order logs—what I was using was largely the same as what I use for my daytime experiments. And when I told Texan Simon that I would handle the science of my cells from here on out, he simply nodded, and I was grateful for his uncharacteristic tact.

I did get asked about the bags under my eyes and my physical state.

Usually by Nadia. "I'm not going to lie, you don't look too well, Abby. Are you taking care of yourself?"

Even Petra, albeit wordlessly: I came in one morning to find a bakery-style blueberry muffin on a brown paper towel on my desk. Petra was peering through the gaps in the row of bottles on her benchtop shelf, with a nonchalant offering of "they gave me an extra this morning. If you want it."

I was always breathless, it seemed. I'm pretty sure it was from my constant state of fear—my fear that my experimental results would be overturned by the next set of data, and that this cheerio trail of clues to my past would be moot.

Ha-joon once told me that some birds don't realize that the rocks they are sitting on are not real eggs.

What if the glimmers of hope were actually mirages? Something nonexistent materialized by pareidolia? I shooed away the doubts the way I would toss a spider in my apartment out the window with two pieces of paper: gingerly, from a distance, afraid of getting too close or ohgodforbid *touching* it—both things that I cannot bring myself to crush.

I was terrified.

Nadia thought this was all hyperthyroidism and kept insisting that I go see an endocrinologist.

"If you keep this up I really *am* going to drag you to one," she said. "Don't you doubt it."

I didn't doubt it.

Once, my nose started bleeding from sleep deprivation while I was transferring liquid cultures of my cells. I didn't realize it until a drop of blood fell into one of the open flasks and bloomed open in a swath of red tendrils.

I looked up. Nadia hadn't noticed. I grabbed a tissue and pressed it against my nose, and when I pulled it away—in those red-on-white blossoms like Rorschach blots—I saw faces again. I saw Iseul's face made out of my blood, and it unsettled me so much that I almost fell over.

My brain's disorienting tendency to visualize faces in inanimate objects continued without pause, but miraculously I also continued to discover a newfound ease in finding patterns in my scientific data as I did earlier with my endosymbiont's genome sequence. Patterns jumped out at me with incredible speed, effortless, even at a cursory glance at images or numbers or charts—the timing at which molecules are produced by the bacteria, the peaks on mass spec chromatograms, the links to known modulators of neural circuits. Image analysis is a piece of cake, I can do the bulk of it in my head.

Again, no way is this just bereavement hallucinations.

I'm suspicious at first—my brain is just seeing what it wants to see—but when I crunch the numbers and do the statistics to back up my intuitions, my fears are allayed.

In breathers between experiments, when I am forced to wait for incubations to complete, I often wonder at this newfound ability. The uncanny knack for finding patterns began after Iseul's death, I think. Not long after. I am not sure what about Iseul's death could have triggered such a change, some alteration at the level of the brain's neurons seems so sci-fi, but

I'm not complaining—science has never progressed so quickly, with time spent poring over data sliced down to a sliver.

★ ★ ★

I still go to orientation events for first-year PhD students, even though I've been at this university for five years already. It's not entirely of my own free will; Simon and Petra push me to go. It'll be good for you, they say. Spend time meeting new people. Spend time having some fun.

The unspoken is *Spend time doing anything but wallowing in grief.*

At these events, my ears are filled with stories, some new, some old hat.

A PI who has a whispered reputation for getting drunk and flirting with first years. Another who makes it a point to never attend diversity and inclusivity trainings. Another who kicked his fifth year out after she refused to come hang wallpaper in his house. Another who is so old and tissue-paper-frail that a gust of wind come winter might just bowl her over for good. (Don't rotate in that lab, her current two students are racing against the hourglass's slipping granules as it is.)

Doesn't end there, the fourth-year raconteur says in a way that's not entirely without glee. It's not just the biosciences departments, it's an interdisciplinary multidepartmental zoo: in physics, just down the road, there's someone who's been accused of sexual harassment at two former institutions but somehow got hired here and is doing who knows what in his basement-level office. Probably superpositioning himself onto things that don't explicitly involve quantum mechanics, some-body says.

In the philosophy department on the other side of campus, there's somebody who's married a former student forty years his junior. A Hedonist, no doubt. Hey, who here can do some quick stats, because Diversity Guy and Basement Physics both have porn star 'staches and that's something of a correlation, right?

It's almost entertaining hearing the stories told like no one knows who these people are—and it's true that no one does yet, except for me.

Is this how it would feel, if I were a disembodied spirit? Looking down so knowingly at the sleeping physical form, so picturesque-peaceful, from which it rose?

Hand-wavy stories of people drunk on posttenure power. What was it that Nietzsche said? Somebody from a liberal arts college remembers: it was, like, everything that increases the feeling of power in man is good, and happiness is the feeling that power increases. Well that's sexist as fuck.

C'est la vie, welcome to academia.

Some more drippings of horror stories from past years, told like scary campfire stories sans the actual campfire (safety regulations). Hydrofluoric acid spills and dissolved bones inside of a sack of skin. What a poor dumbass, what was he thinking? Not a careful bone in his body. Well, actually, *no bones,* after that incident. Somebody takes the fat opportune moment to snipe: fluorine and calcium are like PIs and the tenure track— it's all high-affinity and collateral damage.

More stories of phage contaminations wiping out year-long experiments. Detonating centrifuges, mistakes, explosions. A large and positive correlation constant between those last two things.

Amid all the stories, I finally call Ha-joon and catch him in a good moment. It's still a short call. At first he's angry that I haven't tried harder to call, but as we sit together the hurt quiet gives way to a different quiet in which we try to bend into each other's presence through a telephone. The closest anyone has come to transmitting warmth through a phone—here it is. He says there is a kestrel outside his bedroom window eating a mouse. He says the brick building outside his window is streaked with faint white mineral deposits, and it looks like dried tears. He says there's a pair of sun-bleached sneakers dangling on the electric cables outside, and the way they swing side-by-side in the wind and slap each other is making him think of Iseul and me.

Then we are quiet again. I print out that picture of the damselfly Iseul and I last took at the wetland and slide it into an envelope and mail it to Ha-joon at the post office west of the university, my phone pressed against my ear the whole time so that Ha-joon accompanies me.

★ ★ ★

As fall freezes into winter, the other members of my cohort rotate through labs, go stir-crazy from going through three-hour safety training after three-hour safety training, try to avoid PIs whose labs don't pass the Bechdel test. Days are stained shades of coffee mug rings and Coomassie Blue.

My cohort takes a group weekend trip to the beach. I stay home. Then my labmates are friendly, suggest an outing to the coastline only a week later. I decline. Sorry, I say. They look crestfallen and stung. Their attempts to bond over the seaside are well-intentioned but dredge up things I would like to keep buried in the deep sea—the only water I can look at now without my skin going shellac with icy sweat is tap water.

At night, over mugs of *yuja* tea, never forgetting a day to turn on that air purifier from Iseul, I re-enact in my head the days of being free to go where I pleased with Iseul. The evening hours that once were home to coastline drives and shared chicken at park picnic tables with grease-slick fingers and nighttime road-tripping are filled instead with the white light of my computer screen eating away the night's dark—partially because there is work to do and partially because I do not want to give that reserved allotment of time to some other person. It would be traitorous, I think.

★   ★   ★

These winter months, work became a lifeline for me.

In single-minded obsession, I found sweet amnesia. It was shelter, a bivouac made of smoke and mirrors. Mirrors—I still avoided those, of course. When I looked in the third-floor bathroom mirror to check the bags under my eyes, on one of those mad-panic days when I thought the data I'd just gathered would overturn my previous findings, what I saw in my face both dredged up familiarity and nauseated me to the core.

Of course it was a familiar look, desperation.

Of course I knew what it looked like. I'd seen it so often in my adoptive mother's face. But seeing this thing I'd sworn off displayed on my own face—risen to the surface from subcutaneous haunts—it felt repulsive. Felt like I was wearing prosthetic skin. *Not my skin, that mask, with those dark-circled eyeholes.*

One time I followed her to work. My adoptive father was having a fit in the living room so I ran after her as she was leaving for her night shift, and I pressed against her despite her hesitation and her attempts to push me back inside.

At the hospital entrance she told me to stay in the patient care unit one floor up. I was not to be with her in the emergency room. "It's scary here," she said. "Go to the nurse station upstairs. Be a good girl. Tell them you're my daughter. They have coloring books."

I went up the stairs. But I didn't push past the door onto the patient floor. I waited a few minutes at the top step, listening to the pinging sounds from the elevator breaching the walls and reverberating in the concrete stairwell, and then scrambled back down and pushed back into the emergency room and slipped behind one of those baby-blue cubicle curtains. I shrunk down below the empty bed when two nurses approached the adjacent curtained space. She'd said it would be scary—I wanted to know how my mother dealt with fear here. At our apartment, she tried to color it in with silence, with feverish hoping. Would it be the same here?

The loudness that took over that initial quiet was all so sudden. I saw a man being rushed in, abdomen shiny in once-internal red and pink. Through the flurry of people and carts laden with monitors and cords I tracked the darting movements of my adoptive mother—who could barely lift a finger at home except to pray—as she brought over an IV pole, an oxygen tank, monitors. And then this short and intense history repeated itself when another man walked in complaining of stomach pains. And again, with a girl leaking from cuts on her face and arms. She was my age—my age, my dark brown hair, my skinny wrists sticking out from under that terry blanket, my adoptive mother crouching beside her tweezing glass shards from her injuries. I watched them. I couldn't decide who looked more out of place. I thought of the glass walls that have always stood between me and my mother.

How could she possibly work here?

As I watched her moving around the doctors and other nurses in her meditative trance, I began to think that she had sent me upstairs because she didn't want me seeing her like that, caring for strangers. Didn't want me to see her become someone she could only be within the walls of this building, someone she could not be within the walls of an apartment in which she lived with her husband and adopted daughter.

I went up to the patient care floor above. There, I sat cross-legged in a chair beside a talkative nurse who made photocopies of patient records and sifted them into labeled folders and told me about her daughter, who also sometimes followed her mother to work—"Oh, sweetie, she's just your age!" In the time I waited for my mother's shift to end, listening to stories of a different mother and daughter—suddenly hating the Xerox machine—the question changed. How dare she work here?

When my mother emerged from the stairwell and met my eyes, her strange expression answered my questions.

It's scary here, she had said.

I agreed. Not the blood, but the real scary thing here: that look on her perspiring face, which no longer appeared so frail. Gone was her cornered expression, replaced with a strange lust, an undeniable euphoria. It instantly reminded me of that man's stomach leaking out onto the lining of other organs: things that I couldn't have imagined within the same biological space.

I knew then why she always worked so many shifts, why she seemed to find every excuse to be here. It was the chaos spiked with adrenaline and espressos from the reception desk machine—a chaos she knew how to navigate, for once—and the febrile air thick with the smell of isopropanol and with the pain of others—which distracted her from her own. She liked seeing other people in various stages of falling apart. She liked seeing their disbelief that it could happen all so quickly—the right turn of a car, the leap of a flame, the shot of a gun—*I know just how fast it happens,* she could think, with a touch of elevated pity, clucking her tongue in a motherly way—such a foreign but enjoyable feeling in her mouth. The mangled pieces strewn left and right seemed to grant her an ugly reprieve, seemed to tell her that she would be okay, of course she'd be okay, just *look* at the state of these people, you're doing just fine.

I never asked to follow her to work again.

We all have our own secret lives. She had hers, inside the hospital. I have mine, inside the lab, inside my own cells.

★   ★   ★

Months into this fever-dream-like science delirium, I finally found confidence in my results—only when my replicated results all told the same story over and over. Science, after all, is not so much about proving an idea, but trying every which way to prove it wrong, before you can dare to believe it. That is what I did: over and over with silent fear each time.

To learn how exactly the endosymbiont works, I needed to move beyond my own skin cells. I chased after the animal facilities staff, who injected the isolated endosymbiont into cells of model organisms. Mice, and also zebrafish, to peek into those glassy see-through larvae.

An experimental result: RNA molecules migrate from the bacteria to the host cell. Again to convince myself, I checked everything: different chemical probes, different assays, different imaging conditions. I reserved a time slot with the multimillion-dollar cryo-electron microscope deep in the basement of the imaging facility—a very expensive first date—and I saw that lacy, loopy RNA with my own eyes.

Only in mouse embryos with two X chromosomes—females have two X chromosomes, males have one X and one Y—would the endosymbiont survive to mouse adulthood.

Only the females could possess the endosymbiont.

It was clearly not a pathogen. Broadly, females with the bacteria fared better than females without. There is some kind of mutually beneficial relationship. So yes, it is likely an endosymbiont.

Only when I exhausted all means of proving it all wrong could I begin to let down my guard. Then began the golden hours of thinking, *Can it really be?*

Only then could I finally pause to catch my breath.

But not before Nadia really did follow through on her threats. She grabbed me on my way into lab one morning and dragged me a floor down to the mouse endocrinology lab, where she watched with crossed arms as her fifth-year friend ran a full blood panel on me. The results indicated nothing wildly unusual, which surprised even me—I was so sure my body was out of whack. The slightly high LDL I laughed off on the packets of x-tra cheesy crackers Nadia liked to sneak me.

But this is all beside the point, which is my data on my endosymbiont-containing cells.

I had been so deep in the breathless thrill and speed and hunger of it all that only once I fell out of my lab chair dozing and twisted my ankle—physically forced to slow down—did I stop to think about what it all meant.

★　★　★

As I sit on the ledge of a planter, in the winter darkness outside the biosciences building, waiting for the three third-floor lights to go dark, I look over all the disparate data that I have organized into PowerPoint slides. Data from my own cells, followed by data in lab animals. I move these pieces around, and they click perfectly.

It takes a moment to process this all. Once they all slot together in my head, I'm overcome with a dizziness. I almost fall off the planter ledge.

In this very small slice of time, I am the only living person to know this truth. It's my secret little discovery.

20

Here is what I know about my bacterial endosymbiont. In a nutshell:

It is maternally inherited.

It only survives and takes effect in embryos with two X chromosomes. This means it is only in organisms born female.

It then ends up inside the adult brain tissue and some skin tissue.

These are the results from my work on my own cells (November), on microbial genomics (November—December), and on lab animals (December—February). It appears that the bacteria alter the neurons in that brain tissue, shift the motions of molecules in those cells in an effect that ripples out into "cognitive enhancement."

Like my enhanced pattern-finding.

What remains to be done, then, is confirmation that this bacterial endosymbiont also exists in other women.

III.
WHEN YOU GIVE A CELL A CELL

Identity in biology is a matter of nesting dolls.

Life is divided into three branches: Eukarya, Bacteria, and Archaea. Eukarya includes people. Bacteria includes my endo-symbionts. Archaea includes a lot of oddballs. (And I won't touch the hair-trigger topic of whether viruses should be considered alive or not.)

One does not exist without the other. Take ecosystems, for example. The human gut is home to countless bacteria and archaea. Petrichor, the smell of rain, is from a volatile compound produced by soil bacteria for self-serving purposes of attracting insects that buoy them from place to place.

The interconnectedness goes even further than skin-deep. An endosymbiont is a cell that lives inside another cell in harmony. Examples of famous endosymbioses: Rhizobiales *bacteria and legume roots, and* Wolbachia *bacteria and forty percent of all insects on Earth. Some partners can still be separated, while others cannot live without the other.*

Over millennia, these relationships grow ever more intimate and interdependent and the blurry line that separates "me" and "you" disappears. Eukaryotes arose when an archaeal cell merged with a bacterial cell. The mitochondria, which were once free-living Alphaproteobacteria, *and chloroplasts, which were once free-living cyanobacteria, have been integrated into the gestalt of their eukaryotic hosts.*

21

HOW TO KNOW IF the endosymbiont in my cells is also in other women's cells?

My lucky break for science comes in the form of a paper flyer, taped onto the lamppost by the bus stop near the biosciences building. It's warped from exposure to rain and the ink has bled, but I can still figure out enough information to make my heart pound.

It's soliciting volunteers to donate skin cell samples for a multinational study on melanoma, and my university is the central hub. Bigshot PI one floor below my lab is regarded as the world's leading expert on melanoma. He is always on the news for fancy large-scale multi-omics this and that. One look at Bigshot PI's lab website, which has been recently updated, and a quick conversation with a postdoc from that lab who also waits at the same bus stop, and that is enough to confirm that everything I need is here.

The melanoma study is fed by a massive collaborative research grant that multiple labs at my university, across the country, and in other countries have reeled in together. The grant is for a ten-year study on predisposition to and risk factors for skin cancer. Labs will solicit skin cell samples from many volunteers in their respective countries, perform analyses to sift out red flags written into the genome, and then pool the multinational data. Frozen samples of all cells will be preserved in a basement freezer at my university.

One of the collaborating countries is South Korea. A big lab at the National University of Seoul. This means that hundreds, if not thousands, of cell samples from random individuals in Korea are on their way to this university.

Of those multitudes of cells, there is the possibility that some may also contain endosymbionts.

Meaning, a relative, perhaps.

Meaning, my mother, perhaps.

★   ★   ★

I get access to all that genome-sequencing data from the Korean volunteers. This I accomplish by convincing Texan Simon to talk to his friend in the melanoma lab, and soon I can log in to the cloud repository.

I sort out all of the individuals who have indicated that their assigned sex at birth is female, but it becomes clear that there is no easy marker of bacterial presence among their sequences.

"Tough luck," Simon says. "Looks like you'll have to go through the actual cells manually." He shakes his head sympathetically at the thought. "That is an awful lot of cells."

So that is what I do.

Over the course of several weeks, I retrieve samples of each of the hundreds of cells from Korean women from the massive freezer room, carefully writing down their ID numbers, plucking out their RNA, and checking each for the presence of the endosymbiont.

I've made a chemical probe that fluoresces only when bound to the endosymbiont's RNA—a blip of light means a match, a jump of my heart into my mouth. But I still have yet to see that light, to have my heart skitter.

⋆ ⋆ ⋆

Genes like these live a nomadic lifestyle. These are bits of DNA or RNA that spring up, up, and away from their original genetic hometowns. Sometimes they end up just down the genetic road, other times in an entirely foreign cell. Mobile genetic elements are a rowdy, fidgety, lawless bunch.

They never quite know where they belong.

Like us, Iseul. You, an immigrant, and I, an adoptee, are not unlike mobile genetic elements. All three of us never quite fit in any one place. Or perhaps we feel like we could exist in too many places.

Where we do belong, it seems, is in flux.

⋆ ⋆ ⋆

It becomes harder to hide the evidence that I am working on a secret project. The countless microarray plates I go through— each tiny well for each volunteer's cells—take up a lot of space in the lab's biohazard disposal bin, and I begin to stash them in my own drawer so that I can take them down to the waste disposal center myself at night. Texan Simon watches this all with a quiet concern, but never says anything.

The physical evidence of strain isn't getting any better either. Nadia's urges to go see a thyroid specialist grow ever more persistent.

"Not getting much sleep nowadays, eh?" British Simon comments one day. When I shrug, he adds, "And it's only your first year. Imagine what a state you'll be in when it's your fifth or sixth."

The annual lab safety inspection comes around in February. I have never been so jittery for something so routine. As long as there are no clear violations of safety rules—the ilk of uncleaned spills, sharps lying around, or unlabeled bottles, especially if they contain suspiciously colored liquids—the inspectors glide through the lab, make neat tick marks on their clipboard charts, and send an approval along on its merry way. Even so, as the short man with the round glasses comes toward my impeccably clean bench, my heart rate soars.

He can see through my wan visage, see through everything. Like in the dreams of swimming through dark oceans in which my skin and flesh fall away: see through to bone. He knows I'm a fraud. He knows I don't belong.

The inspector, of course, does not see nor think any of that, and continues along to the next bay after a sweep of his gaze.

22

THE FUNNY THING ABOUT trying to understand life from the past is that you must extract that information from death: fossilized bones, footprints unmoving in stone, forever-still bodies of small creatures enswathed in amber.

Funny. I was head over heels into prehistory when I was a small child.

When I was little, after elementary school, I learned from afternoons spent within library books about prehistoric creatures. On land, there was Spinosaurus, the largest of carnivorous dinosaurs. In the skies, feathered archaeopteryx and membranous pterosaurs. In the seas, pipe-necked plesiosaurs and saw-toothed Onchopristis and bottle-nosed ichthyosaurs.

I knew the order in which they evolved. I knew all the names, could classify by genus and order, would rattle off the eras in which they roved about the earth. Fan-backed lizards were of the Permian Period, tiny shrew-like mammals of the Triassic, lush cycads of the Jurassic, the much-overhyped T-Rex of the Cretaceous.

For me, it was never a matter of "How pretty you are today," or "How nice your pink dress is." All too common words that fall on girls' ears. I never cared for those.

Not that I heard those words often.

It might be a universal truth that small children can be described as adorable as a blanket statement, but I don't recall having ever heard those words as a small child myself. After Iseul and I graduated from college, we spent a day leafing through old photo albums, comparing our photos since elementary school to the shiny new ones of us in our gowns and caps. Iseul always looked the happy kid, the same round cheeks as today and the curly wild hair that is an oddity for a Korean. What a contrast to the other child in every photo—the other child looked precipitous, like a small bird poised for flight at a moment's notice. I wouldn't say she looked like a prey bird, no, there was too much yearning in her eyes. She looked hair-trigger-ready to react to something, to grab at something, to hold onto something. She looked like a small falcon, maybe. Something that clings to more of its hungry dinosaur ancestry.

I wouldn't know if I still look the same; I never look in the mirror for long enough to know.

But I think my eyes all those years back must have shone and sparkled like the sun when the old librarian commented that I knew more about dinosaurs than he could ever dream of knowing.

After school most days, I walked half an hour to the public library, where I waited until my mother or father left work and came to pick me up. There, I had a corner that I called mine, with a little stool shaped like a mushroom, nestled between the shelf for *560 Fossils & Prehistoric Life* and the shelf for *570 Life Sciences*. It was where I sat cross-legged and pored over Earth's flora and fauna. It was there where I learned of the remarkable intelligence of cephalopods, the never-ending strangeness of single-celled organisms.

I couldn't pronounce the long Latin names, of course. In the Yoon household speaking mostly Korean, and not speaking much at all in the years that came before then, I hardly knew how to pronounce *pronounce*, as it were.

Those, the old librarian used to teach me. He didn't talk much. He just knew where all the books were like the back of his wrinkled varicose-veiny hand, which you knew because he smelled like them, the spice that wafts out when books are opened and the spines crackle softly.

"*Ik*-thee-uh-sor," he would say.

The half-dolphin, half-dinosaur prehistoric beasts with the needle-nose plier jaws.

"Triassic to Cretaceous," I'd say. Try-*as*-ik. Kruh-*tay*-shuhs.

"That's right. A smart one, you," he would say, and hand me another book on life in soil, and another book on the birds of North America. "What a wonderful scientist you'll make some day."

How catalytic he was.

★　★　★

Catalyst: something that speeds up a reaction without itself being consumed. Small quantities often have an outsized effect. Critical to the rise of all lifeforms.

★　★　★

The night after graduating from college, I dreamed that I was an ichthyosaur. Except with each moment I cut through the black waters of my dreamscape, I shed a layer. Thin layers of skin at first, slipping off like shed clothes, ghost-like. Then layers of muscle, red sinew peeling back against the water coursing past my skin, and tendons and branched blood vessels fanning out like roots pulled from the earth. All soft casework lost and nothing but bone armature, I swam.

23

As I FORGE ONWARD with my science and deeper into my past, I'm flighty and jumpy and snappish, and a traditional Korean story about a vase from the sea plays out in my mind on endless rewind:

One day, a fisherman husband went out to sea, but all he pulled up in his net was a strange vase. He brought it back home anyway, and after the initial disappointment, he and his wife realized that it was like a genie lantern: it would grant exactly three wishes. They first wished for plentiful rice—rice grains flowed out of the vase and filled the whole room. They next wished for wealth—gold and gemstones spilled out of the vase and filled even the next room over. Overcome with excitement and greed, the wife had her husband go back out to sea and find another vase just like this one, and while he was gone, she wished for eternal beauty—the vase did her bidding. As she admired her new self in her mirror, she commented aloud, *oh how I wish I could have another vase just like this one!* But a fourth wish was against the rules, and so the magic was undone and the rice, wealth, and beauty vanished as fast as they had appeared.

A double-edged thing, that vase from the sea. Luck on one edge, disaster on the other.

I can't shake the all-eclipsing sense that I, too, am walking a fine line between luck and disaster.

★   ★   ★

The first blip of light comes somewhere between the 500th and 600th sample I process.

At two in the morning, a single well lights up with a flash of green light. Endosymbiont-positive. The person who donated these cells is endosymbiont-positive. I've found a potential relative.

I judder out of my drowsiness and repeat the well. Green light again.

My pulse is in my ears.

And then the others follow quickly, little specks of green lighting up the dotted microarray plates like will-o'-the-wisps in a marsh.

It turns out that the Korean lab has been soliciting volunteers from different geographical areas in turn, and this recent batch of cells is from volunteers from the Mulhwa Islands, a huddle of islets a way off the eastern shore, once disputed territory between South Korea and Japan.

★   ★   ★

I try to convince the melanoma lab person to give me access to the identities of these individuals.

"That would be a complete violation of data privacy," he tells me. I already know that. "In any case, we don't even have that information with us. You'd be better off asking the labs in Korea. Not that they would share that information either."

So I find the contact info for the lab closest to the Mulhwa Islands on the Korean mainland. I find the email addresses, the phone numbers, write them down on a sticky note, even write them down on an electronic note as a back-up, but I balk.

I think to myself: would I really want to embarrass myself with my broken Korean? But this is stupid and I know it. It's just a half-hearted attempt to override the surge of real panic that rises deeper in me, the dread that creeps up sudden like a riptide and clogs my throat:

If I do find my birth parents, what do I even want from them?

As I draw closer to answers, I realize that I don't even know what I want in them.

★   ★   ★

I dream that night that I am swimming in the Precambrian seas.

Huge alabaster-white creatures paddle through the waters with feathery appendages, jellyfish oozing past, and a creature that floats by looks like an uprooted ocean-bed fern. Layers of greenish bacterial mats coat surfaces like prehistoric frosting.

This is unlike my old dream of swimming in which my skin slips away. In this new dreamscape, I move from Precambrian seas forward in time into Cambrian seas, the era in which the first hard-shelled organisms emerged. Glassy diatoms with silica shells, trilobites with calcium carbonate carapaces. Rigid exteriors galore. Nobody likes being poked in the soft parts.

When I wake up in the middle of the night, I push back my sweaty covers and go to my fridge. I take the dead blue nudibranch out of the freezer and out of the paper bag, just to make sure that it's still there.

When I leave for the lab the next morning, I take the thing with me. I bring it to the lyophilizer in the lab—a fancy freeze-drying machine with plastic bulbs sticking out of the cylindrical drum at odd angles, in a way that reminds me of the sea slug itself with all of its protrusions. I hold my breath, open the sea slug's plastic container, tip the carcass into an empty bulb, screw it into the drum, and let the machine have at it.

Two days later, I return to the machine and collect Iseul's freeze-dried sea slug. It's tiny and shriveled and looks like an invertebrate raisin.

It will keep like this, as long as I put it somewhere safe and avoid touching it—just as I have been doing with the Korean lab contact info sticky note on my desk. That note is carefully stuck onto the base of a gooseneck lamp, angled toward my chair so that I will see it every time I sit down.

Later when my mind wanders while pipetting, I wonder what would happen if I put a locket clasp on it and wore it around my neck like people do with rabbit feet. It's a stupid thought. It sounds like something my adoptive mother would have done, propping up her life on insubstantial hopes and superstitious strings of chili peppers.

There is the sound of shattering glass behind me. I turn, and Petra is stooping down to pick up beaker fragments.

"*Fils de putain*," she says.

I know that one. *Son of a bitch.*

"Amen," I say.

Petra has an endless arsenal of Louisiana Creole curses, and I've picked some up over the last year. She once said that her mother fired curses left and right just as quickly as she whipped up food left and right to feed Petra and her brothers and sisters. All part of a balanced diet.

"*Fils de putain* is right," I say. I am thinking about the freeze-dried sea slug.

Petra looks confused.

She once told me that when she was a grad student, her qualifying exam committee told her that anything except English was unprofessional. She had never separated Creole from English as an undergraduate and went into grad school speaking a mix. Her committee was the first to frown at her. *Do yourself and your career a favor and learn to speak proper English.*

"At first, I did as they said," Petra had said. "I got into the habit of thinking thrice before saying anything: the second time to make sure it wasn't stupid, the third time to make sure it was nothing but spotless English. And then I realized a year in that *this* was stupid. The way I speak has no bearing on the quality of my science. So when Stanley told me the same thing when I came here, you know what I told him?"

I'd shaken my head.

"*Bec mon cul.* It means 'kiss my ass.' But he didn't know that."

★ ★ ★

When I take a coffee break between experiments, I spot Kwan-sik perched on the edge of an armchair in the lounge area outside of lab. She is facing the side of the building with the glass wall.

It always looks as though she is waiting for someone—people's significant others or friends often wait in the lounge—but no one walking by in lab coats ever seems to acknowledge her. No one seems to see her, really, absorbed in their own thoughts of their ongoing science.

Who does she wait for? I often wonder. What does she wait for?

Sometimes, the way she waits reminds me of the girl from the upper bunk of the youth shelter, who sat scooted up against the metal frame of the bed watching me as I left with the

Yoons, miles between us even as we were mere feet apart. Sometimes all of the waiting reminds me of my adoptive mother, but then I scratch the thought because they don't share quite the same tinge of desperation.

Is that how I look?

I make my way over and sit down on the lime sofa. I try to find a comfortable position on the wavy-shaped thing.

"Whoever designed this sofa is either a masochist or a sadist," I say.

She turns and regards me with her water-well eyes. She says nothing.

I pull out my phone and open up the microscopy images of my own endosymbiont-containing skin cells that I've saved onto the photos app. The edges of cells and DNA are all illuminated in fluorescent colors, like a birds-eye view of towns decked in holiday lights. I proffer her my phone. She doesn't take it, but she looks.

"Isn't it beautiful," I say, in Korean.

She smiles.

It's like a crack splitting through wood, a break in her until-now stoic veneer.

I look again at my images. Working with the cells day after day until it all becomes so routine, like brushing teeth or habitually scratching at a scab that never heals, it is so easy to forget how beautiful they really are, these little pinpricks of cells from my own skin.

Kwan-sik reaches out and puts a feather-light hand on mine. She says nothing, but the afterglow of her smile still lingers on her lips and in the corners of her eyes. The dark inkwells of her eyes, always so inscrutable—they look a little less sad today.

★ ★ ★

When I go home that night, I take an empty jar of *yuja* tea syrup lying on my countertop, wash out the sticky dredges, slide in the dried sea slug, and set the jar beside the gooseneck lamp on my desk for safekeeping. On the silvery lamp base, the sticky note with the contact info for the Korean research university stares back at me.

I reach for my phone and dial quickly. I don't call the university.

"*Yeoboseyo?*" Hello?

Her voice sounds so strained, like someone's put *yuja* fruit pulp into a cheesecloth and squeezed everything out.

"*Umma,*" I say.

A pause.

"Abby-*ya*, is everything okay?"

I realize that my voice must sound the same as hers, for her to ask that question first.

I cut to the chase. "*Umma,* I'm looking for my birth parents." I am leaning forward with my elbows digging into my desk, my ears straining to hear what she will say above the sound of my heart.

And she says, "I was wondering when you would."

I can hear her smiling through her words, almost like my ears are being cradled, and when I hear her smiling like that, the relief I feel is euphoric.

"Oh god," I say. The feeling is delirious. I let my shoulders fall back to earth. "Oh god. I was so worried."

"Abby-*ya,* of course you want to know. You are a scientist, after all. It's a part of you to seek answers. You didn't think that searching for your birth parents would change anything with me and your *appa,* did you?"

"I was so worried. I thought it would make some kind of divide."

"Oh, Abby-*ya*."

"I was so worried."

"Abby-*ya*, we are still family, no matter what."

"I know, I know," I am saying. I'm so stupid. Of course it doesn't change anything. "I wanted to tell you, so many times. I was just so worried. It's so stupid."

"Is this why you stopped calling us?" Her voice is so gentle and so close, even with the thousands of miles that separate us.

I speak quickly, so that I don't stop halfway through. "I was so worried. The fact that I'm still alive and your own daughter Iseul is not, and then the fact that I'm searching for my birth parents, I thought it would turn you away from me. I thought I had to reject you first before you could reject me. I thought it would hurt less that way."

It feels like an out-of-body experience, finally saying those long-trapped words and watching them hang in the air before me.

"Abby-*ya*, no matter what happens, you are our daughter. No matter what happens, we love you. These things don't change. I don't care what you do."

Umma is crying.

I probably am, too, but my cheeks are so flushed red-hot with sheer giddy relief and a wave of such happiness that I wouldn't be able to feel any tears there, if there were any.

"Is *Appa* there?" I say.

"Yes. Your *appa* is here, sitting on our bed behind me. You were on speaker. He is finally crying, the big softie. He will never admit that, though." She lets out a soft laugh.

The proof is in the odd scratchiness of his voice when he speaks.

"Abby, don't ever think such nonsensical things," *Appa* says. "A smart person like you, there is no need to think things like that."

"I love you, too," I say, and then I too am laughing.

I tell them how I discovered a bacterial endosymbiont in my own cells, how I have been using them as a genetic link to search for my birth parents, how I could find my birth mother this way, and how they have led me to a Korean island called Mulhwa-do. I tell them that I have reached a dead-end with data privacy. I tell them that I have been seeing faces in things like graffiti paint speckles and TV screen static. I tell them that I miss Iseul. So, so much. That I can't stop missing her. I tell them all this, and it feels like I have shed skin, like the swimming ichthyosaur dream.

★   ★   ★

Appa calls me the next morning.

His voice is hoarse with sleepiness. 9:30 a.m. here—as I make myself coffee in the lab lounge area—is 2:30 a.m. across the Pacific.

He tells me that he got in touch with some of his colleagues at a mainland university close to the Mulhwa Islands. A long-time collaborator and one of his good friends works there, and he is a data scientist who has been involved in the melanoma project. *Appa* told him about my search for an important person on the islands, and the friend has agreed to reach back out to the women who donated samples for the project, to ask for permission to share their contact information. The friend will send me the contact info when he has it.

I almost spill my coffee.

"I hope you don't mind that I went ahead with all this," *Appa* says. "You were asleep and I didn't want to wake you up."

"*Appa*," I say, shaking my head. "I could shout from the rooftops right now." If only the biosciences building had an accessible rooftop. In this moment, I could climb up onto a ceramic-tiled roof of a traditional Korean building and peer up close at all of the *mak-sae* engravings accenting the ends of the tile rows, and regardless of whether they are *mak-sae* with the floral designs or the ones with the too-generic faces that unsettle me, I would still feel entirely secure.

I look out across the atrium through the glass wall of the biosciences building, where I can see the concrete sidewalk outside beginning to speckle.

"*Appa*," I say. "It's raining."

The droplets pitter-patter against the windowpanes. It's like the rain that fell when the Yoons first took me from the youth shelter, the rain that fell the first *Chuseok* filled with rice cakes steamed on pine needles, the rain that fell when Iseul announced that the whole family would be turning one Korean year older together on Lunar New Year. *You're twelve years old in American years, and thirteen years old in Korean years.*

It's raining, and it sounds like the feather-footsteps of sprites dancing.

I remember something.

"It's Lunar New Year tomorrow," I say. "The family is turning a year older together."

A note to self:

Inside of each of our cells is a crisscrossing highway system of little tubes and fibers and threads. The microtubules dance. To move the cell and ferry cargo along inside, they shrink at one end—where the subunits crumble off—and grow at the other—where new subunits hop on. The rates of crumbling-off and hopping-on are the same.

This phenomenon is called dynamic instability.

A cell cannot grow nor divide without instability. I suppose this might apply not only at the level of the cell, but also at the level of the organism. The necessity of instability in our lives?

♦ 24 ♦

LUNAR NEW YEAR MAKES me think about how even the littlest planets exert gravitational pull.

How even peripheral figures in a person's life can exert gravitational pull with such unexpected force.

The gray-eyed girl at the youth shelter that one night, for instance.

After lights out, the girl on the upper bunk of the bed shimmied down the ladder, sending the metal framework creaking and groaning under the shifting weight. She jumped off the last few rungs, landed with a cat-like lightness by the foot of the bed, and then regarded me with the unblinking gray eyes that would emblazon themselves into my memory for years to come.

"What are you thinking about?" the girl finally asked, after a long silence. She was standing there in a little pool of white from the streetlight outside the window, unmoving. Her eyes were the color of nighttime clouds backlit by the moon, or the surface of the sea on a cloudy day, I thought. Then when the girl moved an arm to scratch her neck, the big yellow smiley face on her pajama shirt crinkled, the brow furrowed as though just as confused or shaken or perhaps angry as the people in the room.

When I didn't respond, the girl simply shrugged, and then sat down on the mattress beside me. She tucked her legs to one side and watched me knead the hexagon-patterned fleece blanket between my fingers.

"Do you think it's any good to learn that another more beautiful world exists out there—" here, she paused to wave a broadly gesturing hand at the window, the motion encompassing all of Earth "—if you can never ever have it?"

Another silence. Just the soft sliding sound of fabric between fingers.

I knew the girl was looking straight at me. I kept my eyes focused on the fleece blanket and said, carefully, "What kind of world?"

"Anything. Anything can be a world you want. Music. Flowers. Maybe even a whole new planet. With nice aliens, even, if you wanted."

I slowly looked up, and when I finally took in the girl's face, I thought I saw a replica of my adoptive mother's look of such desperation that I felt a sudden need to recoil away, or a need to lean in and grab her arm and never let go. Or maybe the other way around. The compulsions came in such fast succession that I was unsure of their order, or maybe they were simultaneous.

Instead, I stayed still, and asked, "Is that what you were thinking of? That there might be more beautiful planets out there that you want but can't have?"

Fabric sliding between fingers like Earth's plates at a fault line.

"No, I wasn't thinking of planets. I was thinking of mothers. Like the one you said is coming for you because you pressed that button." She pointed at the wearable call button on my wrist. "The mother of your friend." The mattress creaked as the girl swung her legs over the edge, kicking her feet in the air. "Whoever she is, she must be a good mother if she has extra room in her heart for you too."

Then she stood up, and the motion seemed so abrupt amid the thick and heavy fall of her words on my ears that I flinched. The girl returned to her bunk, where, save a brief rustling of blankets, she was silent the rest of the night, as I pried out a bedspring and used the pointy end to carve hexagons into the cracking wall-paint all night long, as morning arrived and with it, Iseul and *Umma* and *Appa*, and as I turned at the doorway and waved a little at her before being whisked away into the warmth of a new world.

Years later I would still be thinking about this, some part of me still waving in perpetuity at the girl, at the shelter, at a past life, still waving like the paw of one of those beckoning cat figurines. A drawn-out approximation of a goodbye. So, perpetual motion machines do exist in real life.

IV.
CAMBRIAN
EXPLOSION

Do species exist?

For one, there is much debate among microbiologists over whether bacterial species actually exist. Microbes like to play pass-the-baton with genes carried on mobile genetic elements; they can pick up DNA pieces and slip this genetic flotsam and jetsam into their own genomes. Sometimes these pieces are the remains of another bacterium who met an unfortunate end, or sometimes they are actively donated from another living cell. It's finders keepers.

Who's to draw the boundaries and say what is a separate species?

The cutoff for the species boundary is 95 percent similarity in genome sequence. It's all just classification of living beings—if there is one thing that humans like to do but are no good at, it is classifying.

This is especially true for "self" versus "other" classifications.

I SEND A SURVEY out to the endosymbiont-positive contacts from *Appa*'s friend. It's simple.

> *Have you ever experienced a traumatic life event? If yes, when?*
> *Have you experienced unexpected changes in cognitive abilities? If yes, when?*
> *Has anyone else in your family experienced both of the above?*
> *Are you or any family members from South Korea? If so, from what region?*

With each contact's email address that I copy and paste, I wonder which of these, if any, belongs to a person who is so close yet so far from who I am.

★ ★ ★

Over the course of the week, I gather the pieces from the survey results, and a montage of collective female trauma and grief emerges. A sixty-year-old woman whose husband passed. A twenty-four-year-old rape victim, a graduate student who was assaulted for being Asian. A forty-four-year-old victim of domestic abuse. A thirty-two-year-old who had her second stillbirth. A nineteen-year-old college student whose emotional support animal died.

For women who *do* possess the endosymbiont, there is something about anguish that kicks the endosymbiont within the brain's cells into action. This is universal, it seems. Given the likelihood of a traumatic event occurring in one's lifetime, I reason that women who are born possessing the endosymbiont will have it awakened one way or another.

Once it does become active, it appears that the effects are varied. I don't know much about neuroscience—Petra would know more—but it seems that different parts of the brain have been affected in each individual:

The sixty-year-old widow claims that her deteriorating memory has reversed. The early signs of Alzheimer's have vanished. She now remembers the smallest details with utmost clarity—*I paid 1,037 won for each liter of gas Tuesday last week at 2:30 p.m. It's incredible. I never forget where my car keys are anymore.*

The graduate student claims that she has discovered an ability to pick up new languages with stunning ease, fluency in a matter of days. She now speaks fourteen languages with near-native fluency, and is currently learning five more.

The domestic abuse victim claims that she has suddenly experienced an ability to focus for extended periods of time. She no longer needs her daily cup or two or three of coffee.

The would-be mother claims that she is able to multitask—*It's real. Efficient multitasking isn't a myth!* She says that she is able to take conference calls while writing up annual reports and also messaging her husband about organizing a dinner event with extended family, with no hitches in any of the three tasks.

The mourning college student reports that she can suddenly do complicated mathematics all in her head. She feels that she has found an affinity for numbers. Perhaps she should switch her major from history to something more quantitative, she says.

The case for myself is clear as well: a sudden enhancement in pattern recognition, after the death of my sister and closest friend since childhood. Pattern recognition also underlies my seeing faces in random markings, my near-boredom with games like Sudoku and SET, and my ability to discern relationships among experimental data points with effortless ease.

Not just bereavement hallucinations, after all.

The correlation between possessing the bacterial endo-symbiont, experiencing a traumatic life event, and discovering a change in cognitive ability is astonishing. It's as though the bacteria are wired into the human fight-or-flight response. I wonder if it can cause changes to our genomes that can be inherited—like transgenerational genetic changes induced by trauma.

My enhanced pattern recognition, the other women's enhancements in memory, in language-learning, in mathematics—at the root of this all is of course the bacteria, altering women's neurological activity at the molecular level. And yet, I can't help but feel arcing up within me a swell of awe at what seems otherworldly.

In short, like all of biology, it is something of a miracle.

✦ 26 ✦

THE DISCOVERY OF MIRACLES extends beyond the lab, too.

I find myself reading Korean folklore. One of the books Iseul left behind in my apartment is a thin volume of condensed folktales, with the *Hangul* version on one side and the English translation on the opposite page. I begin reading it on a whim one night, and discover that many of the stories center around death and grief.

There is a story about a prince who dies of a broken heart, after seeing the spirit of his estranged daughter. Another about a man who kills a harmless snake, which then exacts a posthumous revenge plot in which the man kills his own son. Another about a young woman named Jjil-le who loses her father, goes searching for her only sister in the winter mountains, and dies of grief and exhaustion in the snow—a white flower blooms in that spot in the spring, hence the existence of the *jjil-le* flower. Another about a disobedient frog who only regrets scorning his mother after she dies, and then sits by the creek voicing his mourning—hence, frogs croaking. Another about a man who becomes bound to the earth and separated from his ethereal wife, and in his sadness, turns into a rooster—hence, roosters crowing at the skies.

In these stories and their characters, in the disorderly fantasy and lack of logical connections between events, I find a strange comfort. It is so different from the comfort that I find in hard numbers and empirical evidence in science. It is a small miracle.

★　★　★

And another follows it.

One day, I find Kwan-sik sitting on the lounge area couches again when I go out to make myself some coffee. I ask her why so many Korean stories are about grief, why every other character is in mourning. This is how I learn about the concept of *han*.

Han (한) is an amorphous concept with no direct translation into English.

In a little country steeped in five thousand years of colonization, war, bloodshed, and divided families, it is a people living on a trail of sadness that stretches from the distant past to the present. The trail begins with Mongol invasions, American Imperialism, then the Japanese occupation during which the Korean language was forbidden on pain of death and hundreds of thousands of women were taken as slaves, all the way to the present-day 38th parallel that rends a people in two—and so a deep-seated sorrow and resentfulness ties together the open wounds of history. *Han* simmers in the elderly who have lived through the bloodshed, is passed down to younger generations as an intangible and burdensome legacy. So long as the North and South are divided, *han* will persist as a history of resiliency amid sadness, sometimes also a hope.

Korean stories, songs, movies, all have a thread of *han* that runs through like a bitter vein. The media that is often exported from the country to the rest of the world, full of bouncy songs with candy-pink veneers and visages of babyish bubbleheaded mascara girls and dramas that end in rosy colors, is very different from the media consumed by its inhabitants. Songs about sadness fall into a genre called *bal-la-deu* (발라드), a loanword of "ballad," and are among the most popular. The most popular films do not end in gilt Hollywood-esque afterglow, but tragedy.

If you ask several Koreans to define *han,* the chance is very high that someone will say it runs in the DNA of the Korean people. *It's genetically inherited from our ancestors.*

Han is derived from the Chinese character for "sorrow." Coincidentally, the Korean word for Korea is *Hanguk* (한국), the second half *guk* meaning "country." Similarly, *Hangul* (한글) is the word for the language. The *han* here has a different etymology, but it is not uncommon to joke—either smiling wryly or not smiling at all—about a translation of Korea into "country of sorrow."

As one writer noted: the English "the birds sing," when translated into *Hangul,* is "the birds cry."

★   ★   ★

I ask Kwan-sik if she has a favorite story.

Kwan-sik's response is immediate. "Yes, of course." Her pale eyebrows cinch together, as though affronted by the alternative.

"When I first immigrated here with my husband," she tells me, speaking in such rapid Korean that I strain to follow, "neither of us knew what to make of how strange everything was. We knew nobody, except for a contact in New York who taught us how to get visas.

"As we tried to find our way among strangers while knowing little English, folklore was a comfort for me. The familiarity, you know. When my husband died in an accident—riots in the city—it was again folk stories that were the familiar comfort. And it was stories that led to me another gentle soul, years later. He was a much-loved librarian. We were very happy. He died peacefully two years ago."

Her eyes are kaleidoscopic sadness.

"He also loved my favorite folk story. Somehow, he had never come across it before in his many years of reading and storytelling. It's something I keep close with me, ever since coming to this country."

Once upon a time, there was a young woman named Yun-ok. Her husband, who had once been so gentle and loving, had come back from the war changed. He was angry, bitter, violent, and Yun-ok feared for her own life at times.

Longing for the loving husband she once knew, and doubtful of her own abilities to bring him back, she sought out the help of a healer who lived in the mountains. When she asked him for help, he told her that he could make a potion that would restore her husband's old self. For him to brew this potion, Yun-ok would need to bring him a whisker from a live tiger. There was no alternative.

So Yun-ok devised a plan. Early the next morning, she filled a bowl with rice and meat sauce and trekked up to a mountain cave where a tiger lived. Very carefully, she approached and placed it down among the grasses near the entrance, quietly so as not to wake the sleeping tiger, and returned home.

When she went up to the cave the next morning, another bowl of rice and meat in hand, she saw that the bowl from the previous day was empty. She replaced it with the new one, and again made her way back home.

For months, Yun-ok did this every morning. She never saw the tiger—she only saw its paw prints leading out of the cave and circling around the emptied bowl—until one morning she noticed that the bright-eyed beast was watching her from its cave as she set down a fresh bowl of food. In the following weeks, the tiger listened for the sound of her approaching footsteps and came out of its cave a little more than each previous day, until one fateful morning it came right up to her.

Yun-ok reached out a hand and very gently, patted its head—a turning point, after the months and months of slow-growing trust that had built up.

One day, as she fed the tiger and patted it to the rhythm of its deep rumbling purr, she cut off a single whisker. She ran to the healer's abode, waving her precious whisker in one hand. The healer looked at her in disbelief, and then asked her how she did it. Yun-ok, breathless, told him her story, how she very slowly earned the trust of the tiger with patience over the span of many months. She placed the whisker proudly in the healer's outstretched hand.

The healer looked at it, and then threw it into the fire behind him. Yun-ok stared in horror but before she could say anything, the healer spoke first: "Yun-ok, you no longer need the whisker. Tell me, is your husband more dangerous than a live tiger? If a wild beast like the one from which you took that whisker would respond to your patience and persistence . . . would your husband not respond, too?"

Kwan-sik leans toward me, and her eyes have lost their limbo-like sorrow. They are fierce.

"Never forget, you have agency," she says. "You have the ability to do what you want. Never forget that."

Her voice stays level but the regret gives itself away in the way she casts her gaze down once the words leave her mouth.

I tell her that I won't forget.

"Good," she says. "Good. Because I learned that too late."

Then she speaks even more quickly, as though afraid she won't speak otherwise. Confessions are subject to the law of momentum.

"I was angry for most of my life, you know. Angry that I was born with heart murmurs and hip dysplasia. I've had a limp since I could walk. I was angry—at passersby who stared, at my parents who had wanted a son so badly they gave me a man's name. Angry at neighbors who tried to carry my groceries for me, at my husband who tried to help me up the stairs, at that pastor of the neighborhood's chapel, who whispered prayers after me as I went by. All because I couldn't figure out what I was angry at, all because I was angry at myself."

A look of far-away amusement spreads across her face when she sees my surprise.

"Not what you expected? From the quiet janitor?"

I shake my head.

"You know, agency isn't the ability to do anything you want. It's different. It's bigger than that. It's keeping a little breathing space between you and your thinking, so that there's always a little room to spare for new thinking, and for others' thinking, too. My first husband taught me that. My second husband taught me that a second time, him and all his stories. And then I stopped being so angry."

She bows her head.

"I tell you this because I saw your name." She gestures to my name badge—Abigail Rodier—hanging at my hip. "I had twins, many years ago. I was too young. I was foolish. I didn't know what I was getting myself into. I gave them up for adoption. I moved to America in shame and anger. And now, years later, I worry if I passed all that anger I had onto those twins. What if they are as angry today as their mother once was? I wouldn't wish that legacy on anyone. Inheritance of the past—it's a terrifying thing, isn't it?"

She gestures at the break room coffee machine.

"I tell you this because whenever I saw you standing over there, staring away, all those times—you looked so lost and hurt. I imagined my own lost twins in your face. Would they also look so lost, so hurt? The thing about anger is, you yourself might eventually forget it, but it stays with those closest to you. Like dog-earing pages in library books. You can unfold it, you can try to rub out the line with your nails, even. But you can't erase it, that mark you've made on what's around you.

"And so I tell you all this as I wish I could tell my twins: you have agency. Even over your past—because even that's all folded inside the present. Everything we call past, we once called present, anyway."

She flaps her hand at me. "But, who am I to tell you what you are? I'm not one to give advice. Foolish . . . But better foolish than angry."

She starts humming to herself again, massaging her ankles with her hands.

I am quiet, unsure what to do with these emotions laid bare to me. It's always Iseul who's the one to connect emotionally with people, not me, the stony scientist.

I remember something Kwan-sik said earlier. "You said your second husband was a librarian?"

"Yes, he was. He was so loved by all the patrons, especially the children. He often read to them. He was the famed storyteller of that library."

"It wasn't San Oligo East Public Library, was it?"

Kwan-sik raises an eyebrow. "That's the one. You knew my husband?"

"I think so." I'm thinking of ichthyosaurs and the mushroom-shaped stool again, the old librarian who handed me books and taught me how to pronounce words. "If he's the librarian I'm thinking of, he was very important to me in my childhood."

Kwan-sik smiles.

She says, "I carry many stories with me, between all the ones he shared with me and all the ones I brought myself. I have no children to pass them onto—I could never bring myself to have children again because how could I trust myself to be a good mother? So when young people like you ask for them, I'm happy to share."

When my phone alarm rings to remind me that I have a time point coming up, Kwan-sik waves a papier-mâché hand toward the lab. "Go. Go on and do your science." She rises to her feet, joints crackling with the weight of a life's worth of stories, and reaches for the mop propped up between the side of the sofa and the yellow cart.

"And when you face hardships," she says, "you can skip the whisker step, Abigail."

I pause, and then I reach out and squeeze her hand gently. "Abby," I say.

She smiles again.

When I return to the lab and pull on my lab coat like a second skin, I wonder when it will be that I, too, am so comfortable living within my own stories that I would be willing to share them in the way that Kwan-sik has.

◆ 27 ◆

Iseul's former boss calls me. She tells me that she would like to publish Iseul's unfinished sea slug trafficking ring piece posthumously, as a tribute to Iseul and her writing. She has received permission from the Yoon family to publish it, and would like to know what I think.

"Iseul talked about you often," she says. "So we'd specifically like your permission, too, before publishing anything. I'll go ahead and email you the draft as it is. Take a look at it."

When she sends the email and I open the file, it's clear to me that the piece is a work-in-progress. Like writerly macramé, she's tied together a pharma corruption exposé, the link between some implicated higher-ups and military bases, the dragooning of civilians into the business in their desperation to make ends meet, the chemotherapeutic-producing sea slugs, a little Korean island where the creatures thrive. If it were anyone else, it could have passed for a finished draft, but knowing Iseul's writing and the melody it has when she decides it's final, I know this is still in its early stages. In its early stages, her writing sounds like a conversation she might have when slightly tipsy; when finished, her writing sounds like song lyrics. Her early writing often includes Korean words that have no direct English translation, words for things like the color palette of autumn leaves, or the word for the stifling sense of congestion when one is unable to speak their mind. Next to these words, she leaves a little note—"replace me later"—and forges onward with her writing.

I think about the stories *Umma* and *Appa* told about their halting English when they first came to America, about Kwan-sik's similar experiences, about Petra once hushing her Creole voice, and my own Korean always rough around the edges, the "Konglish" chimera of two languages I often spoke in the Yoon household. When Kwan-sik told me stories in her heavily accented English, I thought it sounded like the fireplace in the Yoons' old home here in San Oligo—crackling, warm.

I read the piece again. It sounds like unfiltered Iseul to me, just a bit tipsy, like she's been celebrating with champagne.

I tell the newspaper people that I think they should publish it. I tell them not to change a word of it. Publish it exactly as it is.

Maybe this is a better way to finally say goodbye to Iseul.

★   ★   ★

I convince the postdoc from the bigshot melanoma lab to follow the lead of *Appa's* friend and solicit volunteers who are willing to fill out my survey. It's not easy, and I wish that I had Iseul's uncanny ability to connect with any human being, but eventually he agrees when I tell him that I have a potential lead on the chemical backbone for cancer pharmaceuticals—at last, I can hand off the little vial from black-market man to a chemist.

When I sit down to parse the information that comes in from the melanoma study cell donors worldwide, it becomes clear that there is a strong link to the Mulhwa Islands in South Korea, Mulhwa-do. The pattern is self-evident.

There are some endosymbiont-positives that come up in other locations: a woman in Marseilles, another in Vancouver, and another in Los Angeles and in San Jose. Doing some digging, it's clear that these are all women who have come from Korea or are descendants of Korean immigrants. They all link back to Mulhwa-do. There must also be many more who have either not been sampled by the melanoma project, or those whose dormant endosymbionts have not yet been awakened.

It appears that somehow, a subpopulation of women from this Mulhwa-do island must have initially acquired this endosymbiont. It's impossible to tell now how many years ago the merger happened—I would need to do more experiments to trace the timeline back.

But whatever I do, my work is fated to be contentious and met with skepticism beyond my own. I know that. So much was done in lab-animal embryos—I watched the strange RNA migrate from the transplanted endosymbiont into egg cells, watched the shifting and shaping of the protean landscape as cells harboring the bacteria shimmied along what would develop into the brain and spinal cord. A human endosymbiont put into mice or zebrafish won't behave exactly the same as it does in humans. It's an outsider there. But for obvious ethical reasons, this can't be replicated in human embryos.

If rumors of my work get out, I will be the only one who takes my findings seriously. At best, it will be seen as intriguing. At worst, it will be dismissed as sensationalism dressed up as science, all hype and no substance, and I will be labeled an exhibitionist. A fraud parading around in a lab coat.

But the thing is, I have already felt like that for so long—like I have been parading around in the wrong skin, in the wrong place.

So I find that I don't care about the labeling. There will be no difference there. The only difference will be in potential discoveries outside of the lab. A different kind of biological knowledge.

If this leads me to an answer to my origins question, my birth mother, so be it.

My work may be fated to remain enclosed within zebrafish and mice, my data locked within the wombs of these surrogate mothers, but here is something I can say with far more confidence in this moment in time: of all the endosymbiont-positive women on Earth, I am the only one to know our shared reality.

★   ★   ★

After dinner, I bite the bullet and align the genome data for all of the Mulhwa-do women from the melanoma study. I write the computer code to crunch through the numbers and get all of the percentages, and then I pull up my DNA testing results from all those years ago when I mailed my spit. I punch in my own numbers and wait until the computer outputs the ID numbers of genomes with similar figures.

There are three that are similar to mine.

My hands are already shaking.

I pull up my own list of endosymbiont-positive ID numbers. I search for the three ID numbers.

One comes up as positive.

I stare.

Donor #88.

She has my DNA. I have her DNA.

Even now, my gut instinct is to reach for my phone to call Iseul, even before I have processed what is happening— *especially* when I can't process what is happening. When I see my shaking hand lift up like that of its own accord, possessed by the ghost of habit, my heart wrenches even harder.

Eighty-eight is my DNA mother.

I pull up the survey responses for Donor #88. It's written in Korean, which I can barely read. I paste the responses into an online translator. It only takes a glance over the translation for something like vertigo to wash over me.

Have you ever experienced a traumatic life event? If yes, when?
Yes. I gave away my newborn child twenty-four years ago. The American soldier abandoned me afterwards.

Have you experienced unexpected changes in cognitive abilities? If yes, when?
Yes. I have been seeing patterns in things. It began shortly after.

Has anyone else in your family experienced both of the above?
Yes. My sister. She also sees patterns.

Are you or any family members from South Korea? If so, from what region?
Yes. Mulhwa-do.

Once in elementary school, I fell off the play gym structure trying to take a picture of a crow perched on a bar above for Ha-joon and mashed my skull on the plastic slide below. My head rang like a gong at the slightest noise for a week. Iseul had to tell everyone around us to be quiet or else.

My head is ringing the same way now.

Here is my birth mother. Here, on my screen, our shared DNA, shared internal space.

★   ★   ★

As the night hours slip away into incremental light, I am still echoing the responses in my mind.

I can't get this out of my head: *I gave away my newborn child twenty-four years ago.* It is so short, so matter-of-fact, so uncere-moniously simple for an action with consequences that are all but simple. How can you bundle up the span of twenty-four unmoored years of a person's life in nine words? It is like reducing the moon outside of my window—which is still loi-tering in the pinkened early sky—to a two-dimensional pho-tograph, a flattening into a glassy-smooth likeness stripped of all its accumulated pockmarks and abrasions.

★   ★   ★

In the days that follow, I am lost—and it turns out not only inside my head but also in real life, when I step out of the glass elevator to my lab's floor still staring at the translation on my phone. I realize that I have walked down the wrong hallway once I run into someone's back. As I become aware that this hallway lacks the framed newspaper clippings on the universi-ty's Nobel Laureates that line my lab's hallway, Kwan-sik turns, and steadies me as I stumble and drop my phone.

"*Aigoo,* look who needs some more sleep." She sets aside her mop and leans down to retrieve my phone, and makes as though to hand it to me until she sees what is on the screen. When she looks up, her pained face is a window into a whole universe unspoken.

"That translation is not so good," she finally says.

She returns my phone, wraps my hands around it.

"The translation is not 'I gave my newborn child away twenty-four years ago.' It is more 'Twenty-four years ago, I *had no choice* but to give my newborn child away."

I look at the Internet translation again. How long I have spent with these sparse words, trying to extract from them a personality in order to reconstruct a mother.

"There is more uncertainty in those words," Kwan-sik says. "There is a sense of helplessness and being forced by the circumstances."

There is something in her soft expression that craters into my chest. I overlay the hesitation and the near-apologetic tone in her words atop my rendition of Donor #88, like it is my own mother who is feeling what Kwan-sik is, and it is as though this missing common piece of our pasts arcs between us all. It is paradoxical, that such negative space can bring people together.

History stipulates that in the wake of disaster, new life emerges.

The Great Oxygenation Event: photosynthesizing microbes started producing oxygen in massive quantities. Early Earth's atmosphere filled with oxygen for the first time. Most other bacteria at this point were incapable of tolerating oxygen. They all died. This was Earth's first mass extinction event.

And yet, life came back, the stubborn thing.

I wish I could tell you this. You died that awful night at the beach but somehow, I'm still moving forward. I haven't moved on, but I am moving forward. Somehow, in the wake of disaster . . .

✦ 28 ✦

I EMAIL *APPA'S* DATA scientist friend and ask him for the name of Donor #88. He says that he will ask for her permission.

Never have I sat by my computer with my heart leaping at every ping of an incoming email.

★   ★   ★

But I had made a fatal mistake, in all my breathless rush: I forgot Stanley. I'd thought that he couldn't touch me because he was away for a scientific conference.

What I didn't know was that Stanley does sporadically monitor the lab keycard access logs, and that these rare occasions typically occur while he is away for conferences and wants to make sure that everyone in the lab is still coming in and making progress.

I have just set up an experiment for my daytime salt slug project, and I sit down at my desk to wait when I get an email from Stanley. The subject line is RESPOND. Inside, he writes that he looked at access logs from recent months and noticed a peculiar trend in my history.

Why have you been going to lab at all hours of the night, for several months on end? Because I see no progress in your salt slug research output. I would like an explanation.

I stop reading the email. It's hard to suppress the rush of panic, and my breath comes out quick and shallow.

This must be because Stanley didn't win that major award that he thought he was a shoo-in for, the one that a researcher at a different university won in his stead. This must be why he's decided to scrutinize measures of people's productivity out of the blue.

I look back at his email, and the next paragraph wants me to explain why I've been repeatedly ordering reagents that have nothing to do with my salt slug project. *Why did you order this compound twelve times in the past three months?* It was to make my fluorescent probe that detects the human endosymbiont.

Dumbass, I say to myself. With Stanley away so frequently, flying halfway around the globe for a conference and then again for another and probably with no sense of circadian rhythm all throughout, I'd assumed he wouldn't bother to check keycard access, never mind the lab ordering logs that Tomás the lab manager keeps so neatly organized.

His email has one more line.

What have you been doing and where are the results?

★   ★   ★

Stanley does not understand when I email back to tell him that I have significant results, but that they cannot be published. He writes, *how can you have publishable results that cannot be published?*

I write that it would be easier for me to explain in person. His email response pings quickly. He is returning from his conference tomorrow, would like to see me in the afternoon.

If my work on the endosymbiont altering women's brains is published, I know that news outlets will pick up on it and aggrandize it into flashy headlines screaming of female super-powers found only in select women.

Women around the world will naturally want to be tested for the endosymbiont.

A thought will inevitably cross people's minds: would they *want* to go through more traumatic events, to see if they have the endosymbiont, to see if the endosymbiont will kick in? I think of Iseul's investigative piece on the sex-trafficking ring. In dark and terrible corners of the world, bad people will do things to women and girls to shake potential endosymbionts into activity—*does she have it or not?*—in all forms of contemporary unfreedom: child trafficking, sex trafficking, modern-day slavery.

That night I try to put together my case. Perhaps Stanley can only be convinced by solid data, like a proper scientist.

He will see this indisputable data, and know that it cannot be published in good conscience.

★   ★   ★

"The data is indisputable," I tell him the next day when I walk into his office and seat myself.

I slide my laptop across his desk, let him scroll through my carefully prepared slides as I speak. When I finish, he is quiet. His brows are knitted together in one conflicted caterpillar.

"It's indisputable," he repeats. "You're certainly right there."

I nod. "So you understand why I can't agree to publish this in good conscience."

He leans back and links his fingers behind his head, rocks back and forth, eyes fixed at a point above my head.

"This would make waves, that is for sure," he says.

From the look in his eyes, my hope disintegrates. If anything, seeing my data has had the opposite intended effect.

"It's good work," he says. "Solid. Solid science."

He is clearly not understanding. I say, "Yes, but it's solid science that could be terrible for society. Imagine what people could and would do to girls and women. Imagine if biotech and pharma were to try to capitalize on this. Imagine the effects on wealth inequality, on—"

"Social stratification, social mobility, income inequality. Yes, yes, I'm aware." Impatient. One leg bouncing. He is not listening anymore. He is tapping his fingers on his desk, one leg bouncing. Underneath his hand is a hard copy of a grant application, and I realize what is going through his head. A big finding like this would surely bring in all the grant dollars and awards.

"So, what would *you* propose we do?" he says. "Keep this all quiet? The point of science is to spread knowledge and inform. You can't do either if you keep your findings under lock and key. Be reasonable, Abby. Somehow, you've managed to discover something about humankind, something that potentially affects other women across the planet, and you're going to keep a fundamental fact about their biology from them? Women have a right to know about their bodies, Abby, and I think you believe that too."

Stanley obviously does not know about my ongoing search for my birth parents—I have never told him, of course—but his words hit a soft chord, and I can't speak because I reflexively swallow air.

He takes my momentary silence as a concession.

"You'll write up the paper, yes?" He spins my laptop back toward me.

I am still dry-swallowing.

"Good," he says. "I'm glad we're on the same page."

He picks up the snow globe sitting by his desktop monitor. It is a rendition of the Great Salt Lake, a cut-view that depicts its brine layers in shades of blue. It houses a little figurine of a salt slug, which itself is home to brown beads meant to represent the bacterial endosymbionts.

He gives it a lazy shake. The little world inside of it is upended.

★ ★ ★

When I get back to the lab from Stanley's office my hands, too, are shaking. Everyone is out for lunch break, no one is here to see me fluttering like this.

The way Stanley asks questions with only one correct answer usually doesn't bother me. I don't let it. But today it brings back my adoptive father's voice.

Where is your mother tonight, Abby? Why does she avoid our home, like it's all my fault? You don't think it's all my fault, do you, Abby?

The shaking is so bad that I can't pick up my pipette to collect samples for my time point.

Why is it always so quiet in our home, Abby? As if it's all my fault? Don't tell me you believe that shit too.

I try to curl my fingers around the pipette, but it's going to fall out. I move my arm quickly to send it away, far away. It clatters to the ground at the end of my bay several feet away, and skitters across the vinyl until it hits the base of an incubator.

"You okay?" Petra's saying something, but I'm watching the pipette tip rolling back toward me, snapped free.

I realize I just threw my pipette. I just threw it, the way things used to get thrown around in my old home. I hate people who throw things like that. I can't stand people who throw things. People who throw things, slam doors, break delicate objects in bouts of emotion. I press my shaking hands against my stomach trying to quench their Brownian motion within all of the memory-tumult.

Someone puts a hand on my shoulder. I flinch.

"Abby, what's wrong?"

If I don't look up and I stare at the floor instead, I can pretend that it's Iseul beside me. Iseul's curly dark hair instead of coiled locks, bright brown eyes instead of hardened gray, half a foot shorter, a pen tucked somewhere on her person.

So then I tell Iseul-not-Petra.

I tell Iseul about everything she missed since she left. That I discovered how my bacterial endosymbiont works, that I keep seeing patterns like faces everywhere, that I'm not the only one whose brain's been warped, there are some other women with the bacteria too, and that's how I'm going to find my birth parents, and did you know that the faces on the ceramic *mak-sae* circles aren't always smiling . . .

By the time I reach my conversation with Stanley, my hands have stopped shaking.

"It's complete gaslighting, complete bullshit." I say. "What kind of rhetoric . . ."

I finally look around and I'm no longer in my bay with my lab bench. Someone moved me away, I'm sitting in a chair in the tissue culture room, the door is closed, and the only other person in here is not Iseul, it's Petra.

The look of horror on my face must have been evident. Petra leans forward from her chair and puts her hands on my shoulders. She looks different, her perpetual look of iciness gone.

She shakes her head sadly. I can smell her perfume. It's some kind of citrus. Lemon. I smell it and it reminds me of *yuja* tea, and I see Iseul again, and a wave of fresh longing and calamity comes over me.

"Who is he to speak for us and our bodies," I say. The faltering crackling of my voice suddenly sounds to me like the fireplace Iseul and I used to sit beside, cupping mugs of tea in our hands.

I try to speak but the words die in my throat.

Petra knows this lockjaw. I know that she did her undergrad in physics and then went to grad school in synthetic organic chemistry, and after those years, is now completely unfazed by Stanley's antics.

Scientists like to say—often with a lofty affectation—that to be a scientist is to accept a lifetime of learning and relearning, as new data upturns theories and redefines what was once thought to be fact. It is a lifetime of paradigm shifts. It is a lifetime of being on your toes, of asking why, rooting around for answers, sometimes finding them, and then rewiring neural connections in your brain to fit them in. Change is the lifeblood.

Funny, then, that some cultural undercurrents of science don't seem subject to that kind of change. These kinds of data points add up. In this thrilling, maddening, prideful, curious little hijinks that is called scientific research, the most important data often lies outside of the experiments.

Petra casts aside her carapace of protective professionalism that years as a woman of color in academic science has engendered around her like a second skin.

"You know what to say when Stanley does something like that?" she says.

"Hm?"

"*Bec mon cul*. Kiss my ass. And then you just move on living your best life." She shrugs. "You ever hear what Stanley said to Nadia? When she finally told him she was pregnant?"

I shake my head.

"She could barely even hide her pregnancy at that point. She finally told him, and he said, 'I'm all for family-comes-first. But I do also understand that pregnancy is a choice.' And that wasn't even because he was trying to get tenure—not that that would have been any kind of valid excuse."

I'm not surprised. "Sometimes I wonder if spending too much time around chemicals really has turned his brain. It's a thing, chemical encephalopathy. Or maybe it's the 1960s asbestos in these walls."

"Yeah, well, the research world is a place where you don't need to be a good person to go far. All of the easy ways out. And then once you're as big and famous and good at reeling in awards and grant dollars as Stanley, the university isn't going to get rid of you anytime soon. I wonder what they've done with all of the incident reports I've filed—probably thrown them out. But I still file them all the same, more for the cathartic value than anything."

"What about you?" I suddenly feel compelled to ask. "Have you ever thought about having a family?"

Petra looks surprised, then lets out a short laugh. "I can't have kids now and expect to have a career." She turns her head away, but not before I see the bitterness. "My wife and I are waiting until I leave this place."

She waves a hand in the direction where the salt slug tanks are in the main room.

"Interesting correlation, don't you think? His life's work on invertebrates and his own spinelessness." She gives me a wry smile. "Grow a backbone, am I right?"

Here's something morbidly fascinating.

Some endosymbionts of arthropods are merciless manipulators of their hosts' reproduction. From fruit flies to wasps to butterflies to crustaceans to spiders, Wolbachia endosymbionts dwell in the cytosol, the watery jelly within each cell.

The bacteria are clever. They can only be propagated through a lineage via egg cells, and so they have devised strategies to ensure that female insects are favored.

These are some select Wolbachia strategies: Transmogrify genetically male offspring into females, by meddling with hormones to produce ovaries and eggs. Tamper with sperm so that only embryos from bacteria-containing eggs will survive. Turn their hosts parthenogenic, so that eggs are not reliant on fertilization by sperm in order to develop into adults. Terminate would-be male embryos—and the hatching female siblings consume their remains.

◆ 29 ◆

I'M STILL A MESS of nerves the next day.

When I go into lab, the place on my lab bench where I had anesthetized salt slugs yesterday with magnesium chloride solution is ringed with white smears, marking places where some solution had spilled and the water evaporated to leave behind a white deposit. I make the mistake of looking at it and in those irregular shapes I see a chimera of the faces of my adoptive father and Stanley.

Petra hears me from the next bay over when I curse.

"Hey." She's come over, still holding a liter flask of media. "Take it easy today, yeah?"

I'm trying to pull on some gloves to get going on experiments, but my hands are shaking and I can't get my fingers in.

"It's just his usual ego-induced lapse in judgement," she tells me. "Self-confidence is like arsenic, and Stanley has spent too much time around his arsenic-full salt slugs."

"How hard do you think it would be to just arsenic him away," I mutter, and Petra gives me a sympathetic look.

"*Bec mon cul* or arsenic, take your pick."

Arsenic, which dissolves in water to be colorless and odorless, had a seventeenth-century fanbase of fancy-wigged

Frenchmen with far too little real hair on their scalps and far too much megalomania underneath. It was historical Official Murder Powder, used for seizing the throne plus other hijinks with a homicidal slant. A classic since the days of Roman Emperor Nero and his not-so-good-natured brotherly scuffles.

British Simon taught everyone all that. His closet history-buff mouth moves of its own accord after Friday happy hours. *Inheritance powder, it was called, can you believe it. Arsenic-happy arseholes hahaha.* (Someday, British Simon will find out about everything he's taught all of us. Texan Simon has the soliloquys recorded, for future extortion purposes.)

When I do manage to get some gloves on to prepare salt slug slides for imaging and take them over to the microscopy room, the shaking has faded away. The rhythm of doing routine lab work is what calms my nerves, once again.

From science, I have also learned that life has a penchant for flaunting the odds, perching on the cusp between viable and lethal in a way that reminds me of Humpty-Dumpty.

Biology is the original Danse Macabre.

The body uses arsenic to make and process a special little amino acid building block of proteins called methionine. Some species of unicellular green algae are encased in a membrane of arsenic-containing fats, some of which even have little shards of RNA. In the absence of oxygen, some bacteria rejigger respiration to use arsenic.

I arrange a glass slide on the confocal microscope, and then flick off the lights.

The slide glows.

(With arsenic, scientists have even devised ways to make molecules light up the dark.)

Paracelsus may as well have been talking about confidence. "All substances are poisons . . . and the right dose differentiates a poison from a remedy."

It's a prickly thing. Everything can be a poison at the right dose, even water.

An ocean's worth of water: multitudinous.

I think back to the article I read a few months ago about the adoptee in Denmark, who was reunited with her birth family after posting a picture of a tattoo she'd always had on her inner left wrist. I think of that story, the catalyst that compelled me to make those calls to embassies and pastors, that led me back to that drop-box that once sheltered a baby whose cells sheltered bacteria, and in this moment, I think for the first time that maybe Stanley's insistence on publishing my human endosymbiont findings wouldn't be the end of the world.

Stanley would want to submit the paper first to a preprint archive, before taking on the switchback path of big-name peer-reviewed journals. Effectively a researcher's version of planting the flag. I know my work isn't likely to be accepted to a peer-reviewed journal quickly, if at all—the claim of a human-cognition-controlling endosymbiont is too fringe, too sci-fi to be met with anything but skepticism from the global scientific community. It will be dismissed as contamination, as an artifact of poor microscopy technique, as deceitful tampering with statistical measures. Journal submission reviewers will demand more experiments, more stringent controls, a sample size far larger than the one I was able to scrape together. So, it would be some time before it would be seen as science. I ease my worries about the ethical dilemmas that had sprung to mind earlier. People in science won't take my work seriously for those scenarios to pan out anytime soon.

The primary outcome of the preprint submission, then, would be media attention. And Stanley would never turn that down, because edema of the ego is an intractable condition.

But the media hubbub that would be generated—that noise could, like the Denmark adoptee story, serve as a catalyst for bringing people together. A connective tissue between adoptees and biological parents.

A frisson of anticipation goes down my spine as an imagined scene plays out in my mind's restless eye: somewhere, my birth mother reads of my endosymbiont discovery, recognizes her own symptoms, sees my name, sees my face, perhaps she has been following my stumbling progression through life unbeknownst to me, perhaps something will click when she sees the bridge of my nose, my chin, the furrow between my eyebrows, my eyes. I know from looking at old photos of Iseul and me that eyes, even when reduced to two-dimensions, spill secrets—would she look into my eyes broadcast on a grainy screen and find a pixelated reflection of a calamity within herself?

It's a long shot. But for the hope-parched, the line between possible and delusional is thin.

This is because delusion is soluble in reality.

Like how arsenic is soluble in water, I think.

I open my laptop when I return home, pull up all of the microscopy images and the spreadsheet tables filled with numbers like honey in comb. It's time to pull this paper together, I think—when two pings from my laptop startle me out of my thoughts.

Melanoma-lab postdoc has emailed me with a happy update. He ran Iseul's black-market chemotherapeutic through a machine that can be used to ID all of the compounds in a mixture based on their individual masses, and it appears that the results are promising. Potential new drug leads. He will be running some follow-up experiments and will keep me posted.

The second ping is from *Appa's* data scientist friend, who has also emailed me back.

He has received permission from Donor #88.

Funny, he writes, I forgot that she was the one person who said that if anyone ever asks for her name and contact info, we should share it. It was odd, now that I think back to it, but we had all forgotten until now.

Her name is Sun-ah.

She lives on Mulhwa-do, in the east side of the main city in the rural outskirts.

30

IT'S LIKE A TIME bomb lodged in my chest, this new knowledge of who and where my biological mother is.

In the days that follow, I can't decide what to do with it. The obvious option is to defuse the tension: just go find her in person. But defusing bombs is risky business, I could hurt myself trying, wound my heart. On the other hand, sitting passively for too long is dangerous too.

I spend a lot of time staring at the ceiling.

It's a strange pace of life, now that the past months' delirious focus on this sole goal of discovery—*find out who she is*—has come to an end. The giddy adrenaline tide that buzzed in my head and puppeteered my limbs forward is gone, and in the quiet of its absence, I realize how exhausted I am.

And Iseul—the silence just amplifies my wish for Iseul to be here.

There is a corner in my apartment still piled with Iseul's belongings. A few books, balled-up socks, her mug with the quill-shaped handle, her chenille sweater whose sleeves we once used to wipe our laugh-cry tears, a jumper cable, a bra that has taken on the contours of my body—things she left behind and things I once borrowed, all of which I'd meant to return to her. Bric-a-brac-turned-memorabilia. I don't touch this fossilized ecosystem of our interdependence.

The only exception is that translated compendium of Korean folktales. Tonight after dinner I find a strand of her hair when I sit down to read another folktale, my nighttime ritual. It is lodged between the pages detailing the myth of *Magohalmi,* the giant grandmother goddess who made the Earth by sculpting mountains and oceans, canyons and islands.

It's a gray hair, curly and shoulder-length, prematurely gray, and I set it on my desk beside my laptop, unable to take my eyes off it, my chest compacting itself all small and tight like the apricot pit I spat out minutes ago.

I know this folktale already. Before *Magohalmi* can build the Earth, she has to wait for the male deities to first create the universe, the sun and the moon, heaven and hell. Ha-joon, Iseul, and I had come across it years ago when the family went to a Lunar New Year festival downtown. Ha-joon had been least impressed as we flipped through the book of ink paintings.

"Well, why can't *Magohalmi* do any of that bigger stuff herself?" he'd said. "How come she has to slow down for those guys?"

★   ★   ★

Hey little mister, I text Ha-joon.

The texts we send each other are never long conversations. They're not supposed to be. They're little check-ins. Are you still alive? Because I am.

As I struggle to write this endosymbiont paper, I leave my phone directly beside my laptop. Every time the flickering of my desk lamp bulb reflects off the screen, my eyes leap over in the hopes that my phone is lighting up with a response from Ha-joon.

Sitting at my desk and trying to write up this paper on my endosymbiont, I think of Iseul's gray hair again. Lines of past, present, and future come together—the past entangled in the present, like Iseul's hair in my belongings—as I trawl through my data. I fantasize about how the world could react down the line to this news of an endosymbiotic bacterium that alters the human brain at the molecular level, that rewires neurons and enhances cognition in a certain lineage of women. A genetic change caused by grief that is inherited in a matrilineal fashion.

Could this someday presage a reversal to age-old trends of the sex-selective abortion that haunts parts of Asia? No more small bones of female fetuses found discarded at the bottoms of wells? Would this someday spell the end of workplaces without separate rooms for pumping? Of Stanleys everywhere who have a habit of roping in the women scientists whenever a lab event needs to be organized?

I think of the first Precambrian fossil discovered in England, a fern-shaped sea creature, credited to a schoolboy named Roger Mason because when a school*girl* named Tina Negus discovered it a year before in 1956, people dismissed it as folly. The fossil was named *Charnia masoni*. Who in their right mind would believe that a girl could make such a ground-breaking scientific discovery?

I pause. This preprint will generate plenty of noise. For me, that is the point. The preprint sits just within the limits of what sounds far-fetched, not yet stepping into the territory of the ludicrous. The premise alone has just enough of one foot in reality and one foot in possibility. Even if new evidence later trickles in that raises skeptical eyebrows everywhere to no point of return, the media will already have gushed about "the superpowers of women." No point of return there, too. The world will already have been swept up in the intrigue.

If new data overturns my findings, if skeptics never believe it, so be it. I and endosymbiont-positive others will be just as we have always been: competent as is.

Petra once revealed to me her paper-writing process. This was the secret to her incredible output, her bevy of quality first-author papers: "Whenever I am infuriated, I revenge myself with a new diagram." She said those were Florence Nightingale's geeky words of wisdom. "Worked for her in the 1800s, still works for me now. Ageless. Whenever Stanley slights me in front of all his male colleagues, or whenever a collaborator speaks over me in a presentation, or takes credit for my work, or my idea, or whatever, you name it, first thing is I respond appropriately"—here, she smiled elliptically, and images of knocking snakes with lab equipment and *bec mon cul* came to my mind—"and then I make myself another drop-dead gorgeous figure for a paper in the works. It's a super-power, you know, channeling all that crap into something useful. I call it patriarchy recycling."

I go to the kitchen to make myself a cup of tea. As the water boils, I stir around the *yuja* syrup within the jar, sliding the bits of pulp up the walls. The pareidolia kicks in and the pulp turns into Iseul, Ha-joon, and me sitting together on Ha-joon's bed, a field guide to birds between us as always. I blink at the three of us overlaid on the syrup jar, the past emblazoned on the present.

When I return to my desk, I see my phone screen lit up. It's Ha-joon.

Hey

Got the damselfly pic in the mail today

It's a good one

And then the next text he sends is entirely unexpected.

Did you know that Umma was once a grad student? In evolutionary biology?

"What?" I say out loud. I send, *What?*

Last week I was going through our filing cabinets to find one of my medical records and instead I found her acceptance letter from 1995. Seoul University, I had no idea. Did you?

Umma was a science grad student? *Umma,* who used to tell me that I should not be a scientist for the sake of having a family, being a mother, being a wife?

I type back quickly. *No, no idea either. Did you talk to her about it?*

Nah. But I heard her talking on the phone to our halmeoni *about how she still blames herself for something ages ago . . .*

And so I learn that young *Umma* had gone to grad school as a statement that, yes, women in the Korea of the 90s could in fact do as well academically and career-wise as men. A statement that all of the daughters born before a precious long-awaited son could do just as well outside of the home as that coveted male baby of the family. She'd become so caught up in her studying, spurred by stubbornness and spite and the need to prove—until her older brother was hit by a bus in a fatal accident. So deep in her studies, she hadn't noticed nor responded to any attempts at contact until a full two days later.

I didn't know we had an uncle.

And then I remember that argument between *Umma* and *Appa* that I'd overheard one of the days not long after I joined the Yoon family. I remember the anger *Umma* had when she felt *Appa* was not spending enough time with the kids. The fear, rather, that something, god forbid, would happen, and he would regret it and blame himself.

I realize that this was why *Umma* had kept up with what I'd interpreted as sexist discouragement to stay in science. She'd just wanted to protect me, was afraid that her past would repeat itself in my present.

She'd never really doubted my abilities.

I return to writing my paper, and I find that my writing comes easily now.

31

W HEN THE PREPRINT PAPER gets out, it's a stone dropped into still water.

It's meteoric.

The headlines scream "Brain-warping bacteria make women smarter," which reads like something flashy written hastily by a disingenuous journalist, except this time it's not only flashy but also accurate.

TVs and radios are abuzz with news pundits, commentators, hosts of talk shows, all with viewerships of millions, all splashing around in the endosymbiont story. Politicians make blustering comments on C-SPAN. One channel airs a special of an interview with an endosymbiont-positive woman, who, sitting with her arms and legs folded in a velvet armchair, describes her "origin story" (a buzzword these days). She says her endosymbiont kicked in one day—no, she couldn't recall a precise moment of intense distress, it must have been cumulative, yes—and then she found herself suddenly clearheaded. That ability to intensely focus on tasks at hand hasn't changed, from pulling everything together to get herself out of an abusive relationship, all the way to her increased productivity as a software engineer today—she just can't believe the level of her output these days, it's remarkable.

The media response is so much more than I had expected for a fringe preprint.

Ancestry and DNA testing companies are climbing all over each other to be the first to develop a new rapid test for the endosymbiont. Labs at other institutions begin to work to reproduce my results. Letters arrive from various offices for research integrity, announcing imminent compliance-check visits for the taxpayer-funded grants that fuel the lab.

And then the paparazzi. Outside of the biosciences building, it is a feral landscape of cameras and extension cords and silvery reflecting panels and overhead light diffusers.

I can't step outside anywhere near the ugly concrete building without being encircled by reporters who thrust microphones into my face, their voices like Vaseline, their cameras turning after my fast-walking form like little turrets. I walk with my head down, hoping that avoiding eye contact will drive them away. When that doesn't work, I start moving about the campus through the underground tunnel system that utilities and facilities staff use to transport tanks of liquid nitrogen and carts loaded with the dead bodies of lab mice.

Of course, the more I evade them, the more persistent they become. They adore it, this cat-and-mouse game. A figure of intrigue, so elusive. Irresistible. They lionize the slippery figure.

In the rare slivers of time when I surface from the underground to hurry to the entrance of an inaccessible building or the bus stop, I think of owls who dare fly in the daytime. Ha-joon and his field guides taught me: such owls are mobbed by crows.

The visibility is so isolating. Never have I felt like such an outcast.

Sometimes I dream about crows mobbing owls.

Other times it's still dreams about strange undersea creatures.

The insomnia is the same as ever, if not worse.

The pareidolia, however, has changed. On things like rain-speckled pavement or cereal flakes or soap foam, I still see faces of people I know, but I also see amorphous vaguely female faces: my brain tries to guess what my biological mother Sun-ah looks like. What features of my own face will hers mirror? Is she the parent with the widow's peak—the dominantly inherited allele that I carry—or is it my biological father, or is it both?

In lab, Petra often asks me if I am okay. It's discreet. She makes the quiet comments as she passes me when I am weighing out powders in the corner of the lab with the reagent shelves.

"Do I really look that harrowed?" I say.

"Yeah, you really do."

I usually shrug.

There is fan mail from around the world, too—or as close as it gets to fan mail for scientists. We sent a note to the melanoma study donors whose cells I tested, informing them that they could contact us for their results if they wished, and now I get occasional emails from women around the world who possess the endosymbiont:

I am a physicist. You wouldn't believe the sudden drop in microaggressions in my workplace. Doesn't matter if you've tested positive or not, people regard women—or, rather, anyone who is deemed to have the physical appearance of a woman—very differently.

I am an athlete. No one believed me when I said I was sexually assaulted by my coach. That all changed when the

*endosymbiont news broke, and I could prove that I had
enhanced long-term memory.*

*I am a sociologist. I study implicit biases, and I'd like to
repeat the famous Jennifer vs. John study, in light of this new
finding.*

*I am a small business owner. I'm in my third trimester.
It's a bright future for my daughter. I can't wait for her.*

*I am an analyst at a think tank. After six years on the
job, I finally got my first promotion.*

I am a graduate student in philosophy.

I am a stay-at-home mom.

There is also hate mail. Email, mostly, from misogynists of
all sorts, but physical, too.

I arrive in lab one day to the sight of the head of the biosciences administrative office, who is scowling and standing by
my bench with her arms full of envelopes and sealed manila
envelopes and bubble mailers. She glowers at me as I approach.

"For the love of god, pick up your fan mail," she says. "Are
you going to make me come deliver it to you every day? There
is absolutely no room for anything else." She pushes the pile
into my arms and turns on her heel, leaving in her wake stray
envelopes fluttering to the ground.

I dump the pile onto my desk and pick up the fallen strag-
glers. Texan Simon watches me, clicking his pen against his chin.

"I'd think twice about opening any of those," he says. "I
doubt all of them are just media folk singing your praises and
begging you for an interview."

"Oh yes, anthrax spores," I say. I'd meant it as a joke, but
then I think again. "You think people would really send something like that?"

"You never know."

I pull open a drawer and push everything in, careful to toss out the ones that do not have return addresses.

Another frightening evening, I think that the loud shouting at the base of my apartment building is a mob of people coming after me—in my head are images of people from the alt-right propagandists that emailed me last week, telling me to "go back to the home country, yellow peril"—but I realize after sitting motionless on my bed that it is a group of teens arguing about sports. It's another sleepless night.

When I am getting ready to leave for lab the next morning, I think about how abruptly Iseul's life ended.

I register to have my brain donated to science when I die.

★   ★   ★

A neuroscience group at my university offers to collaborate with us. Soon, their preliminary data suggests that the endosymbiont modifies the amount of myelination in different parts of the brain—the wrapping around the brain's communication cables that affects the speed of info transmission. Different combinations of lifetime traumas cause increased signaling in different regions of the brain for different people, hence the rise of different enhanced cognition-related abilities.

They use *Aplysia*, a genus of sea slugs historically used for studying learning and memory, the same ones that Petra uses.

An evolutionary biology group presents their theory of how the endosymbiont first ended up in Mulhwa-do women. The endosymbiont is a member of the *Rickettsiales* order, which includes pathogens transmitted by tick bites, so they say that the origins must involve someone who was bitten by an infected tick. They say that they are collaborating with researchers at a university in Seoul to sift out which endemic tick species it may have been.

There is a movement in scientific funding, as more taxpayer dollars and private endowments are allocated to researchers studying endosymbionts (to the despair of cancer researchers).

The world also stirs with people keen on debunking the whole endosymbiont hubbub. There are rumors that they are backed by the alt-right. They search for alternative correlations with lack of sleep, predisposition to Alzheimer's, not enough exercise, too much red meat, vitamin D deficiency. They all draw a blank. The ground is shifting under them.

★　★　★

Even in a world rattling in the aftershocks of the endosymbiont news, I find that the myriad distractions aren't enough.

When I come home for the night, I sit at my desk and try to imagine what Sun-ah looks like. What does a mother look like? When I can't come up with anything, I stare at Iseul's freeze-dried sea slug sitting inside its glass jar. I metabolize memories.

Sometimes I wrack my brain but can't remember if her hair smelled more like raspberries or strawberries or if that shampoo also had a floral note, and if so, what kind of flower, and then cold panic percolates through my body as I scrabble after the fading memories.

Every night I sit by the glass jar and try to remember as much as I can, because if I don't, the memories will slip away like retreating ocean waves through open fingers. It's a cruel thing, the protean nature of memories. I think to myself: if only I could freeze-dry them with the lab lyophilizer and keep them in jam jars, too. I would line my apartment with floor-to-ceiling shelves like the ones that *Appa* filled with books and vintage film reels and inhabit them with the memory-jars and build myself a glassy museum.

The night that I think alt-right mobs are outside the window, I pull out the full-length mirror I keep in a closet and look hard in it, despite my aversion to mirrors.

Unlike memories, the physics of light reflecting off mirrors are immutable law.

As I change into my pajamas, I check that each rib is still there, the curved edges softened by pale skin. An isolated mirror can't play tricks.

And then I notice: I have always been chronically underweight, but in the last few months I have put on a fine lamina of soft padding. I am ever so slightly less spidery, less spiky, I no longer bear quite the sharp angles nor the stork legs. I look more feminine than I ever have in my life. There is something of the inklings of a curve at my hips. For the first time in my life, it hits me that I carry the physical patina of a woman.

For the first time in my life, I stand in front of a mirror and look for a long time.

Perhaps this change unfolded with all of the extra food that *Umma* and *Appa* have been shipping me, reminding me to never miss a meal no matter how much I argue the superior value of a successful experiment. Or maybe it's something about my activated endosymbiont.

Or perhaps this is how I have always looked, and I just didn't realize it.

No matter the cause, I find that I hate the newfound vulnerability I feel in seeing what I look like.

In knowing the exact placement of each rib, the exact location where my collarbones meet, the exact curve of my hipbones, there's no space for uncertainty. I think of the frog I dissected in high school, with its three-chambered heart. There's no liminal space in precise anatomy.

Flayed open to the world, it's hard to hide secrets.

It's 3:48 am. I can't sleep. Lots of random thoughts. Writing down all this crap that I would have texted you.

The average person is home to just as many microbial cells as human cells.

Knowing that, how would you define "I," "me," and "my"? I'm at a loss—or rather, my microbes and I are at a loss.

And Schrödinger's cat is both alive and dead until you open the box and look inside and, in that instant, seal its fate. I like this one. Since I never actually saw your body after that beach night, I can say that you're alive. Since I've never met my biological mother, I can say that she's a wonderful and loving person who would welcome me with open arms. I can keep saying. I can keep saying.

Reality, I am learning, is whatever you want it to be, made malleable by memory.

✦ 32 ✦

I WAKE UP EARLY the next morning and get to the biosciences building by six thirty. The first place I head for is the third-floor lounge area, where I know Kwan-sik will be making herself a cup of tea before getting to work.

She has her back turned, standing by the counter swirling a tea bag around in her mug with a spoon. She is humming. It's the same sad tune that she hummed when she first asked me if I knew what *han* was. It's the same sad tune that she hums to herself in the morning when she opens the supply closet and wheels out the yellow cart of cleaning supplies, and again in the evening when she pushes the cart back into its home and closes the door, and it reminds me of birds that vocalize at the rising and setting of the sun—in Korean, the birds cry.

"Kwan-sik," I say, sitting down on the wavy sofa. "Can I ask you something?"

Kwan-sik doesn't turn around but she grunts in between her humming. I take that as a yes.

"How do you say, 'I am searching for my mother' in Korean?"

She turns. There is a look on her wooden face that tells me she knew this was coming all along. With her gray shawl and

the long-handled spoon with which she stirs her tea, Kwan-sik
has the presence of an augur.

I ask, "How do you say, 'I am searching for my mother.
Her name is Sun-ah. Do you know where I can find her?'"

She regards me over the rim of her mug.

"So you remembered the tiger's whisker," she says. "Do
you have a pen?"

I pull one out of my bag, a red ballpoint, and hand it to
her. She reaches for one of the yellow napkins left over on the
counter from another lab's party, begins writing, and says each
character out loud as she writes. She passes me the napkin.

제가 엄마를 찾고 있어요. 엄마 이름은 선아입니다.
엄마를 어디에서 찾아야 하는 지 알고 있나요?

"You should know what it looks like, too," she says.

As I run a finger along the characters, the elevator doors
hiss open beside the lounge. Stanley steps out. He regards me
impassively, but when he looks at Kwan-sik, he dips his head
slightly in acknowledgment as he continues toward the hall
with the faculty offices.

I turn to Kwan-sik in surprise.

"My husband knew him," she says. There's something of a
faint smile at her thin lips. "It's an interesting story."

She comes over to the sofa and sits on her usual edge, beckoning me with one knotted hand.

"Stanley was at the San Oligo East Library many years
back with his little daughter. My husband saw them. It must
have been before Stanley divorced his wife, since she took the
two kids—I haven't seen them around here since.

"Stanley's little girl liked fairy tales. My husband knew
that her favorite book was a story with an elf that could

magically fix anything broken. She loved that character. So on this day, Stanley and his daughter were looking for a new storybook to read, and when his daughter wasn't looking, he tore some pages out of a book. He called her over, pulled out a bottle of glue from his pocket, and made a show of fixing it."

I am having a hard time imagining Stanley interacting with a small child, never mind his own small child.

"Your husband saw this all play out?" I ask.

"Yes. But he didn't say anything, because what he saw was a brokenhearted father trying to win his daughter's love. Stanley only noticed him standing there afterwards."

Kwan-sik gives me a sad little smile.

"My husband took care of the book once they left. The only living people who know this story to this day are Stanley, me, and now you."

"So he knows that you know."

"Yes. But there is one other thing." Her smile is less faint now. "There is a Korean children's story about two brothers. The younger one is poor and older one is rich. The story goes that the younger brother finds a swallow with a broken leg and takes care of it until it can fly away. To thank him, the bird brings him great wealth. The older brother is jealous, and he lays traps that catch and hurt the swallow, and he makes a show of freeing it and helping it. When the bird returns, it brings him nothing but devastation.

"We had an English version of this children's book at home. After I heard about the things Stanley said to an international second-year regarding her work—'pretty good considering your minority status'—I brought the book with me to work and left it outside of Stanley's office door. A gift, if you will. At the time I thought it was deserved and rather funny.

Now I think maybe it was too cruel." She waves a hand in the direction of the offices. "In any case, he treats me with caution now. Caution is the poor man's attempt at respect."

"Presumably to keep you quiet."

"Yes."

She sets her mug down on the coffee table, gestures at the yellow napkin with her red writing in my hands. "You're leaving soon to search for your mother?"

I give a hesitant shrug. I fold the napkin in half. "I want to be prepared."

"Good. Let me tell you one more story."

Today, I learn of the folklore behind Korean dragon mythology.

★   ★   ★

Korean dragons are benevolent entities that bring the rainy season and water-laden clouds to farmers and their parched crops and make life possible. They are called *yong* (용) and they are powerful and revered creatures that live in the seas, rivers, lakes, and mountain ponds. They are serpentine with no wings, with antler-like horns and a long beard and four-toed limbs with claws like those of eagles, one of which carries a magical orb. This orb is called a *yeouiju* (여의주).

But they do not start off like this. They begin life as aquatic snakes called *imugi* (이무기).

The path to dragonhood is varied.

Some say an *imugi* must wait a thousand years.

Some say an *imugi* must keep an eye on the skies and catch a falling *yeouiju*.

Each fully fledged dragon has its own origin story.

★   ★   ★

When I return to the lab, I end up sitting in my chair staring out the window, transfixed because to my eyes, it looks like a vaguely fox-shaped cumulus cloud is being wind-swept into a female figure, into Iseul, with her wild curly hair, and I start to trace the shape with a finger when I realize that the dark outline in my peripheral vision is Stanley standing by my lab bench with his arms crossed.

"Abby," he is saying, and the way that he says my name suggests to me that he has already said it several times to my unhearing ears.

I look up at him. My eyes are still unfocused and so the two sides of his face are melding together in my field of view, and he has become a blurry cyclops.

"Abby, can I ask what you are doing?" he says, and his voice is fatally slow—I know immediately this is the end of some kind of line for me—and even so, I can't focus and bring myself back to Earth.

"Practicing casual astral projection," I say. I can hardly say that I am hallucinating my dead friend.

He tells me to come with him to his office, where he asks me for my progress on the salt slug bacteria's RNA.

From days and nights steeped in my own cells and their own bacteria, I have nothing to show for the salt slugs. I am still stuck on the same experiment from ages ago. It was probably something with the salt concentration, I remember saying to Petra. I never followed through on the bacteriophage hunch I had on the day Iseul and I last went to the wetland, after stumbling across the mystery of my own cells.

Stanley's leg is bouncing again.

You're wasting my grant money, he tells me. You're wasting my time. You're wasting all of our time. He tells me that my work on my endosymbiont is all fine and dandy, but he needs results on the salt slugs. He tells me that he is transferring my salt slug project to Petra, whom he says has been much more productive even with her many other ongoing projects. He says that she will finish it from here, and she will get credit for the publication.

His leg is still bouncing, or my eye is twitching, or both. Stanley has just pulled years of my work out from under my feet. But I find that I am surprisingly unaffected by what is a heavy blow to any scientific career. It is a loss, but compared to other recent losses, it seems to pale in significance.

You're not taking ownership of your own project, he tells me. It's gathering dust. You need to take ownership. You need to show some initiative.

★ ★ ★

He is unsatisfied, but that does not matter to me; he will not send me away from his lab, not with this preprint. Even if he were threatening to kick me out of the lab, it wouldn't scare me as it did before, when I'd needed a means to pay for college, when I was desperate for all of the equipment and resources I would need to bootstrap my way into my past, to pursue that thread to my birth mother that I'd whipstitched together from my cells and Iseul's help and scientific creativity.

But now—now, I already know where that thread leads. I hold one end, and the other end lies in Mulhwa-do, where there is a woman named Sun-ah, who is my biological mother.

I am an origins-of-life scientist, and through science, I have found my life's origin.

I have done the most meaningful science I have ever done.

The lab has served its purpose.

It's when I flip through Iseul's book of Korean folktales, back in my apartment, that I finally feel a rush of emotion, unrelated to Stanley or the lab.

In the corner of one full-page folk painting is a blue-eaved building wreathed in peach blossoms, and hanging from the entryway lintel is a yellow rectangle bearing red characters in sweeping brushstrokes.

I recognize that rectangle.

It's a near-replica of a strange piece of paper I found in my backpack the day before my adoptive mother left for good. It fell out at school when Iseul and I sat down for lunch: a yellow rectangle of paper with red Chinese characters, an illustration of a growling tiger, and oddest of all, a three-headed hawk with one leg. I'd thought the paper was something that had come along with the Chinese takeout from the previous night, didn't think much of it when the wind picked it up and carried it away across the middle school's courtyard, never to see it again.

I now move a quick finger across the pages of Iseul's book searching for an explanation.

That piece of paper was most definitely not something from the takeout restaurant.

The book calls it a *bu-jeok* (부적). A footnote on the English translation side explains that it is a piece of paper inscribed with characters and symbols believed to ward off evil spirits and misfortune, to usher in healing and well-being. The yellow of the paper repels bad spirits, and the red of the ink represents good luck. And that bizarre hawk (삼두일족응), which would never have appeared in Ha-joon's bird field guides—a symbol that grants protection against calamities caused by water, fire, and wind.

I freeze up at that. The words "water calamity."

My adoptive mother had left a *bu-jeok* with me. A talisman for protection and rebirth. That yellow paper with red writing that flew away in the wind—it was her wordless goodbye.

★   ★   ★

That night, I make up my mind to go find and meet my biological mother.

Show some initiative, as Stanley had said.

Alone in my kitchen, spooning Nutella from the jar, I say out loud, just as Kwan-sik taught me: *"I am searching for my mother. Her name is Sun-ah. Do you know where I can find her?"*

The inside of my mouth feels thickly coated, and I'm not sure if it's just chocolate hazelnut spread.

I dream of oceans again. Tonight, the ocean du jour is full of prehistoric dinosaurs. An ichthyosaur snaps its needle jaws.

Amidst all this water-soaked history, I am calm.

♦ 33 ♦

I T'S ONLY MIDDAY WHEN I head out of the lab the next day—
far earlier than I would normally leave—but today I only
went in to wish Petra luck with her newly adopted salt slug
project. I found myself handling the situation well: with a
newfound ebullience, as though the previous night had quietly
carbonated my heart, I gathered my notebooks, saved my data
and spreadsheets and papers onto a flash drive, and passed it all
neatly into her arms. I told her about the possible bacteriophage inside of the salt slug bacteria, which I suspected was the
reason my experiments had not been working, and that I really
do think she should tinker with the salt concentration before
imaging the RNA.

"If you try it, let me know how it goes," I told her.

For once, Petra was at a loss for words. She just nodded,
her rapid-fire repartee nowhere to be found. Seeing someone
else's science hamstrung like this and feeling the prickle of
unwilling complicity dulled the sharp edge of her tongue.

Petra thought I was pretending to take all this in stride for
her sake. But my heart really was light, luminous, surprising
even me. Knowing the existence of the *bu-jeok* did something,
and it lingers in my thoughts like afterglow, that good-bye in

the form of a talisman for protection and rebirth from my adoptive mother. I am illuminated by the light from three mothers, it seems—my adoptive mother, my *Umma,* my biological mother.

I wouldn't be bothered by Petra's silence, anyway. From all of the times I called *Umma* and *Appa* to tell them about my birth parents search only to find my own tongue in knots, I know that feeling only too well.

I bounce on my heels to keep warm in the chill wind as I wait for the bus. It's peaceful. The paparazzi are nowhere to be found today. Across the street, the winter-bare trees that flank the east side of the biosciences building are becoming cherry blossom candelabras.

On early spring days like this when sunlight stretches long into evening, Iseul and I might have walked down to the canal south of campus, where the flattened dirt path is stippled with young flower petals this time of year. She might pluck a bulrush seed pod and poke me with it, as she did in elementary school, trying to make me laugh, as we wander through a colonnade of willows, wild grasses, and white coneflowers.

Nostalgia: sometimes, the past can taste so favorable—a Stockholm syndrome in which the captor is the present. I skip lightly through the memories like I am skimming sweet cream off of milk. If I dwell too long, if I think about how I must enjoy the budding spring alone, the luster will oxidize. Among phantasmagoria, I tread lightly.

In a way, it's all like the forgotten bacteriophages that have cost me my salt slug project.

Bacteriophages are little viruses that infect bacteria, and they are the planet's tiniest and most successful predators. Start with one phage that infects one bacterial cell. The phage makes hundreds of copies of itself, they all burst out of the unfortunate host, and each of those replicas repeats the process. They are merciless assassins: a single misplaced bacteriophage can lay waste to a microbiology lab.

Even so, some of the most delicate language in science comes from phages.

Phage ghost: the hollow husk left over after a phage has sent its genes ribboning through a cell. This tiniest of exoskeletons then drifts away into interstitial oblivion—I picture a spacesuit that has lost its way among planets, and there's a vague sense of self-recognition.

Eclipse: a quiet, as the phage then deliberates inside of the cell. It takes time, devising a stratagem and marshaling all your macromolecular foot soldiers, the way it took me so long to reach this point.

Headful packaging: some phages assemble themselves by filling their proteinaceous shells to the very brim with coils of DNA. This is a literal manifestation of cramming as much knowledge into your head as possible.

Iseul would like that last one, I think. She used to sleep at night with storybooks under her head, up through middle school, sometimes in high school, and then afterward whenever she was particularly worried. *They have a lot to say,* she insisted. *And this is the only time there's enough room for all of it in a person's head, with all the thinking that goes on in there when you're awake.*

That made me pause.

Even years later, Iseul has me pausing at even terminology.

Some terminology in biology is like turning over stones—the stones that Iseul and I used to look under in the backcountry mangrove forests of our childhood days. There, very carefully, we found the littlest high-rises, made of sphagnum moss and inhabited by a populace of many-legged creatures and no-legged creatures. There were whole storybooks underneath.

At the corner down the street, the bus is turning onto the road that runs through the natural sciences complex. I look up at the concrete biosciences building.

In a workplace where people peer at the secrets of life at the smallest scale—the beating of worm hearts, the molecules of deep-ocean denizens, the whirling of electrons—beautiful bright things are not exclusively found in and between cells.

In between sadness, I can see what is luminous.

★   ★   ★

When I return to my apartment, I call *Umma*. I tell her I'm coming.

I tell her I'm coming to Korea. I tell her I know how to find my biological mother. I tell her I'm thrilled, I'm terrified, I still can't believe it, I still think it's a dream—what if it *is* just a dream, because ever since Iseul died, I can't tell what's a real pattern and what's imagined, what's delirium, I can't tell what the difference is between having insomnia and keeping vigil. Why is everything so messy, why does each thing bleed into the next?

Umma listens to my deluge with her timeless patience. When I finally run dry, she speaks.

"Abby, do you know what this is called?"

I shake my head in silence.

"It's called being human. What else? That's what it is."

If we were together in person, I know that she would reach over and tuck the loose strands of hair at my temples behind my ears.

"Nobody's story is all that tidy," she says.

Never before have I known so intimately that amid chaos, life finds a way.

In earthly matters, turbulent flow is the norm, and orderly laminar flow is the exception.

The blood in your veins, the air in the room, the atmosphere near the surface of the Earth, the air near cumulus and cumulonimbus clouds—it's all turbulent. It's chaos. Turbulent flow is critical to the formation of raindrops—life on Earth can thank turbulence for rainfall.

Living organisms have adapted to life in a turbulent world. Wings, fins, skin, scales, the shapes of bodies and cells, these are all giveaway signs of adaptation to turbulence.

Amid chaos, life finds a way.

♦ 34 ♦

I TAKE THE NEXT soonest flight to Incheon International Airport.

As I wait at my gate—baseball cap pulled down low plus a pair of large sunglasses, obscuring my face from any nosy travelers who might be aware of the endosymbiont news hubbub—I call Nadia to ask her to teach Petra salt slug care 101. She's in a good mood, laughs a little, doesn't ask me why. "Now the salt slugs will have three mothers in the lab," she says.

The flight is fourteen hours of jittery heart and inability to fall asleep, even when the cabin lights are off and there is no sound but soft snoring and engine humming blending into one tone of white noise. I cannot tell if the thundering in my head is from this droning noise, or if it is my own blood flowing chaotically.

I hail a taxi. It is a quiet ride. The driver doesn't seem to recognize me from all the media coverage. I stumble over my Korean when I give him the address and again when I thank him. When we pull up to the address, as I step out into the metallic heat, a middle-aged couple emerging from a little bakery watch me. Their stares are not unfriendly, not confrontational, but something about them is discomfiting.

I make my way toward the narrow alleyway that leads to the Yoons' home. An old woman hobbling along the sidewalk peers at me as I walk by her. It's the same gaze as before; it's not antagonistic, but it's not necessarily welcoming.

Prickling under the gazes of passersby, I think maybe my hair has become disheveled while dozing during the taxi ride here, but when I glance at my reflection in the dark storefront window glass of a hair salon closed for the evening, it hits me that it's not just my sleep-mussed hair or the sleep-deprived bags under my eyes or baggy traveling clothes or any other physical temporaries. It's not my appearance in newspapers or on television. Instead, it is the fact that I do not look quite like all of these people walking around me in this quiet part of town, a less-trafficked area that sits on the more rural outskirts of Incheon.

What these people see when they watch me walk by are the same foreign shapes that I saw in my face as a child, the telltale signs that I could not find in either of my adoptive parents' faces back in our apartment. These people see the shapes that I couldn't find in my full-Korean adoptive mother's face: the sharper edges, the higher nose bridge, and the eyebrow curvature, plus the color of my hair that leans more toward brown than black and my tanner skin.

I hadn't noticed it back at the airport, which was full of international travelers against the metropolitan backdrop of Incheon, but here, in a little corner of a tiny country where everyone looks so uniformly Korean, I am like the idiomatic sore thumb. When a friendly shopkeeper locking his store's door greets me, I don't open my mouth to respond, lest people hear my stilted Korean, and it puts not only their eyes but also their ears on alert.

Having lived my whole life in San Oligo, a place full of all sorts of people where you would be hard-pressed to find

WE CARRY THE SEA IN OUR HANDS 265

anyone who would bat an eye at someone's physical appearance, this intense scrutiny is as unsettling as it is new. I cannot blame them for staring—how rarely they must get any foreign visitors in this part of town—but I walk faster all the same.

But I am strangely unbothered. That luminous feeling still within me leaves no room for such worries.

I hurry up the alleyway incline and find the house. It is rust-colored brick, crammed into the space between two slanted white homes like an afterthought, the whole complex built on a steeply inclined road that is crisscrossed overhead by electric cables. "X" marks the spot, I think as I look up.

To me, their new home is more fitting than their old apartment in San Oligo, which was straight and flawless as though subjected to architectural orthodontics. Here, the crookedness, the slight worn edge, it reminds me of the electric fireplace that always struggled to start, the hot spills of kimchi stew when I carried the pot too quickly to the dinner table, the misfired good intentions of *Umma* advising me not to pursue science. It is a manifestation of foibles, and so it feels closer to home, I think.

I raise a hand toward the doorbell, hesitate. All of the jumbled thoughts come pouring at once, and I stiffen, shivering. How will the Yoons react, Iseul dead and their adopted daughter alone and alive on the steps before their home? Their adopted daughter, a fish out of water in this little country, with nothing but a small suitcase by her side.

I press the doorbell.

When the door opens, it's *Appa* standing before me. His face is as stoic as ever, his curly gray hair sticking out at odd angles in comedic contrast with the rest of his solemn appearance, the same as ever. He looks down at me. I can smell kimchi stew in the house behind him.

I am still struggling to come up with words to say, when he speaks first.

"Come here, you," he says gruffly, and he pulls me into an embrace. It's warm and full and soothes away the fears that had kept me all stiff, melts the lacquer of ice that had cinched my chest. "We missed you. We worried about you."

I hear the rapid flip-flopping of house slippers behind *Appa*.

"Oh my goodness, is that Abby? Has Abby arrived?"

Umma appears, and she's in the same floral lace apron as ever.

"Oh, Abby-*ya!*"

And then it's one very long group hug. Standing like this, there could be an earthquake now and I would still feel whole and stable. The ground beneath my feet is more present than ever, alive. Like the kind of earth that Iseul and I used to play in. Like the kind of living ground that is crisscrossed with tree roots and brocaded with fungal mycelia, pocketed deeper below with earthy sanctums that are home to burrowing beetles and sleeping mice.

And then I am whisked to the dinner table, where Ha-joon is laying everything out. I'm stunned to see him standing and moving. I think of Iseul's bullheaded hopefulness, of things working on the sheer basis of belief.

"Hey, you." I slip into English. I pull Ha-joon into a hug. True to *Umma*'s words from our last call, his bony frame is less pointy than I remember it. "I missed you, little mister. Look at you, up on your feet and everything."

Ha-joon's hug is strong. "You're seeing it all with your own eyes."

I tussle his hair, and he squirms and pushes me away, laughing. "I still hate it when you do that."

"I know."

"I'm not so sure you can call me 'little mister' anymore either. I'm, what, half a foot taller than you now?"

Umma hurries in with another bowl of stew, waving her ladle at Ha-joon. "Oh you'll always be 'little mister' to your *noona,* don't you think otherwise. Come now, everyone sit down before the food gets cold."

Appa comes in with a chair he has taken from another room. It's blue, a clear outlier among the three beige wooden ones that clearly are a set with the round, beige, wooden table. Three chairs for three surviving family members. I wonder if the table had come with only three chairs, or if a fourth had been moved away.

But I'm pushed into one of the beige chairs, and then *Umma* is spooning me way too much rice as always, and I'm sent back in time to high school dinners when there were five members around the table, and I notice that Ha-joon still avoids eating the beans and lentils buried among the rice, and then I'm laughing, and it's all beautiful in its imperfection.

We're together around a table, even if it's not the same as before.

We're eating together, Ha-joon is no longer bedridden thanks to the special treatments he has been receiving, *Appa* is doing very well at the university here and his promotion has given them the financial means to afford Ha-joon's treatments. I tell them how I found my birth mother through science, how I will go find her tomorrow.

It's a sliver of time coated in dreamy sepia overtones.

When they show me around the home, I notice very quickly that nearly all of the photos with Iseul have me in them, too. We move down a short hallway with walls mosaicked with framed photographs and the mostly crayon drawings of our childhoods. I stop in front of a watercolor painting of a beach. Iseul painted this in middle school, with a dollar-store kit whose oval of black paint fell out as soon as we opened it, so the scene is candy-bright with no shadows. The dark bluffs we had stood above at Strand Beach aren't here, replaced instead with the color of sunshine. I raise a finger toward the outcrop where I had parked our car, barely daring to touch, and *Umma* knowingly pulls me into an embrace.

Ha-joon also reads my expression.

"Here, come to my room," he says. "You should take a look at what I'm learning in biology class these days. It's just your thing. RNA and the Central Dogma. The stuff of your dreams, not mine." Ha-joon gives me a quick grin, and I laugh a little.

"Okay, let's go to your room," I say.

When we pass by another small room with the door ajar, *Appa's* home office, I stop. On a paper-strewn desk is that mystery forest-green folder: back when the whole family lived in San Oligo, I saw this forest-green folder on his desk, saw *Appa* rifling through it and reading with a focus so intense that he was oblivious to my curious presence. When I asked him what kind of important work was in it, he said, "The most meaningful things in my career." And then he paused, wrote those words in permanent marker on the cover, and returned it to a filing cabinet.

Now, when *Appa* nods permission, I lift the cover of the green folder.

It's full of cardstock notes and store-bought cards.

After all of these years of thinking it was a collection of ground-breaking data, I see that in reality it is full of thank-you messages from former students, some written in pen, some printed, one even scrawled in purple crayon. A slip of paper with the most softened edges from frequent handling is one I recognize: *Happy Father's Day! I liked learning about bird eggs from you.* My own pencil middle-school handwriting.

I glance at *Appa* in surprise. "It's not data? Not key findings? Records of groundbreaking discoveries?" I close the folder again and touch the writing on the cover. "'The most meaningful things in my career?'"

Appa gives me a quizzical look. "Why would data and key findings be the most meaningful things from my career?"

He asks the question like he's genuinely bewildered, and I realize—how much more obvious could it have been? The way *Appa* sat by Ha-joon's bed and taught him about birds and flight mechanics, the way he taught us on the occasional bird-watching trip, the quiet pride when I came to understand a concept he taught me. I think back, and I recall the shine in his eyes, and the memories shift like light refracted by water.

On the way to Ha-joon's room down the hallway, there is a room with a queen-sized bed with two pillows and two adjacent nightstands, on top of which are two matching balsa wood boxes. Those were from a sixth-grade woodwork workshop. One painted blue—mine—and the other painted yellow—Iseul's. I open the blue box, and inside are shells and stones we'd picked off beaches, a snail shell, seagull feathers, a smooth pebble, pressed wisteria flowers. When the family was packing to move back to South Korea, I urged everyone to throw away the stuff for sake of practicality, but Iseul wasn't able to bear the thought—"No one is going to throw away pieces of our childhood, not under my watch"—and so memorabilia strung with our shared stories made it across the ocean too.

This uncannily clean room is itself really something, too. It's like an immaculate museum diorama of a domestic setting that is, ever so realistically, a bit rumpled, like someone is still living in here and has only just left to fetch a snack from the kitchen, or run to the bathroom, or go tell a joke to a sibling. An uninhabited space that the Yoons tried their best to give the semblance of habitation, filled instead with that inevitable melancholy of historical museums and dollhouse displays.

Ha-joon has evidently tuned into my thoughts again.

"So you'll visit us more from now on, right?"

When I don't respond, he elbows me.

"I know what you've been doing all this time, putting all your earnings into my medical bills. You don't need to do that. I mean, look how much better I'm doing. I'm *standing*." He spreads his arms out in a self-referential gesture, wiggles his fingers. Then he gives me a serious look. "Buy that plane ticket from now on."

I throw an arm over his shoulders and pull him close. "Yeah, little mister. I will."

★ ★ ★

In Ha-joon's room, once *Umma* and *Appa* have left to tend to the kitchen, I notice that the books on his bedside table have changed since San Oligo.

"What's the bookworm reading these days?" I say.

I turn the stack to read the titles on their spines. Underneath one lone field guide to South Korean birds are books on comedy: books written by comedians, books about comedians. I lift them up, and the smiling faces on their covers meet my sudden sadness with their pearly-white mirth.

I stare at Ha-joon. This hits me like a physical blow, that he has replaced many of the birdwatching books on his nightstand after Iseul's death: that he has been trying to figure out how to translate the lines written in English into humor that can spill from *Umma* and *Appa*'s eyes, trying to figure out how to fill an Iseul-shaped rift. I look at the books, and I see his effort to reach for the laughter entombed deep and forgotten inside everyone's chests and set it free.

Ha-joon tries to shrug. He rotates the stack of books so that the titles face the wall again, so that no one walking into the room can glance and know what they are.

I hug him for a long time after that.

For once, he doesn't mock-groan and resist.

★   ★   ★

I insist on sleeping on the sofa, after much argumentation. I sit down and pull up one of the fleece blankets from the enormous mound that *Umma* has placed on one armrest.

Umma sits down beside me as everyone else heads into their rooms for the night. Our combined weight on the same cushion tilts us toward each other, nestling us together in a fabric dimple.

"Abby-*ya*," she says, taking one of my hands between hers. She sits there, as though thinking of how to arrange what to say. In that pillowy silence I feel an overwhelming urge to lean my head on her shoulder, and then *Umma* instinctively reaches a hand up and strokes my hair, and then I am no longer in the present. I'm rewound back to when I was twelve—twelve in American years, and thirteen in Korean years, as Iseul said so chirpily over that dinner—and stumbling into the Yoons' warmth, so parched for that warmth of a family that can argue and misunderstand but still love.

"Abby-*ya*," *Umma* murmurs. "You're a good scientist. You know that, right?"

I lift my head up to look up at *Umma*, and I'm startled to see how weathered she looks.

She cups a hand under my chin, lifts it up a touch to look into my eyes. "You're a good scientist. Don't let anyone tell you otherwise. Not even me."

Then she continues stroking my hair. "I don't care what kind of science you're doing, how many papers you publish, how famous you become or don't become. It's because your heart is in the right place. Because you're a good daughter. A good sister to Iseul and Ha-joon."

I smile over a tight throat and say, "It's because I don't pick the beans out of my rice, isn't it?"

Umma snorts, gently pretends to slap my leg in scolding.

"Abby-*ya,* when I look at you, sometimes I see three time-lines. My own *umma's,* mine, and yours. That made me afraid, before."

At that, what Ha-joon told me returns to my mind, about *Umma* and her brother's death and her own *umma.*

"But Abby-*ya,* you are not me, nor my *umma.* You're here right now, a daughter, a sister, a friend, a scientist—and, really, anything else, whether there's a word to neatly describe it or not."

She pulls me into her arms.

"Whatever you do, it will be meaningful to you. And as long as that's true, everything will be okay. Everything will be okay." And we sit there like that, hearts tethered to each other.

When *Umma* finally pulls back, she puts both hands on my shoulders, squeezes firmly, and looks into my eyes with such a fierce love and conviction that even after she has left to go to bed and the home is quiet, save the cricket-chirping outside, I am still feeling their kinesis deep within my chest.

★ ★ ★

When I find that the elephant-shaped wall clock above the kitchen alcove reads one in the morning, still sleepless I push aside my blankets and wander back to the hallway lined with pictures.

There's a microscope I drew when I first learned how to use one in middle school science class, except here a stick-figure Yoon family is sitting together on the slide underneath the objective: *Umma* in her floral kitchen apron, *Appa* and his curly gray hair, Ha-joon in his wheelchair modified with a bookstand, Iseul and her broad smile, and me, with my arms spread in the air as though asking for a hug, or perhaps offering a hug.

Drawing-Iseul's smiling mouth is closer to her chin than in real life. But then I wonder if this is what Iseul would have looked like as a sixty-year-old. By then, would her aging skin have slipped just a bit down her face, to fit Drawing-Iseul's geometry? As a seventy-year-old? Crows-feet ravines, skin growing thinner and looser like the scrim fabric of our room's curtains, maybe. An eighty-year-old? Cheeks sinking inward and lips thinning, like a receding tide? She would have lived to be at least a hundred. Because she always ate *tteokguk* on New Year's and *miyeokguk* on birthdays. *They promote longevity,* she'd say to me when I'd shrug it off myself. *Come on, you're not gonna live to be a hundred at this rate. I'll outlive you. You just watch me.* And yet, here I stand, watching Drawing-Iseul's static agelessness.

A door creaks open down the hallway, startling me.

When Ha-joon emerges from his room, unaware of my presence in the hallway, I'm surprised again at the sight of him out of bed and walking on his own.

"Look who's still up. Night owl?"

He looks alarmed when he sees me. "Oh Jesus, you scared me." His arms are hidden behind his back.

"Why the guilty look?"

Ha-joon glances in the direction of *Umma* and *Appa's* bedroom—the door is still closed and quiet—before stepping out, carrying something round in his arms.

"One of *Appa's* old film reels," he says, showing me, and I stare at the bronze reel like it's a revived corpse. "I hid one before he threw them all out, before we moved."

He waves a hand in the direction of the kitchen. "I spilled some hot chocolate on it so I'm gonna go wash it off. But why aren't *you* asleep?"

I tell him it's not nightmares, this time.

"Really? No ocean, no mirrors?"

I shake my head, and Ha-joon considers this. "You know, 'it only takes two mirrors to make a labyrinth.'"

I give him a funny look. "When did the little mister get so wise?"

"Who says I wasn't wise before?" He sticks his tongue out. "Wise enough to quote Borges in my English essay just a second ago. The dude had nightmares about mirrors, too."

He moves on to the kitchen, and I hear the tap turn on.

There's something that's warmed in me knowing that one of *Appa's* reels is cared for by Ha-joon. A kind of prophetic tingle. The same electric warmth shared by my microscope drawing hanging on the wall. I squint at the piece of taped paper again, at the knobs and screws I was so careful to draw, at all five little people sitting together on the glass slide, stick-figure smiles unaware of the passage of time.

A microscope—such as the confocal microscope that I used to discover the endosymbiont in my cells—depends on two or three internal mirrors.

And what a labyrinth that has led to, I think.

I breathe slowly to feel that warmth fill my lungs.

I have thought often again in recent months: Is it good to learn or dream of another world you want desperately if you cannot have it? If I cannot have a world in which Iseul lives on, if I cannot have a world in which Ha-joon is completely cured, if I cannot have a world in which my history is not spliced together from so many disparate, disorienting pieces.

Dreams: perhaps dreams are like salt on the soul if the soul were a tongue tasting all the world has to offer. I cannot live without them, existence would be bland without them, but they will desiccate me if I dwell too long.

When I first looked at my cells within cells through a microscope, those few surreal months ago, I was reminded that there are worlds within worlds, too. If I just know to look, I think. Even in this one home world I have, this one home, there is an infinity of fractal worlds unfolding within.

★   ★   ★

When I make my way back to the sofa and draw the blankets up around me, I notice that on the wall above my head is a framed photograph of elementary school Iseul and me playing at Strand Beach.

My last conscious thought is that *tomorrow, I will go find and meet my biological mother.*

I fall asleep under the watchful gazes of our childhood selves. I dream of nothing.

I WAKE UP BEFORE the sun rises in the morning. It's a two-hour taxi ride to the shore where boats frequent the waters between the mainland and the Mulhwa Islands.

Before I leave, I pull Iseul's cellphone from an inner pocket of my suitcase, leave a sticky note message on it, and place it on Iseul's desk in clear view, where *Umma* will find it soon. I leave with my right hand in my pants pocket, where I rub the yellow party napkin scrawled with Kwan-sik's red Korean between two fingers, my own good-luck talisman, the exact colors of a *bu-jeok* like the one my adoptive mother left me, until it is worn thin and soft like new skin.

★ ★ ★

It's a squid-fishing couple who agree to take me out to Mul-hwa-do, early morning. They're seasoned sailors, skin mottled from the sun and salt-stiffened white hair like piles of seafoam, and they beckon me to follow as they shuffle coils of seine nets along the docks. The entirety of the wharf is quietly bustling with people who bear the ocean-rimed look of years of life on water. The sun only rose fifteen minutes ago, but people who spend time at sea are an early bunch.

"You might feel sick at first," the husband says to me, as they help me onto their boat. Their hands are lined with calluses from years of pulling rope. "Best to look far into the distance if you can."

The husband begins unmooring the purse seiner, and I follow the wife into the main cabin. Inside, it smells even more like the sea: there is squid drying on a kerosene stove, and the wife turns the flat strips over with a pair of tongs. She is silent; perhaps because it is early morning, but more likely because the sound of the sea fills the air already and leaves no space for human words. It's a glass-like music. I wouldn't want to break it.

She gestures toward the wide window at the opposite end. I sit down on the window seat, where I can feel the engine trundle to life below me. For the rest of the ride, I look out to the mirror-like interface where cloudless sky meets sea, trying to decide if my biological mother and I, too, will look this remarkably similar.

★   ★   ★

The Mulhwa Islands are an atoll formation, a small cluster of coral-encrusted islands that encircle secluded ocean water, like a geological cell membrane. As we approach, I can see the mountains. They are painted in sweeping brushstrokes of dark green, which peel away into sheer black cliff face palisades a mile away. Everything glistens with ocean spray.

The seiner pulls into the southeast main quay, where the coral has been cleared to allow boats to dock. The engine put-puts to a stillness, and the wife helps me up onto the deck and then onto the pier.

I thank her, tell her I will return at sundown as agreed.

"Your hands are bleeding," she says.

She shows me her palms, flecked red.

I look down and there are small raw crescents in the flesh of my own palms and there is red under my fingernails. I didn't realize that I was making such tight and anxious fists the whole trip to the islands.

★   ★   ★

I read online that Mulhwa-do has traditionally been a matriarchal society. *Haenyeo* (해녀) women have been the breadwinners for hundreds of years: these are the diving women who take to the sea for hours each day, collecting harvests of seafood and returning to land only when their nets and baskets hang heavy with enough to feed their families and to sell.

Other island provinces like Jeju-do have since shifted more toward the tourism industry in recent years, but Mulhwa-do has not strayed from its history.

As I walk onto the shore, girls who look no older than ten or twelve run down from the close-packed houses further up the sandy incline, wearing wetsuits, diving masks dangling from the crooks of their elbows, swimming fins and *mangsari* (망사리) nets clutched against their flat chests. There are older women waiting by the water—most of them look over seventy—who guide them around the sharp coral and help them pull on their equipment.

I think back to when I was twelve, the age of these girls. Twelve was when I took my first science class in middle school and learned about molecules.

I can hear a woman holding a sickle-shaped tool explain how to pry abalone from rocks to a group of girls, miming the subtle motions. She is calling to everyone else—they will together enter the water. I squint at them. No, my birth mother will not be one of these *haenyeo* here—she is older than twelve, younger than seventy. Not much of a clue otherwise.

Not far away from the *haenyeo*, merchants like the squid-fishing couple are unloading crates of their deepwater catches that the *haenyeo* cannot reach from holding their breaths and diving. Squid, in particular—the squid fishers trawl through the depths throughout the night and then set up shop during the day in the city market.

One by one, the *haenyeo* enter the water and slip away under its surface.

What do they bring back from the ocean? When they return, their *mangsari* nets will be laden with marine invertebrates: conches, clams, abalones, oysters, sea squirts, and sea slugs.

★   ★   ★

The part of the city closest to the main quay is full of tall apartment complexes and multistory buildings of irregular heights, stacked next to each other like books lined on a shelf. I weave through the sleepy streets, following the instructions that my phone reads to me toward the other end of the city.

That is where I am supposed to ask for the head *haenyeo,* who will know where my birth mother is.

I don't need my phone to navigate once the concrete buildings collapse into low-lying homes with exteriors made of packed clay and stacked stone, where there is no cell signal. The tall cityscape melts away closer to the center of the atoll— the central pool of seawater encapsulated by the island ring— and is replaced by folk villages sprouting from the spaces between huddled alder trees. As I walk forward it is like moving backward in time. I count the endless *mak-sae* that adorn the ends of the curving tiled roofs—the ornately engraved capstones that end each row of tiles. Some have patterns of the sea and its creatures. Some have smiling faces. I search for my own face in their merry ceramic visages.

"Lost?"

A woman with a sun-browned face looks at me from behind a low stone fence that wraps around her home. She is filling large chestnut-brown earthenware vessels with vegetables. A small child clings to her left leg, partially hidden as he peeks out at me. His eyes are round and wide as he stares.

"*Umma*, look at her!" he says to his mother, pointing at me.

The woman shushes him, scolds him for being rude, and then turns back to me, smiling apologetically.

"Newcomers don't often come wandering around here," she says. "Can I help you find someone?" Her Korean has a thick accent that sounds almost like warbling, intonations pinched and pulled at places like clay.

"I'm looking for the *haenyeo bul-teok*," I say in Korean. *Bul-teok* (불턱) is the word for the headquarter building where all of the diving equipment is stored, where the women return between dives to eat meals, recoup, and nurse ears ringing from the ocean pressure.

Under the little boy's stare, I am a novelty museum specimen, and under the woman's benign but nonplussed gaze, I am more aware of my stumbling Korean than ever before. I can see the woman thinking, what could this strange half-Korean girl from America possibly want from a *haenyeo*?

She gestures down the dirt path that snakes past a congregation of alders and a thatched roof home. "You take that path, and it will lead you to the center of the atoll. When you see the water, you will see the *haenyeo*. You can ask them from there."

True to the woman's words, when the clear waters of the atoll's center come into view, there are many *haenyeo* milling about in wetsuits. Some emerge out of the water pulling nets full of shellfish, others emerge out of a low stone-brick building—the *bul-teok*—to head into the waters. Some stand in the shallows, tending to cultivated seaweed that grows in long ropes on wooden latticework buoys. Further up the sand are row after row of wooden frames filled with seaweed slurry that will dry into thin flat sheets under the sun.

When I approach, the women turn and stare at me.

I ask the nearest person where I can find the head *haenyeo*. The Korean words I had practiced inside my head on the long flight feel crooked in my dry mouth, but the woman seems to understand and nods and gestures for me to follow.

By the *bul-teok,* several women are standing drying themselves off and laughing about something, pointing at a small vase-like object in one of the nets lying on the ground. The people of Mulhwa-do have a thick accent to their Korean that I struggle to understand through rapid-fire conversation, but I pick up enough pieces to know that they are talking about the sea vase folktale, in which the fisherman brings a magical vase back from his fishing trip that turns out to contain a genie and to bring devastation to his greedy wife. The *haenyeo* find it amusing that one of them has brought back a vase from the seafloor, a switch in gender roles from the original tale.

I'm ushered into the *bul-teok,* past the wooden planks engraved with Korean that I cannot read. Inside are rows and rows of nets and buoyant baskets and crowbar-shaped tools for prying mollusks from rocks, hung on the stone walls and stacked neatly underneath. Large earthenware vessels line one wall.

She calls to an older woman hanging baskets on the wooden racks, hurries over to speak quietly in rapid, accented Korean, gestures at me, and then exits.

The older woman looks at me with a curious smile. She must be at least eighty, I think, with her crêpe-like skin folding in on itself in a way that reminds me of old window glass that has flowed over time, like the windows of my childhood library.

"How can I help you?" she says. Her voice is surprisingly deep.

I knead the napkin on which Kwan-sik's looping Korean spells out the words looping in endless ouroboros repeat in my head.

"I am searching for Sun-ah. Do you know where I can find her?"

She nods. "I do."

She hangs up the basket she is holding and slips past me out of the building.

I sit down on one of the earthenware vessels. I am not sure what I am expecting. In my head, I sift through all of the *maksae* engraving faces that I passed by. I try to figure out which one will be closest to reality, which one will shift from ceramic to flesh. The loud beating of my heart ringing in my skull hurts.

The door opens, and one person enters—and it's not the head *haenyeo*.

It's a small woman still in her damp wetsuit, who sets down a net full of her catch on the ground by the entrance. The way she lays it down, moving very carefully, very slowly, is like the way in which a person tries not to move quickly lest she scare away a delicate and timid creature.

Pattern-finding is so easy for me—show me any set of microscopy images, any sequencing data, any collection of numbers, and patterns will leap out as though on springs.

But as I search this new face, search so deeply, I cannot find my own in it. It's rough-hewn, like it's been carved out with the sickle-shaped tool beside her net, surreal like Cubism come to life in Korean skin and bone.

It's a cruel twist of fate, to find something so close and yet so foreign.

I think for a moment, perhaps this is the wrong person? But no—I think of the science I did, I think of the DNA. This is her.

My heart scrabbles for purchase against ribs and flesh, trying its best not to drop to the ground like the lead diving weight belt around her waist that she unfastens and lets fall. When the weight hits the ground, the sound is colossal.

She takes a step closer.

Who are you?

And then her brow furrows with something sad, something sweet, something sacred, and the familiar set of ridges it forms loosens my throat. I notice then that she has a widow's peak.

I have seen both of those before, in the mirror.

"Oh—" is all I can say.

And then I fall forward, or maybe she falls forward, and our arms are wrapped around each other, and both of our throats unclog. I am breathing heavily, trying desperately to suck in all of the words tumbling out of her mouth before they vanish into air: *Oh my sweet one look how tall you are what a woman you have grown into I am so proud of you I am so sorry Oh look at you now Oh I am so proud of you I am so sorry so sorry.*

★   ★   ★

Occam's Razor is the scientific rule of thumb that the simplest explanation for an observed phenomenon is often the correct one. A fourteenth century philosopher named William of Ockham said *pluralitas non est ponenda sine necessitate*. Plurality should not be posited without necessity.

Occam's Razor, of course, posits that this is my biological mother.

★　★　★

I saw you on the news, you know, when you got famous for your endosymbiont discovery. I heard all the women talk about how their brains had changed. I read that you, like myself, like your aunt, had suddenly found yourself seeing patterns everywhere. I knew you were the one, then.

But I don't have evidence that specific changes are familial yet.

But I hoped. When I heard about the mainland melanoma study from the squid fishermen, a study that would put our DNA into a large database, I decided I would do it. Maybe my daughter will find me somehow, I thought. And she did, didn't she? Here, now, why don't we go outside for a walk? Why don't we go for a walk.

Yes, let's do that.

Let me show you the center of the atoll. Let me show you the wonder there. Why don't we do that?

I'd like that.

The center of the atoll is a strange place, a bit separated from the rest of the ocean. The creatures are of a different sort there. You're a life scientist. I think you will like it. Oh, how much you've grown.

★　★　★

An 1871 letter from Charles Darwin to his friend read:

"It is often said that all the conditions for the first production of a living organism are now present, which could ever have been present. But if (and oh what a big if) we could conceive in some warm little pond with all sorts of ammonia and phosphoric salts,—light, heat, electricity &c. present, that a protein compound was chemically formed, ready to undergo still more complex changes, at the present day such matter would be instantly devoured, or absorbed, which would not have been the case before living creatures were formed."

The phrase "warm little pond" stuck in people's minds.

The center of the Mulhwa-do atoll sticks in my mind.

★   ★   ★

I couldn't keep you. I traveled to the mainland, where I heard there was a baby box run by a pastor.

I talked to him. I talked to that pastor on the phone.

He is a good person. But no one could mend the heartbreak that day.

Is that when you realized that you could see patterns better? That something in you had changed?

Yes. From then on, I could read the sea and clouds. I know their patterns. I know when storms will come without needing the weather forecast.

That's the endosymbiont.

A strange thing. Many women here must have it.

Did you name me? Or have a name in mind?

I had always liked the name Hye-rin. But no, I couldn't name you. It would have hurt too much.

Hye-rin. Does it mean something?

It evokes kindness and intelligence, and clear water.

★   ★   ★

It is possible that life arose on warm little ponds on land. A very famous experiment in the 1950s put a mix of gases—thought to resemble early Earth's atmosphere—above a pool of water within a little glass flask. When they sent in electrical sparks, molecular building blocks of life emerged.

Recent bodies of evidence support this idea of land-based ponds over ocean-floor vents as the cradles of *first life*.

But as I walk with my biological mother, these theories slide together over the threshold between abstract concept and lived reality, manifesting simply as the green and blue landscape around me. For me, I think, both are truth. Because for me, each new day—each of many circadian *first lives,* one after another—has been shaped by waters that both gave so much and took so much.

As I finally walk across this saltwater-fed earth under my feet, across Mulhwa-do, I feel for the first time that my life was sewn with intention into the fabric of all Earth's life.

* * *

Look over there—it's a leaping swordfish, did you see it? Oh watch your step, the rocks here are tricky, they're all slippery coated in algae. It takes years of haenyeo *training to walk quickly on them without falling. But look at the water—the sun is shining bright on it today. It's sparkling for you.*

It's beautiful.

Here, come to the shallows. You can dip your feet in—mind your step. Ah—why don't you turn that stone over, the one over there.

This one?

Yes, that one. See what's under it. Do you see it?

A blue sea slug. It's the blue dragon nudibranch.

Something pretty, isn't it? Yes, the creatures in the center of the atoll are of a unique sort. It's a special place.

It's a kind of warm little pond.

* * *

There is a beautiful pond nestled in the crook of a green valley near the center of Mulhwa-do, formed where the freshwater running down from the mountains meets the saltwater from the sea. This pond never dries out, even in times of drought;

legend has it that an *imugi* that lived in this pond caught a falling *yeouiju* became a dragon, and ascended to the heavens. To this day, the dragon watches over the pond from whence it came. It makes sure that rain always falls here, so that its origins never dry out.

★ ★ ★

Do you also go for walks to clear your head?
Do you put your left or right shoe on first?
What about socks?
Shoes on or off in the house? Oh, off of course.
When you make rice, do you make it with just rice or with mixed grains?
That cloud there, what does that cloud look like to you?
When you look at the water, what's the first thing you think of?
Does the water still feel cold?
Are you ever afraid of the water?
Would you rather ask a question or be asked a question?
Questions are endless. They really are.

★ ★ ★

Evening. The squid-fishing husband is waiting in his boat by the shore, pulling on a pipe, the green-stained rope that moors his vessel to the piling coiled in his free hand.

I turn and hug my birth mother goodbye. We look into each other's eyes trying to transfigure this memory into permanence. I try to learn the creases in her sun-spotted face, which are paler white, like sheafs of cloud caught between mountain ridges.

She presses a slip of paper with her mailing address into my hands, squeezes once, twice, thrice, so that I never lose it, and in those seconds, I count the scars on those wiry arms again. On the back of her hand: a raised pale scar that looks like the ragged line of white foam separating sea from shore. From a clumsy mistake with a *haenyeo* tool, she told me earlier, when I touched it. On her left ring finger: a thin slit. From the kitchen knife, she said, when I cut watermelon too fast. I always cut watermelon for the neighbor's sweet daughter when she comes over on afternoons asking for stories. On her inner left forearm: long and snake-like. From a stray cat, who tried to scratch every time I offered it a bowl of milk, until one day it came home with me.

After the cat-scratch explanation, she'd looked at *me*. A long stare as infinite as sand grains, slow as honey, diaphanous as the reality that a scar could materialize as the person standing before her.

Unable to think of what to say, I'd upended my purse on the sand between us: spilling out a highlighter and a red pen running out of ink, crumbs from one of Petra's extra muffins, a luggage tag stub, a faux leather wallet that Iseul bought me in middle school, a one-year-old receipt for two California burritos and two churros and two horchatas. Things in a bag can tell stories about the owner, sometimes like scars, I'd said.

And now, she tucks my hair back behind my ears—there is something about the gesture that makes me start crying. When I brush away the tears, they fall into the sea.

The squid-fishing husband helps me step up onto the boat. As we pull away from the quay, I turn back and wave. Sun-ah— silhouetted against the glow of the city lights behind her amid the fast-falling night, she looks like a mirage.

I sit on one of the wooden crates and watch as the strings of green lights on the boat are flicked on—these lights will lure plankton, which in turn will lure the squid into the seine nets underneath the boat. They are bright green, like the green fluorescent protein that is a stanchion of molecular biology research. In this watery eventide seascape, the boat is a collection of glowing pinpricks.

The squid-fishing wife tries to beckon me into the cabin, where it is warm, but I shake my head. I will sit on the deck. She passes me a cup of tea and leaves to tend to the trawling nets.

Later, when the islands have long since passed out of view and night has fallen, she comes back and says to me, "The two of you looked so alike."

I'm surprised. "You thought so?"

She laughs a little at my expression. "I watched you two walking back to the shore and it was like mirror images, the way you walk."

The salt-licked ocean wind is cold against my skin. I shiver. But inside—inside, it's like a warm little pond.

Iseul, I realized earlier today: you've become something of an endosymbiont.

When an endosymbiont has lived inside of its host cell for long enough, a genetic rearranging happens: it's a process of sharing, merging, being at peace with one another. It's mutual dependence. The lines fade between separate versus *same, you* versus *me, self* versus *other.*

The memories are all there, sometimes with leftover fragments of genes and evolutionary trails of noncoding sequences, the genomic equivalent of faded scars.

No longer so discrete, but very much there.

So much like you, Iseul.

✦ 36 ✦

I RETURN TO SAN Oligo. There are four places I must visit.

★ ★ ★

I visit the wetland. At the crack of dawn, I grab the jam jar with Iseul's blue dragon and the worn *bu-jeok*-like napkin with Kwan-sik's Korean instructions, hop into Iseul's car, and drive to the wetland. I put "The Bitch is Back" on. It's at a tentative volume at first, but then halfway through I roll down my window and crank the sound up to full like a teenager who has just learned to drive.

By the time I kick off my shoes and wade into the chill waters, the rosy glow of the early morning sun has already cast memories before my eyes like a bittersweet trickery of light. The eelgrass tugs at my bare toes. My heart seems to tug back.

This time of year, sea-life comes to the floodplain shallows to feed and to spawn. Baby fish can hide and grow among a nursery of seagrass and plant stems. The sediment here is full of detritus, the remains of once-living things that now feed the roots.

Only a few feet ahead, I can make out the shape of a blue-gill flicking back and forth in the water. He is a nervous but fierce parent. He is guarding his nest, which I cannot see.

There, hundreds of thousands of transparent eggs will be quaking with the movements of the baby fish within.

He must be aware of the long-legged waterbirds picking their way through the water. When the floodplains drain and the watery link to the sea becomes dry land, the birds will hurry in and pick off the landlocked fish who were too slow.

Life moves quickly here.

This is where I would have buried Iseul, if I had been the one deciding.

I carry the Tupperware over to a patch of drier land. In the crook of a willow root, I push apart the sea lavender and dig a small hole, where I place the dried sea slug and the yellow-and-red napkin before replacing the earth. The sea lavender fronds sway back into place.

I take a step back and look. You can't even tell that some-one had disturbed it moments ago.

On the silent drive back, I suddenly start laughing. I had a private burial ceremony for a sea slug. Iseul would find this stupidly amusing too. Hearing my own laughter fill the empty space in the car, I think it's appropriate to call this acceptance with minor revisions—in the parlance of scientists.

★ ★ ★

I visit the library.

I push through the doors that I found so heavy as a child. The glass displays that line the vestibule are filled with picture books about animals, with the same annual decorations of green crinkle-paper grass and tissue-paper butterflies that herald the start of spring. I walk along the library walls, pass by the thick encyclopedias that I liked to ease open to hear the spines murmur, and I peek into the used bookstore in the back of the building, where paperbacks with edges velveteen from age live out their retirement years. Fifty cents, same as ever, marked delicately in pencil on the inner covers.

I move through the library bookcases and find the shelf for *560 Fossils & Prehistoric Life* and for *570 Life Sciences*. The little stool shaped like a mushroom is still here. The large windows on this side of the library are the same as ever, but the abutting sycamore trees have grown even larger and the sunlight filters onto the worn carpeting in irregular speckled patterns. In those sunlight speckles, I see the face of the old librarian.

I loop back to the circulation desk.

"Hi. There was a librarian here several years back, his name—" I realize then that I don't actually know his name. I had never asked, and he had never told me. I had never asked Kwan-sik, either. I remember the creases on his face, the veins on the backs of his hands, the gentleness with which he held books, always so tender with the paperbacks when bending their spines—so vivid even after all these years. But not his name.

The little lady peers at me kindly. "Sorry, who are you looking for?"

I try my best at a physical description. She smiles.

"Ah. You must be looking for Rafael. Rafael passed away two years ago." A small and sad smile. "We all miss him very much. But out of everyone, it's the children that he used to read to who seem to miss him the most."

I nod.

"His legacy fills the library," she says.

★ ★ ★

I visit the apartment I lived in with my adoptive parents.

I don't remember the address, but I do remember the walk from the library from all those times that no one came to pick me up. It's not as long as I remember it, with my grown-up legs and faster stride. It takes me twenty minutes to arrive at the front of the apartment complex, and it looks the same: the beige stucco building with the white gabled roof and window shutters. The thorny natal plum bushes around the perimeter are the same—I suddenly recall the summer I tripped on the sidewalk and fell in. I look up at the third window from the center of the building, fourth floor.

I had spent the next half-hour sitting against the wall outside of my apartment, pulling thorns from my skin. Will bad spirits leave through these holes in my skin, I'd wondered, after reading about trepanning in the library just hours earlier. *Is this why my mother murmurs to herself in prayer each time before entering the apartment?*

That same book of strange facts contained a section about the Rosenthal Experiment: teachers led to believe that their students were gifted would unconsciously treat those students differently, and those students did ultimately succeed—a self-fulfilling prophecy.

The window of my old apartment is stained with evaporated hard water, and the patterns that form before my pareidoliac eyes are like my adoptive mother's superstitious strings of chili peppers. Sometimes, things do seem to work on the basis of sheer belief.

"Ma'am, can I help you?"

A man in uniform is looking at me, a bemused look on his salt-and-pepper stubbled face. I realize how odd I must have looked to the security guard: a scrawny woman in her mid-twenties, leaning down to touch the natal plum bushes, and then standing motionless on the sidewalk to stare up at a window.

"Sorry, got lost in my thoughts," I mumble, and move on.

★ ★ ★

I visit the lab in the evening. It's quiet, save the burbling of the filtration system in the salt slug tanks. Nearby, the salt slugs are all happily green, flourishing under Nadia's care in my absence. When I peer closer, I see that there are strands of tiny pale yellow eggs clinging to the algae fronds in the tank. *Well, hell.* They finally did it. A congratulations to the proud new parents of hundreds of healthy hermaphrodites.

I walk to the -80°C freezer. I've finally decided to add my own sticky note, the latest addition to the lab fails poem mosaicked on the door. I pull it from my pocket, rub it onto a patch of empty space.

The poem's story grows like so:

VIII. Tomorrow
But out of the ruts of my lab record's shame, ("Still I Rise,"
    Maya Angelou)
still I'll rise. ("Still I Rise," Maya Angelou)
I went galumphing back. ("The Jabberwocky," Lewis Carroll)
I am taking the road that all scientists travel by, ("The Road
    Not Taken," Robert Frost)
and that will make all the difference. ("The Road Not
    Taken," Robert Frost)

As I head back toward the door, I notice something on my desk.

It's a print-out of microscopy images. I realize that they are my salt slug cells, containing their bacterial endosymbionts. The images are flawless. Underneath are images of RNA extracted from the cells and radioactively labeled, run out on picture-perfect gels.

There's a sticky note on one sheet. *A little gift for you. Here's more evidence of RNA transfer between the bacteria and the salt slug cells. Turns out you were right all along—there were some strange phages in them, and I just had to tweak the salt concentration. Then it worked.*

It's in Petra's handwriting.

Talk to Stanley and get your project back. It's your project, not mine. Your science baby.

I lift off the note and in the microscopy images underneath, little cherry-colored dots light up the images like red stars. Each dot is a strand of the Houdini-like RNA that jumps around from bacteria to sea slug, which we can demonstrate in very precise concentrations of salt. We can pluck them from the cells, watch them reform elaborate shapes.

There is a Korean idiom to describe tasks that are immensely difficult to do without any luck. 하늘에서 별따기야. To pluck a star from the sky.

In recent months, I have been thinking a lot about things that glow. Nighttime ocean microbes all bioluminescent, my labeled RNA, the probe I made that lit up upon touching endosymbiont RNA.

I've finally made the connection to you.

Let me explain. Fluorescence and phosphorescence are two physical phenomena that both involve emission of light. Both start with a substance getting very excited within: ghostlike motes called photons that can't decide if they are particles or waves are shot up into higher energy levels.

The difference between the two phenomena lies in the timing of how the motes fall from the atomic stratosphere back to the ground. Fluorescence happens immediately: photons burn out real fast and fall back down. Light is emitted like a sneeze. Phosphorescence happens after a delay, so coming back down to terra firma takes longer. It's an afterglow. Light is emitted like a sigh.

Coming back to earth is a process full of different states, of spinning in circles, of reversing direction, of pent-up tension seeping out. But in the end, you find a way back.

When I think of you, Iseul, I think of phosphorescence.

✦ 37 ✦

Iseul's old newspaper published the posthumous piece on the pharma exposé this morning. I am reading it again for the fourth time. The unfinished writing isn't immaculate, but each time I read it I can visualize her.

It also turns out that the content of Iseul's little black-market vial really does appear to be crude sea slug extract. I heard from the melanoma-lab postdoc this morning—not only did he find the compound that is the backbone of existing chemo-therapeutics, but he also found several unidentified compounds that may be the beginnings of new potent chemotherapeutics. It was impossible not to smile when he told me this; even now, Iseul is still nosing her way into my science.

In the lobby full of egg-shaped armchairs, I sit down to write. I pull out my laptop and open the file with my jottings and musings on science, which all begins with an entry on DNA from November and ends on the most recent entry on phosphorescence from just last week. My second lab notebook.

I will write something that isn't so neatly trimmed. It will be a book about stories unfiltered that is still a little raw and bears all of the writer's rough edges like a birthmark.

Something like the stories Kwan-sik told me, and like Iseul's posthumous piece. Something like misplaced love, obsessions, fleece blankets with chemical patterns, fingers sticky with *yuja* tea syrup, finding the earth beneath my feet, unexpected secrets in my biology—all of the cell-like things that make up a person. It's an origins story.

I've finally decided how to say goodbye to Iseul.

It's to wrap all of this shared history into writing.

But it's not really a goodbye. Once an idea is put into writing, it's given newfound life in all of the multifaceted ways in which people interpret it. Iseul said that to me once. So I'm taking her advice and I'm putting both her and the things that remind me of her into writing. There, she will be as dynamic as ever.

I type some words: Prehistoric Earth sucked ass. It was hellfire at first and then it got its act together and was all water and poisons and then, take three, it got a little better.

A very abbreviated timeline of the origins of life on Earth:

  i. *it's all water and poison.*
  ii. *you get a transition, maybe an RNA world, that leads to cells.*
  iii. *you give a cell another cell and get fancier cells.*
  iv. *you get a bunch of new lifeforms.*

I draw a blank. I stare at the ceiling. I make constellations out of the stucco there.

I print out the sparse page anyway. I fold it into its own envelope, write Sun-ah's mailing address on it, tuck it into my bag.

I fidget. These chairs are ergonomic disasters.

What was it that Iseul once said again?

Just write, and don't forget to cite as you go.

I write:

Life is technically radiant. All cells are loaded with mole-cules made of hexagons that fluoresce under ultraviolet light, and some particularly talented bacteria, dinoflagel-lates, fireflies, and jellyfish DIY their own internal fairy lights. But really, Hawking radiation and black-body radi-ation mean that at some level all of us are luminous any-way, from people to black holes.

This is a cute and happy concept. It's very nice and all, but the fact of the matter is—entropy, Murphy's Law, Normal Accident Theory, whatever euphemism you like best—sometimes things just go to shit anyway.[1]

---

[1] firsthand experience

Cite as you go, she said.
Make a sea change, we said.

I MUSTER UP THE courage to visit Strand Beach after lab one day.

Three times, I almost tell the cab driver to turn around. Three times I suppress the urge to shout at him to drive anywhere—I don't care where—anywhere but Strand Beach. But I swallow it down. Some words may have escaped my lips the third time around; the driver looked at me in the rearview mirror, frowning, and said, "We're five minutes away, you really want me to drive forty minutes back to where we started?" So we kept going.

So now I am standing on the overlook where Iseul and I stood not so long ago.

I walk down, tracing our steps along the soft sand, moving through the other beachgoers. It feels foreign, visiting during broad daylight when the ocean is lit by sunlight and not by the nighttime bioluminescence that sometimes haunts my dreams like will-o'-the-wisps.

I walk all the way to the end of the beach marked by ragged black rock cliffs. In the water pooled in those big stones, I see something moving.

It's a sea slug. Brown and green, waving its rippled parapodia around, stretching its neck this way and that as it searches for algae to snack on.

It looks so small, this soft thumb-sized creature, so exposed and vulnerable against the backdrop of turbulent waters and unpredictable land—and yet here it is, at the cusp of that earth and sea, and how far it has ventured out in its determination to live.

When the next waves roll in, I crouch down and put my hands together in the water beside the sea slug. When the waves pull back out, I close my fingers—briefly, I carry the sea in my hands.

ACKNOWLEDGMENTS

To A. M. Homes: a million thank-yous. Your belief in my ability to pull this story together meant so much to me. For each time that I wanted to give up (which was many, many times), you sent encouragement and confidence in many multiples and kept me going. Thank you for your guidance, for your insight, and above all, for seeing a dream through to completion.

To Joyce Carol Oates, for your encouragement and feedback on my writing, from my first science-y story to the first version of this book.

To Erica Spellman-Silverman, for believing in my writing and my ideas, and so fiercely advocating for them. In all of the self-doubt that is so much of sitting down trying to get words onto paper, you bring me back to earth, and then re-energize me. Is all this not the definition of the perfect literary agent? I am so lucky.

To the rest of Trident Media Group, especially Kristen Bertoloni and Michael Pintauro, for all your support and energy, and for making me feel like a legit writer.

To the Alcove Press team, especially to Tara Gavin, for all your enthusiasm for this book and for expertly guiding me through the editing process; to Thai Fantauzzi, Rebecca

Nelson, Mikaela Bender, Dulce Botello, for working your magic in all things production, marketing, and publicity to turn this into a *book* book; and to Amanda Shaffer, for the beautiful cover art.

To Ms. Charlyne Barad and Ms. Leigh Morioka, for encouraging me to write, from third and fourth grade to present day. To Mr. Brady Kelso, for telling me to keep writing after you read the entirety of that very shitty book draft in tenth grade. To Jhumpa Lahiri, Joyce Carol Oates, Aleksandar Hemon, Kirstin Valdez Quade, for the many ways to look at the world. Special thanks to Kirstin Valdez Quade, for all your warmth and extra support across the years.

To those who welcomed me into science. To Victor Nizet, for being all that a lifelong mentor can be, and to Leo Lin, Wdee Thienphrapa, Monika Kumaraswamy, Tamara Escajadillo, and the rest of the Nizet lab, for those special early sparks of curiosity. To Mrs. Elaine Gillum, for what middle school science fair led to, and to Ms. Mitra Moshiri, the best chemistry teacher. To Rebecca Corrigan, for encouraging the trifecta of science, reading, and writing. To Elio Schaechter, Roberto Kolter, and Christoph Weigel, for all your encouragement, guidance, and effervescent wonder with life on all scales. To Mohamed Donia, for all the ways your guidance has led to my growth in and out of science, and the rest of the Donia lab, for the wonderful science-ing community and for being my first story-writing scientific advisory panel. To Jodi Schottenfeld-Roames, for the confocal microscopy; to Jason Puchalla, for the physics; and to Ralph Kleiner, for the prebiotic chemistry and for your extra support. To the Martinez and Fire labs: I'm so lucky to each day be surrounded by people who are the kindest individuals and the most curious and brilliant scientists (yes, I am using the b-word unironically). Extra thanks to some labmates past and present for help during the publishing process: Moamen Elmassry and Eva Sonnenschein, for reading; Zach Kloos, Josh McCausland, Vanya Zheludev, Drew Galls, and Usman Enam, for your thoughts on some science bits; and Christina Rouhotas, for making me feel like myself while also qual-ing.

To Lilah Blalock and Catherine Pham, for being my part-ners-in-crime since kindergarten and for cheering me on throughout this whole book process. To Corr Cooper, for all our hours-long what-ifs and what-abouts and how-abouts and oh-shits, and for being my go-to for all the writing highs and lows and in-betweens. To Andreea Stoica, for being the other half of our collective functional human being, to Alice Egar, for the good chaos, and to Anika Yardi, for your heart, hijinks, and dreams. To Tenzin Norzin, María Nguyễn, Albert Martí, all of my graduate cohort, Metta Nicholson, and Leslie Chan, for making life on campus sweeter. To Vydhourie Thiyag-eswaran, Ellen Li, Nanako Shirai, Michelle Rowicki, Wen Du, Anthony Kang, A. J. Jacono, Jess Montoya, for the good times and help with details in my writing. To Naomi Kellogg, for your lifeline, and to David Vizgan, for being the other life-line. And of course, to my other friends from childhood or present-day, for all your warmth since.

Also to Acacia Denton, Doug Denton, Gina Bravo, Victo-ria Alonso, Deanna Altomara, Sofie Gonzalez, Kirit Limperis, Dan Herschlag, Devaki Bhaya, for making me think or won-der in such a way that those thoughts recur to me when I write, whether it was a conversation we had or just a passing com-ment you made that you probably didn't realize would still be rattling around in my head years later. To the women in sci-ence who took the time to share their stories during the sum-mer of 2020, when I first began writing this story, for your generosity and forthrightness. I hope that my characters live up to your real-life strength. To all of the people with whom I spoke as a CONTACT of Mercer County volunteer throughout undergrad, for sharing your stories and letting me into your lives for a sliver of time.

To my family in Korea—너무 오랫동안 직접 못 봤지만, 옛날에 어렸을 때 한국에서 보낸 추억들은 잊을 수 없을 만큼 아직도 따뜻해요 (이 책에도 몇 군데 담겨 있고...). 항상 전화할 때마다 웃게 만들어서 고마워요.

To 엄마, 아빠, and 형우/Elliott/nugget, for everything, always. So many 사랑s and 감사s. 여기에 모든 것을 그냥 몇 마디로 표현하려고 하니까, so 이상하네. But, no 문제— 허니가 crepes 또 만들어 줘야지.

NOTES

A NOTE ON THE science in this story:
    There's a mix of science in this book. Some of it is "real"—as in, based on principles generally agreed upon by the scientific community (i.e., info found in textbooks) and on scientific publications in peer-reviewed journals. This includes most of Abby's journal entries.

This also includes facts about endosymbioses. For example, endosymbiotic bacteria are often maternally inherited, their genomes often sport group ii intron RNAs and prophages, many are within the *Rickettsia* genus, and they're especially vital to many insects and marine invertebrates that depend on them for nutrients and protection.

The experimental techniques that the characters use are also realistic: 16S rRNA sequencing is useful when identifying unknown bacteria, computational genomics can reveal characteristics unique to particular bacteria, RNA is often visualized by radioactive labeling, some chemical probes fluoresce when they find their target DNA, etc.

Some of the science in this book is "made-up" or more speculative, but grounded in bits of "real" science. This includes the endosymbiont of humans that Abby discovers.

"*Candidatus* Rickettsia mirabilis," the key to Abby finding her biological mother, is a figment of my imagination. To date, there aren't any known bacterial endosymbionts of vertebrates (possibly because the trigger-happy immune systems of vertebrates make it hard for bacteria to hang out). I wanted something that bridges "self" and "other" in a biological, bodily, and collective sense, and a fictional endosymbiont seemed like a way to explore that. It has some realistic features: it's maternally inherited, in the *Rickettsia* genus, loaded with all of the common genomic characteristics of endosymbionts, Gram-negative so that it can theoretically produce little outer membrane vesicles to package up RNA for its host, etc. When it came to imagining how it would get embroiled in embryo development . . . I just tried my best.

The endosymbiont-containing aquatic slug species that Abby studies is also fictional, but its biology is based on some real-life extremophiles. Some experimental techniques are also "made up." As of August 2021, endosymbionts haven't been successfully transplanted into mouse or zebrafish cells, and Petra's fancy new method for precisely visualizing the movement of single RNA molecules in living cells doesn't exist (yet!).

The science inspiration came from a lot of Googling, reading journal articles and *Small Things Considered*, talking to people . . . The timeline of writing this story also overlapped with writing my undergraduate molecular biology thesis on a bacterial endosymbiont of algae. Some science books I read during this time included *The Eighth Day of Creation* by Horace Judson, on the history and origins of molecular biology; *One Plus One Equals One* by John Archibald, on endosymbioses; *The Genesis Quest* by Michael Marshall, on origins-of-life research from the Soviet era to present-day; *Inferior* by Angela Saini, on the biology of gender differences.

I drew from material learned from the lab, courses, and talks. A handful of courses at Princeton were particularly influential: MOL320, for all of the confocal microscopy; PHY108, for the physics underlying life; CHM541, for the nucleotide chemistry; CHM538, for various chemical biology snippets. And Integrative Microbiology at UCSD, which Elio Schaechter and Joe Pogliano were kind enough to allow me to Zoom-sit in on.

But these distinctions between "real" and "made-up" science are maybe not all that important. "Real" science in textbooks and in publications is always revised, anyway. Scientists estimate that upwards of 80 percent of living species on Earth are still undiscovered, including 99 percent of Earth's microbes. The planet's oceans remain as mysterious as outer space. Our own bodies are just as enigmatic—new microbial species are still being named among the trillions of cells that live in and on us. Not to mention that new endosymbioses are being discovered on a regular basis, from within insects to deep-sea tubeworms to sea sponges to microscopic paramecia, and are even being artificially engineered. Within all of these unknowns, it's fun to imagine what new biologies could be (and, maybe, will be) discovered.

SOURCES OF DIRECT QUOTES

THE EPIGRAPH QUOTATION FROM Esther Lederberg is from the Esther M. Zimmer Lederberg Memorial Website.

The writer who noted that "the birds sing" is "the birds cry" when translated into Korean is Lee Oh-young, author of *On Crying*.

The quotation from Paracelsus on poisons is from the U.S. National Library of Medicine website.

The quotation from Charles Darwin's letter to Joseph Hooker is from the Darwin Correspondence Project at the University of Cambridge.

ADDENDUM ON SEA SLUGS

"TAKE THINGS IN STRIDE" would be the mantra of sea slugs, if sea slugs could stride.

There are thousands of species of sea slugs. It's a marine menagerie, a crayon-box palette of creatures that come in all colors, shapes, and sizes, with a biology that is just as bizarre and wonderful as it is varied.

Eating habits:
In a process called kleptoplasty, some sea slugs co-opt the chloroplasts from algae and shunt them into hijacked energy production. Some slugs that eat coral snatch their prey's symbiotic phytoplankton for the same purposes. Others like to live more on the edge: the blue dragon feeds exclusively on the Portuguese man-of-war jellyfish, a highly venomous thing, which you definitely do not want to touch.

Mating habits:
Traumatic mating involves stabbing an accessory stylet into the partner's head, injecting both nutrients and mind-controlling chemicals. Other sea slugs snap off their disposable penises after mating; they have back-ups ready to use within twenty-four hours.

Defensive habits:

Sea slugs that feast on jellyfish and anemones gather up the ven-omous barb-filled cells—the nematocysts—and store them in their own bodies to deploy against predators. Other slugs seques-ter bacterial toxins that algae use to fend off hungry predators, unbothered, and then use them against their own predators. Some disembodied slug heads can grow back a full body, with the two-chambered heart and the wiggling parapodia and all.

No backbone, no problem.